CT
101   Hubbard.
H84
1928a   Little journeys
vol.14   to the homes of
          the great.

RICHARD WAGNER

Little Journeys

To the Homes of the Great

Elbert Hubbard

Great Musicians

The World Publishing
Company

Cleveland, O.   New York, N. Y.

Manufactured in U. S. A.

CONTENTS

CONTENTS

Little Journeys

To the Homes
of
Great Musicians

RICHARD WAGNER

Was ever work like mine created for no purpose? Am I a miserable egotist, possessed of stupid vanity? It matters not, but of this I feel positive; yes, as positive as that I live, and this is, my " Tristan and Isolde," with which I am now consumed, does not find its equal in the world's library of music. Oh, how I yearn to hear it; I am feverish; I am worn. Perhaps that causes me to be agitated and anxious, but my " Tristan " has been finished now these three years and has not been heard. When I think of this I wonder whether it will be with this as with " Lohengrin," which now is thirteen years old, and is still dead to me. But the clouds seem breaking, they are breaking—I am going to Vienna soon. There they are going to give me a surprise. It is supposed to be kept a secret from me, but a friend has informed me that they are going to bring out " Lohengrin."

—*Wagner in a Letter to Praeger*

RICHARD WAGNER

BSURD and silly people make jokes about mothers-in-law, stepmothers and stepfathers—we will none of this. My heart warms to the melancholy Jacques, who dedicated his book to his mother-in-law, " my best friend, who always came when she was needed and never left so long as there was work to do." Richard Wagner's stepfather was his patient, loving and loyal friend.

The father of Wagner died when the child was six months old. The mother, scarcely turned thirty, had a brood of seven, no money and many debts. There is trouble for you—ye silken, perfumed throng, who nibble cheese-straws, test the hyson when it is red, and discuss the heartrending aspects of the servant-girl problem to the lascivious pleasings of a lute!

But the widow Wagner was not cast down to earth— she resolved on keeping her family together, caring for them all as best she could. The suggestion from certain kinsmen that the children should be given out for adoption was quickly vetoed. The fine spirit of the woman won the admiration of a worthy actor, in slightly reduced circumstances, who had lodgings in the house of the widow. This actor, Ludwig Geyer by name, loved the widow and all of the brood, and he

11

proposed that they pool their poverty. ¶ And so before Mrs. Wagner had been a widow a twelvemonth they were married.

In this marriage Geyer seemed to be moved to a degree by the sentiment of friendship for his friend, the deceased husband. Geyer was a man of many virtues—amiable, hopeful, kind. He had the artistic temperament without its faults. To writers of novels, in search of a very choice central character, Ludwig Geyer affords great possibilities. He was as hopeful as Triplett and a deal more versatile. The histrionic art afforded him his income of eleven dollars a week; but painting was his forte—if he only had time to devote to the technique! Yet all the arts being one he had written a play; he also modeled in clay and sang tenor parts as understudy to the great Schudenfeldt. Hope, good-cheer and a devotion to art were the distinguishing features of Mein Herr Geyer.

All this was in the city of Leipzig; but Herr Geyer becoming a member of the Court Theater, the family moved to Dresden, where at this time lived one Weber, a composer, who used to walk by the Geyer home and occasionally stop in for a little rest. At such times one of the children would be sent out with a pitcher, and the great composer and Herr Geyer would in fancy roam the realm of art, and Herr Geyer would impart to Herr Weber valuable ideas that had never been used. The little boy, Richard, used to cherish these visits of

RICHARD WAGNER

Weber, and would sit and watch for hours for the coming of the queer old man in the long gray cloak.

The stork, one fine day, brought Richard a little sister. He was scarce two years older than she. These two sort of grew up together, and were ever the special pets of Herr Geyer, who used to take them to the theater and seat them on a bench in the wings where they could watch him lead the assault in " The Pirate's Revenge."

Richard regarded his stepfather with all the affection that ever a child had for its own parent; and until he was twenty-one was known to the world as Richard Wilhelm Geyer.

The comparison of Ludwig Geyer with Triplett is hardly fair, for Geyer's fine effervescence and hopeful, rainbow-chasing qualities were confined to early life. ¶As the years passed Geyer settled down to earnest work and achieved a considerable success both as an actor and as a painter. The unselfish quality of the man is shown in that his income was freely used to educate the Wagner children. He was sure that Richard had the germ of literary ability in his mental make-up, and his ambition was that the boy should become a writer. But alas! Geyer did not live long enough to know the true greatness of this child he had fostered and befriended ⚹ ⚹

Unlike so many musicians Richard was not precocious. He was slow, thoughtful and philosophic; and music

did not attract him so much as letters. Incidentally he took lessons in music with his other studies, and his first teacher, Gottlieb Muller, has left on record the statement that the boy was " self-willed and eccentric, and not fluid enough in spirit to succeed in music."
The mother of Wagner seems to have been a woman of marked mentality—not especially musical or poetic, but possessing a fine appreciation of all good things, and best of all, she had commonsense. She very early came to regard Richard as her most promising child, and before he was ten years of age, said to a friend, " Richard will be able to succeed at anything he concentrates his mind upon."
The truth of the remark has often been reiterated. The youth was superb in his mental equipment—strong, capable, independent. Had he turned his attention to any other profession, or any branch of art or science, he could have probed the problem to its depths, and made his mark upon the age in which he lived.
In height Wagner was a little under size, but his deep chest, well-set neck, and large, shapely head gave him a commanding look. In physique he resembled the " big little men " like Columbus, Napoleon, Aaron Burr, Alexander Hamilton and John Bright—men born to command, with ability to do the thinking for a nation. ¶ It 's magnificent to be a great musician, and many musicians are nothing else, but it is better to be a man than a musician. Richard Wagner was a man. Envi-

ronment forced literature upon his attention: he desired to be a great poet. He wrote essays, stories, quatrains, epics. Chance sent the work of Beethoven within his radius, and he became filled with the melody of the master. Young men of this type, full of the pride of youth, overflowing with energy, search for a something on which to try their steel. Wagner could write poetry, that was sure, and more, he could prepare the score and set his words to music. He fell upon the work like one possessed—and he was. To his amazement the difficulties of music all faded away, and that which before seemed like a hopeless task, now became luminous before the heat of his spirit.

Nothing is difficult when you put your heart in it.

The obstacles to be overcome in setting words to sounds were like a game of chess—a pleasing diversion. In a month he knew as much of the science of music as many men did who had grubbed at the work a lifetime. " The finances! Get your principles right and then 't is a mere matter of detail, requiring only concentration—I will arrange it," said Napoleon.

Wagner focused on music, yet here seems a good place to say that he never learned either to play the piano or to sing. He had to trust the " details " to others. Yet at twenty he led an orchestra. Soon after he became conductor of the opera at Magdeburg.

In some months more he drifted to Konigsberg, and there acted as conductor at the Royal Theater.

RICHARD WAGNER

In the company of this theater was a young woman by the name of Wilhelmina Planer. Wagner got acquainted with her across the footlights. She was young, comely and all that—they became engaged. Shortly afterwards, one fine moonlight night, in response to her merry challenge, they rang up the " Dom " and were married. They got better acquainted afterward.

RICHARD WAGNER

IT is a fact that Wagner's imprudent marriage at the age of twenty-three has been much regretted and oft lamented. "What," say the Impressionable Ones, "Oh, what could he not have accomplished with a proper mate!"

It is very true that Minna Planer had no comprehension of the genius of her husband; that her two feet were always flatly planted on earth, and her head never reached the clouds; and true it is that she was a weary weight to him for the twenty-five years they lived together. Still men grow strong by carrying burdens; and we must remember that Wagner was what he was on account of what he endured and suffered.

Wagner expressed himself in his art, and all great art is simply the honest, spontaneous, individual expression of soul-emotion. Had Wagner's emotions been different he would have produced a totally different sort of art. That is to say, if Wagner in his youth had loved and wedded a woman who was capable of giving his soul peace, we would have had no Wagner; we would have had some one else, and therefore a totally different expression, or no expression at all. Probably the man would have been quite content to be a village Kapellmeister. His life being reasonably complete, his spirit would not have roamed the Universe crying for rest. The ideals of his wife were so low and commonplace that she influenced his career by antithesis. His soul was ahungered for the bread of life, and stones were

17

given him in way of the dull, the ugly, the affected, the
smug, the ridiculous. Wagner's life was a revolt from
the ossified commonplace, a struggle for right adjustment—a heart tragedy. And all this reaching out of
the spirit, all the prayers, hopes, fears and travail of
his soul, are told and told again in his poetry and in
his music.

All art is autobiography.

Minna Planer was amiable and kind, but the frantic
effort she made at times, in public, to be profound or
chic must have touched the great man on the raw. He
sought, however, to protect her, and at public gatherings used to keep very near to her in order that she
should not fall into the clutches of some sharp-witted
enemy and be lead on into unseemliness of speech. The
scoffs of critics and the ready-made gibes and jeers of
the mob were to her gospel truth; her husband's genius
was a vagary to be stoutly endured. So for many years
she was inclined to pose as one to be pitied—and so
she was. That she suffered at times can not be denied,
yet God is good, and so has put short limit on the
sensibilities of the vain.

But Wagner would never tolerate an unkind word
spoken of Minna in his presence, and once rebuked a
friend who sought to console him by saying, " Never
mind, Minna lives her life the best she can, and expresses the thoughts that come to her—what more do
you and I do? "

18

RICHARD WAGNER

And in his later years, when calm philosophy was his, he realized that Minna Planer had supplied him a stinging discontent, a continued unrest that formed the sounding-board on which his sorrow and his hope and his faith in the Ideal were echoed forth.

Love is the recurring motif in all of Wagner's plays. A man and a woman, joined by God, but separated by unkind condition, play their parts, and our hearts are made by the Master to vibrate in sympathy with the central idea. Only a broken-hearted man could have conjured forth from his soul such couples as these: Senta and the Dutchman, Elizabeth and Tannhauser, Elsa and Lohengrin, Tristan and Isolde, Siegmund and Sieglinde, Walter and Eva, Siegfried and Brunhilde. ¶ Wagner's unhappy marriage forms the keynote of his art. Every opera he wrote depicts a soul in bonds. From " The Flying Dutchman " to " Parsifal " we are shown the struggle of a strong man with cruel Fate; a reaching out for liberty and light; the halting between duty and inclination; and the endless search for a woman who shall give deliverance through her abiding love and faith.

RICHARD WAGNER

LL art seems controlled by fad and fashion.
No fashion endures, else 't were not fashion,
and in its character the fad is essentially
transient. Still we need not rail at fashion; it
is a form of periodicity, and periodicity exists through
all Nature. There are day and night, winter and summer, equinox and solstice, work and rest, years of
plenty and years of famine. Comets return, and all
fashions come back. Keep your old raiment long enough
and it will be in style.

All things move in an orbit, even theories and religions.
Certain forms of fanaticism come with the centuries—
every new heresy is old. All extremes cure themselves,
for when matters get pushed to a point where the
balance of things is in danger of being disturbed, a
Reformer appears and utters his stentorian protest.
This man is always ridiculed, hooted, reviled, mobbed,
and very happy indeed is his fate if he is hanged, crucified or made to drink of the deadly hemlock; for then
his place in the affection of men is made secure, sealed
with blood, and we proclaim him liberator or savior.
The Piazza Signora is sacred soil because there it was
that Savonarola died; John Brown's body lies a-
moldering in the grave, but his soul goes marching
on; J. Wilkes Booth linked his own name with that of
Judas Iscariot and made his victim known to the Ages
as the Emancipator of Men.

These strong men, sent at the pivotal points in history,

are born out of a sore need—they are sent from God. Yet strong men always exist, but it is the needs of the hour that develop and bring them to our attention. Not always have the Reformers been fortunate in their takings off—many have lingered out lengthening, living deaths in walled-up cells. The Bastile, Chillon, London Tower, that prison joined to a palace by the Bridge of Sighs, and all other such plague-spots of blood are haunted by the ghosts of infamy. Before the memory of all those who wrote immortal books behind grated bars we stand uncovered.

Exile has been the lot of many who tried to live for sanity, justice and truth when mad riot raged. Dante, Victor Hugo, Prince Kropotkin and Wagner are types to which we turn. Then there is an attenuated form of persecution known as ostracism, which consists in being exiled at home, but of this it is not worth while to speak ✄ ✄

Wagner was a strong, honest man who simply desired to express his better self. The elements of caution and expediency were singularly lacking in his character. These qualities of independence and self-reliance brought him into speedy collision with those who stood in the front rank of the artistic world of his day, and he became a marked man. His offense was that he expressed his honest self.

In Eighteen Hundred Forty-three, when he appeared upon the scene in Dresden as Hofkapellmeister of the Royal Theater, matters musical were just about where the stage now is in America. In this Year of Grace, Nineteen Hundred One, the great Shakespeare has been elbowed from the stage by the author of " A Texas Steer "; and where once the haughty Richard trod the boards, the skirt-dance assumes the center of the stage and looms lurid like the spirit of the Brocken. Recently a vaudeville " turn " of Hamlet has been presented, where the gravediggers do their gruesome tasks to ragtime; and on every hand we behold the Lyceum giving way to the McClure Continuous, Lim.

Wagner abhorred the mere tune for the sake of tune. " You can not produce art and leave man out," he said. All art must suggest something. Mere verbal description is not literature: it is only words, words, words; a picture must be charged with soul, otherwise a photograph would outrank " The Angelus." Music must be more than jingling tunes and mincing sounds. And thus we find Wagner at thirty years of age boldly putting forth " The Flying Dutchman," with music not written for the text, nor text written for the music, but words and music created at the same time—the melody mirroring forth the soul of the words.

In this play Wagner for the first time sacrificed every precedent of musical construction and all thought of symmetrical form, in order to make the music tell the tale. " The Flying Dutchman " is to opera what Walt

22

RICHARD WAGNER

Whitman's " Leaves of Grass " is to poetry, or Millet's " Sower " is to painting. There is strength, heroic strength, in each of these masterpieces I have named, but the " Dutchman " needs a listener, " Leaves of Grass " requires a reader who has experienced, and the " Sower " demands one who has eyes to see, before its lesson of love and patience and the pathetic truth of endless toil are bodied forth.

Whitman's book was well looked after by the local Antonius Ash-Box inspector of the day, its publication forbidden, and the author incidentally deprived of his clerkship at Washington; Millet did service as the butt for jokes of artistic Paris, and was dubbed " The Wild Man "; Wagner's play was hooted off the stage.

RICHARD WAGNER

VERY man is but a type representing his class. Of course the class may be small and one man may even be its sole living representative; but Wagner had his double in William Morris. These men were brothers in temperament, physique, habit of thought and occupation.

Wagner wrote largely on the subjects of Art and Sociology, and made his appeal for the toiler in that the man should be allowed to share the joys of Art by producing it. His argument is identical with that of William Morris; and yet the essays of Wagner were not translated into English until after Morris had written his "Dream of John Ball," and Morris did not read German

Both men hark back to a time when Man and Nature were on friendly terms; when the thought, best exemplified by the early Greeks, of the sacredness of the human body was recognized; when the old medieval feeling of helpful brotherhood yet lingered; and the restless misery of competition and all the train of woe, squalor and ugliness that " civilization " has brought were unknown.

Wagner's music is made up of the sounds of Nature conventionalized. You hear the sighing of the breeze, the song of the birds, the cries of animals, the rush of the storm. Wagner's essay, entitled, "Art and Revolution," is the twin to the lecture, "Art and Socialism," by Morris; and in the "Art-Work of the Future,"

24

RICHARD WAGNER

Wagner works out at length the favorite recurring theme of Morris: work is for the worker, and art is the expression of man's joy in his work.

In Eighteen Hundred Forty-four, when Morris was ten years of age, Wagner wrote:

"I compose for myself; it is just a question between me and my Maker. I grow as I exercise my faculties, and expression is a necessary form of spiritual exercise. How shall I live? Express what I think or feel, or what you feel? ❧ ❧

"No, I must be honest and sincere. I must, for the need of myself, live my own life, for work is for the worker, at the last. Each man must please himself, and Nature has placed her approbation on this by supplying the greatest pleasure men ever know as a reward for doing good work. I hate this fast-growing tendency to chain men to machines in big factories and deprive them of all joy in their efforts—the plan will lead to cheap men and cheap products. I set my face against it and plead for the dignity and health of the open air, and the olden time." ❧ ❧

This sort of talk led straight to Wagner's arrest in the streets of Dresden on the charge of inciting a riot; and it was the identical line of argument that caused the arrest of Morris in Trafalgar Square, London, when he was taken struggling to the station-house.

Wagner was exiled and Morris merely "cautioned," placed under police surveillance and ostracized. The difference in time explains the difference in punishment. A century earlier and both men would have forfeited their heads.

In all of Wagner's operas the scene is laid at a time when the festivals, games and religious ceremonies were touched with the thought of beauty. Men were strong, plain, blunt and honest. Affectation, finesse, pretense and veneer were unknown. Art had not resolved itself into the possession of a class of idlers and dilettantes who hired long-haired men and fussy girls in Greek gowns to make pretty things for them. All worked with their hands, through need, and when they made things they worked for utility and beauty. They gave things a beautiful form, because men and women worked together, and for each other. And wherever men and women work together we find Beauty. Men who live only with other men are never beautiful in their work, or speech, or lives, neither are women. But at this early time life was largely communal, natural, and Art was the possession of all, because all had a share in its production. Observe the setting of any Wagner opera where Walter Damrosch has his way and get that flavor of bold, free, wholesome, honest Beauty. And yet no stage was ever large enough to quite satisfy Wagner, and all the properties, if he had had his way, would have been works of Art, thought out in detail and materialized for the purpose by human hands.

Now turn to "The Story of the Glittering Plain,"

26

RICHARD WAGNER

"Gertha's Lovers," "News From Nowhere" or "The Hollow Land," by William Morris, and note the same stage-setting, the same majesty, dignity and sense of power. Observe the great underlying sense of joy in life, the gladness of mere existence. A serenity and peace pervades the work of both of these men; they are mystic, fond of folklore and legend; they live in the open, are deeply religious without knowing it, have nothing they wish to conceal, and are one with Nature in all her many moods and manifestations—sons of God!

RICHARD WAGNER

IN the history of letters there is a writer by the name of Green, who exists simply because he reviled a contemporary poet by the name of Shakespeare. Green's name is embalmed in immortal amber with that of Richard Quiney, who wrote a letter to the author of " The Tempest " begging the favor of a loan of forty pounds.

There are several ways of winning fame. Joseph Jefferson has written in classic style of Count Johannes and James Owen O'Connor, who played " Hamlet " to large and enthusiastic audiences, behind a wire screen; then there was John Doe, who fired the Alexandrian Library, and Richard Roe, the man who struck Billy Patterson. Besides these we have the Reverend Obadiah Simmons of Nashville, Tennessee, who, in Eighteen Hundred Sixty, produced a monograph proving that negroes had no souls, the value of which work, to be sure, is slightly vitiated when we remember that the same arguments were used, in Seventeen Hundred One, by Bishop Volberg, in showing that women were in a like predicament.

And now Henry T. Finck has compiled a list of more than one hundred names of musical critics who placed themselves on record in opposition to Richard Wagner and his music. Only such men as proved themselves past masters in density and adepts in abuse are given a place in this Academy of Immortals.

No writer, musician or artist who ever lived brought

RICHARD WAGNER

down on his head an equal amount of contumely and disparagement as did Richard Wagner. Turner, Millet and Rodin have been let off lightly compared with the fate that was Wagner's; and even the shrill outcry that was raised in Boston at sight of MacMonnies' Bacchante was a passing zephyr to the storm that broke over the head of Wagner in Paris, when, after one hundred sixteen rehearsals, "Tannhauser" was produced ✍ ✍

The derisive laughter, catcalls, shouts, hisses and uproar that greeted the play were only the shadow of the criticisms that filled the daily press, done by writers who mistook their own anserine limitations for inanity on the part of the composer. They scorned the melody they could not appreciate, like men who deny the sounds they can not hear; or those who might revile the colors they could not distinguish. And worse than all this, the aristocratic hoodlums refused to allow any one else to enjoy, and would not tolerate the thought that that which to them was "jumbling discord, seven times confounded" might be a succession of harmonies to one whose perceptions were more fully developed.

Wagner himself only escaped personal violence by discreetly keeping out of sight. The result of the Paris experiment was that the poor man lost nearly a year's time, all of his modest savings were gone, creditors dogged his footsteps, and the unanimous tone of the critics, for a time, almost made him doubt his own

29

sanity. What if the critics were really right? ¶ And this, we must remember, was in Eighteen Hundred Sixty-one, when Wagner was forty-eight years of age ✠ That even a strong man should doubt his value when he finds a world of learned men arrayed against him is not strange. Every man who works in a creative way craves approbation. Some one must approve. After the first fever of ecstasy there comes the reaction, when the pulse beats slow and the mind is filled with doubt and melancholy. This desire for approval is not a weakness—it seems to stand as a natural need of every human soul. When the great Peg Woffington played, you remember, she begged Sir Henry Vane to stand in the wings so as to meet her when she came off the stage, take her in his arms just for an instant, kiss her on the forehead and say, " Well done! "

Shallow people may smile at such a scene as this, but those who have delved in the realm of creative art know this fervent need of a word of encouragement from One who Understands.

The one man who held the mirror up to Nature for Wagner was Franz Liszt. Were it not for the steadfast love and faith of this noble soul, Wagner must surely have fallen by the way. Wagner worked first to please himself, and having pleased himself he knew it would please Franz Liszt, and having pleased Franz Liszt he knew it would please all those as great, noble, excellent and pure in heart as Franz Liszt. To speak to an audience made up of such as Liszt, and have them approve, was the sublime dream and hope of Richard Wagner ◈ ◈

Some of the enemies of Wagner, having placed themselves on record against the man, have sought to make out that Wagner and Liszt often quarreled, but this canard has now all been exploded. Such another friendship between two strong men I can not recall. That of Goethe and Schiller seems a mere acquaintanceship, and the friendship of Carlyle and Emerson a literary correspondence with an eye on posterity, as compared with this bond of brotherhood that existed between Wagner and Liszt.

During the ten years of Wagner's exile in Switzerland he received barely enough from his work in music to support him, and several times he would have been in sore need were it not for the " loans " made him by Liszt. He did not even own a piano, and never heard his scores played, except when Liszt made a semi-yearly visit. At such times a piano would be borrowed, and the friends would revel in the new scores, and occasionally talk the entire night away.

When Liszt would go home after such visits, Wagner would go off on long tramps, climbing the mountains, lonely and bereft, sure that the mood for high and splendid work would never come again. Then some morning the mist would roll away, the old spirit would come back, and he would apply himself with all the intense fire and burning imagination of which his spirit was capable.

When the score was done it was sent straight to Liszt, before the ink was dry.

The " Lohengrin " manuscript was sent along in parts, and Liszt was the first man to interpret it. On one such occasion we find Liszt writing: " Your ' Walkure ' has arrived—and gladly would I sing to you with a thousand voices your ' Lohengrin Chorus '— a wonder, a wonder! Dearest Richard, you are surely a divine man, and my highest joy is to follow you in your flight and be one with you in spirit!"

On this occasion, when the "Lohengrin Chorus" first found voice, the only auditor was the Princess von Wittgenstein, who added a postscript to Liszt's letter, thus: " I wept bitter tears over the scene between Siegmund and Sieglinde! This is beautiful—like heaven, like earth—like eternity!" Was ever a woman so blest in privilege—to be the near, dear friend of Franz Liszt and hear him play the music of Richard Wagner from the manuscript, and then add her precious word of appreciation for the work of the weary exile! The quotation given is only a sample of the messages that Liszt was constantly sending to his exiled friend. And we must understand that at this time Liszt had a world-wide reputation as a composer himself, and was the foremost pianist of his time. And Wagner—Wagner was only an obscure dreamer, with a penchant for

32

RICHARD WAGNER

---

erratic music! ¶ The " Lohengrin " was produced at
Weimar under the leadership of Liszt, but even his
magic name could not make the people believe—the
critics had their way and wrote it down.

Yet Liszt lived to see the name of Wagner proclaimed
as the greatest contemporary name in music; and he
was too great and good to allow jealousy to enter his
great soul. Yet he knew that as a composer his own
work was quite lost in the shadow of the reputation of
his friend. At a banquet given in Munich in Eighteen
Hundred Eighty-one in honor of Wagner, Liszt said,
" I ask no remembrance for myself or my work beyond
this: Franz Liszt was the loved and loving friend of
Wagner, and played his scores with tear-filled eyes;
and knew the Heaven-born quality of the man when
all the world seemed filled with doubt."

RICHARD WAGNER

MONG men of worth, no man of his time was more thoroughly hated, detested and denounced than Richard Wagner. Before he became an anarch of art, he was singled out for distinction by royalty and a price was placed upon his head. He escaped, and for ten years lived in exile, his sole offense being that he lifted up his voice for liberty ❧

That is the only thing worth lifting up your voice, or pen, or sword for. The men who live in history are the men who have made freedom's fight—there is no other. These men fought for us, and some of them died for us—Socrates, Jesus, Savonarola, John Brown, Lincoln —saviors all—they died that we might live.

Instead of dying for us, Wagner lived for us, but he had to run away in order to do it. There, in exile—in Switzerland—he wrote many of his most sublime scores, and these he did not hear played till long years after, for although the man could compose, he could not execute. The music was in his brain and he could not get it out at his finger-tips—for him the piano was mute. So now and again Franz Liszt would come and play for him the scores he had never heard, and tears of joy would flow down his fine face; then he would stand on his head, walk on his hands and shout for pure gladness.

All this, I will admit, was not very dignified.

Ostracism, exile, hatred, and stupid misunderstanding

did not suppress Wagner. In his work he is often severe, stern, tragic, but the man himself bubbled with good-cheer. He made foolish puns, and routed the serious ones of earth by turning their arguments into airy jests. If in those early days he had been caught and carried in the death-tumbrel to the Place of the Skull, he would have remarked with Mercutio, " This is a grave subject."

Finally, public opinion relaxed, and Wagner found his way back to Germany. He settled at the town of Bayreuth, and very slowly it dawned upon the thinking few that at Bayreuth there lived a Man.

Among the very first who made this discovery was one Friedrich Nietzsche, an idealist, a dreamer, a thinker, and a revolutionary. Nietzsche was an honest man of marked intellect, whose nerves were worn to the quick by the pretense of the times—the mad race for place and power—the hypocrisy and phariseeism that he saw sitting in high places. He longed to live a life of genuineness—to be, not to seem. And so he had wandered here and there, footsore, weary, searching for peace, scourged forever by the world's displeasure.

¶ The trouble was, of course, that Nietzsche did n't have anything the world wanted. In the time of the Crusaders, the tired children would ask at night-time, when the tents were pitched, " Is this Jerusalem? "

¶ And the only answer was: " Jerusalem is not yet! Jerusalem is not yet! "

RICHARD WAGNER

In Wagner, Nietzsche felt that at last he had found
the Moses who would lead the people out of captivity,
into the Promised Land of Celestial Art.

Nietzsche came and heard the Wagnerian music and
was caught as flotsam in its whirling eddies. He read
everything that Wagner had written, and having come
within the gracious sunshine of the great man's presence, he rushed to his garret and in white heat wrote
the most appreciative criticism of Wagner and his
work that has ever, even yet, been penned. This booklet, " Wagner at Bayreuth," is a masterpiece of insight
and erudition, written by a man of imagination, who
saw and felt, and knew how to mold his feelings into
words—words that burn. It is a rhapsody of appreciation ✠ ✠

Art is more a matter of heart than of head.

The book had a wide circulation, helped on, they do
say, by the Master himself, who confessed that in the
main the work rang true.

The publication of the book sort of linked these two
men, Wagner and Nietzsche. The disciple sat at the
feet of the elder man, and vowed he would be in literature what Wagner was in music. He gazed on him,
fed on him, quoted him, waiting in patience for the
pearls of thought.

Now Wagner was a natural man—a natural son of
God. He had the desires, appetites and ambitions of
a man. If he voiced great thoughts and wrote great

36

scores, he did these things in a mood—and never knew how. At times he was coarse, perverse, irritable. ¶ The awful, serious, sober ways of Nietzsche began to pall on Wagner—he would run away when he saw him coming, for Nietzsche had begun to give advice about how Wagner should regenerate the race, and also conduct himself. Now Richard Wagner had no intention of setting the world straight—he wanted to express himself, that was all, and to make enough money so he could be free to come and go as he chose.

Once, at a picnic, Wagner climbed a tree and cawed like a crow; then hooted like an owl; he ate tarts out of a tin dish with a knife; a little later he stood on his head and yelled like a Congo chief. When Nietzsche tearfully interposed, Wagner told him to go and get married—marry the first woman who was fool enough to have him—she would relieve him of some of his silliness ❧ ❧

Shortly after this, the great Wagner festival came on, and Bayreuth was filled with visitors who had read Nietzsche's book, and bought excursion-tickets to Bayreuth ❧ ❧

Wagner was over his ears in work—an orchestra of three hundred players to manage, new music to arrange, besides the humdrum, but necessary, work of feeding and housing and caring for the throng. Of course he did not do all the work, but the responsibility was his ❧

In this rush of work, Nietzsche was dropped out of

sight—there was no time now for long conferences on the Over-Soul and Music of the Future. ¶ Nietzsche was snubbed. He went off to his garret and wrote a scathing criticism on the work of Richard Wagner. This divine music was not for the intellectual few at all —it was getting popular and it was getting bad. Wagner was insincere—commercial—a charlatan.

Nietzsche was no longer interested in Wagner—he was interested only in Nietzsche.

Literary men do not quarrel more than other men—it only seems as if they did. This is because your writer uses his kazoo in getting even with his supposed enemy —he flings the rhetorical stinkpot with precision, and his grievances come into a prominence all out of keeping with their importance.

In Eighteen Hundred Eighty-eight, Nietzsche issued his little book, " The Fall of Wagner."

After a person has greatly praised another, and wishes to say something particularly unkind about him, one horn of the dilemma must be taken. If you admit you were wrong in the first conclusion, you lay yourself open to the suspicion that you are also wrong in the second—that you are one who makes snap judgments. The safer way then is to cling close to the presumption of your own infallibility, without, of course, actually stating it, and claim that your idol has changed, backslidden—fallen. This then lends an aura of virtue to your action, as it shows a wholesome desire on your part not to associate with the base person, and also an altruistic wish to warn the world so it shall not be undone by him.

Of all the bitter, unkind and malicious things ever uttered against Wagner, none contains more free alkali than the booklet by Nietzsche.

Nietzsche, not being satisfied with an attack on Wagner's art, also made a few flings at his pedigree, and declared that the Master's real name was not Wagner: this was his mother's name, he being a natural son of Ludwig Geyer, the poet—the Jew. What this has to do with Tannhauser, Tristan and Isolde, the Ring, Lohengrin, and Parsifal, Nietzsche does not explain. In any event, the information about Wagner's birth comes with very bad grace from an avowed enemy, who practically admits that he got the facts, in confidence, from Wagner himself. Neither does Nietzsche, the freethinking radical, recognize that good men have long ceased taunting other men concerning their parentage, or boasting of their own.

A man is what he is; and the word " illegitimate " is not in God's vocabulary, since He smiles on lovechildren as on none other. If you know history, you know this: that into their keeping God has largely given the beauty, talent, energy, strength, skill and power, as well as that divinity which confuses its possessor with Deity Incarnate.

Wagner might have replied to Nietzsche in kind, and

39

pointed him out as the product of " tired sheets," to use the phrase of Shakespeare. Wagner might have said, " Yes, I am a member of that elect class to which belong William the Conqueror, Leonardo da Vinci, Erasmus, the Empress Josephine, Alexander Hamilton and Abraham Lincoln! " But he did n't—he did better —he said nothing. Wagner had the pride that scorned a defense—he realized his priceless birthright, and knew that his mother and father had dowered him with a divine genius. Let those talk who could do nothing else: silence was his only answer.

In a year later, Nietzsche was taken to an asylum, dead at the top. He lingered on until Nineteen Hundred, when his body, too, died, died there at Weimar, the home of Goethe and the home of Franz Liszt—another of life's little ironies. It is an obvious thing to say that Friedrich Nietzsche was insane all the time. The fact is, he was not. He was a great, sincere and honest soul, intent on living the ideal life. He wrote thoughts that have passed into the current coin of all the thinking world. When he praised Wagner to the skies and afterwards damned him to the lowest depths of perdition, he was sane, and did the thing that has been done since Cain slew his brother Abel. Take it home to yourself—have n't the best things and the worst that have ever been said about you, been expressed by the same person?

The opinion of any one person concerning any man of

genius, or any product of art, is absolutely valueless. Whim, prejudice, personal bias, and physical condition color our view and tint our opinions, and when we cease to love a man personally, to condemn his art is an easy and natural step. What was before pleasing is now preposterous.

Of course, it is all a point of view—a matter of perspective, and most of us are a trifle out of focus. When we change our opinions we change our friends.

As a prescription for preserving a just and proper view, and living a sane life, I would say, climb a tree occasionally, and hoot like an owl and caw like a crow; stand on your head and yell at times like a Comanche ✂ Robert Louis Stevenson says, "A man who has not had the courage to make a fool of himself has not lived." ✂ The man who does not relax and hoot a few hoots voluntarily, now and then, is in great danger of hooting hoots and standing on his head for the edification of the pathologist and trained nurse, a little later on.

The madhouse yawns for the person who always does the proper thing. Impropriety, in right proportion, relieves congestion, and thus are the unities preserved. And so here the great Law of Compensation, invented by Ralph Waldo Emerson, comes in: The sane, healthy man, who occasionally strips off his dignity and hoots like an owl, or rolls naked in the snow, will surely be called insane by the self-nominated elect, but his personal compensation lies in the fact that he knows he is not.

RICHARD WAGNER

ND now look upon the face of this man! Even so, and upon every face is written the record of the life the man has led: the loves that were his, the thoughts, the prayers, the aspirations, the disappointments, all he hoped to be and was not—all are written there—nothing is hidden, nor can it be. Here was one born in poverty, nurtured in adversity, and yet uplifted and sustained by homely friendships and rugged companions who dumbly guessed the latent greatness of their charge.

With soul athirst he sought for truth, and stubbornly groped his way alone. Immediate precedent stood to him for little, and his sincerity and honesty made him the butt of mob and rabble. His ambition to be himself, to live his life, the desire to express his honest thought, led straight to deprivation of bread and shelter. He had too much sympathy, his honesty was not tempered by the graces of a diplomat—a price was placed upon his head. By the help of that one noble friend, whose love upheld him to the last, he escaped to a country where freedom of speech is not a byword. But misunderstanding followed close upon his footsteps, even his wife doubted his sanity, mistaking his genius for folly, and died undeceived. Calumny, hate, brutal criticism, the contempt of the so-called learned class—and all the train of woe that want and debt can bring to bear were his lot and portion.

Still he struggled on, refusing to compromise or parley

RICHARD WAGNER

—he would live his life, expressing the divinity within, and if fate decreed it so, die the death, misunderstood, reviled, and be forgotten.

And so he lived, working, praying, hoping, toiling, travailing—but with days, now and then, when rifts broke the clouds and the sun shone through, his Other Self giving approbation by saying, " Well done! the work will live."

More than half a century had passed over his head, and the frost of years had whitened his locks; his form was bowed from the many burdens it had borne; the fine face furrowed with lines of care; his eyes grown dim from weeping—when gradually the critics grew less severe.

Advocates were coming to the front, demanding that brutal hands should no longer mangle this man: grudgingly pardon came for offenses never committed, and he was permitted to return to his native land. Strong men and women placed themselves on his side. They declared their faith, and said his work was sublime; and they boldly stated the patent fact that those who had done most to cry Wagner down, had themselves done nothing, nor added an iota to the wealth or the harmony of the world. People began to listen, to investigate, and they said, " Why, yes, the music of Wagner has a distinct style—it has individuality."

Individuality is a departure from a complete type, and so is never perfect, any more than man is perfect. But

43

RICHARD WAGNER

Wagner's music is honest and genuine emotion set to sweet sounds, with words in keeping. It mirrors the hopes, the disappointments, the aspirations and the love of a great soul.

As men and women grew to cultivate the hospitable mind and receptive heart, tears filled their eyes and as they listened they came to understand. Honesty and genuineness in souls are too rare to flout—when found men really uncover before them. The people saw at last that they had been deceived by the savants, blinded by the dust of paid and prejudiced critics, fooled by those who led the way for a consideration. They flocked to see the great composer and listen to his matchless music, and they gave the man and his work their approval. Such sums were paid to him as he had only read of in books. Adulation, approbation and crowning fame were his at last.

Then love came that way and gentle, trusting affection, and sweet, spiritual comradeship, such as he had never known except in dreams—all these were his. His fame increased, and lavish offers from across the sea came, proffering him such wealth and honor as were not for any other living artist.

A theater was built for the presentation of his productions alone; the lovers of music from every nation made Bayreuth a place of pilgrimage.

When the man died—passed peacefully away, supported by the arms of the one woman he had loved—the

RICHARD WAGNER

daughter of Liszt—the art-loving world paid his genius all the tribute that men can offer to the worth of other men ✄ ✄

And now the passing years have brought a confirmation in belief of the statement made by Franz Liszt, " Richard Wagner is the one true musical genius of his age."
¶ Wagner's admirers should, for him, plead guilty to the worst that can be said: he is everything that his most bitter critics say, but he is so much more that his faults and follies sink into ashes before the divine fire of his genius, and we still have the gold. Inconsistent, paradoxical, preposterous—why, yes, of course! Still he is the greatest poet of passion the world has ever seen—don't cavil—passion's consistency consists in being inconsistent.

" Every sentence must have a man behind it," and so we might say, " Every bar of music must have a man behind it." That harmony only can live which once had its dwelling-place in a great and tender heart.

The province of art is to impart a sublime emotion, and that which affects to be an emotion, no matter how subtly launched, can never live as classic art. Honesty here, as elsewhere, must have its reward. Be yourself, though all the world laugh.

I will not say that Wagner was—he is. The man himself in life was often worn to the quick by the deprivations he had to endure, or the stupid misunderstandings he encountered, so at times he was impatient, erratic,

RICHARD WAGNER

possibly perverse. But all that is gone—his mistakes have been washed in the blood of Time—only the good survives. The best that this great and godlike man ever thought, or felt, or knew, is ours—he lives immortal in his Art.

PAGANINI

PAGANINI

For lo! creation's self is one great choir,
And what is Nature's order but the rhyme
Whereto the worlds keep time,
And all things move with all things from their prime?
Who shall expound the mystery of the lyre?
In far retreats of elemental mind
Obscurely comes and goes
The imperative breath of song, that as the wind
Is trackless, and oblivious whence it blows.

—*William Watson*

PAGANINI

OME time ago, after my lecture one night in Boston, I bethought me to call on my old friend Bliss Carman. I expected he would be sleeping the sleep of the just, but I was prepared to rout him out, for although my errand was from a fair, frail young thing, and trivial, yet I was bound to deliver the message—for that is what one should always do.

But the poet was not abed—he was pacing the room in a fine burst of poetic fervor, composing "More Songs From Vagabondia." The songs told of purling streams, hedge-rows, bathers lolling on the river-bank, nodding wild flowers, chirping pewees, and other such poetic proper-ties, which the singer conjured forth from boyhood's days, long since gone by.

This suite of rooms, where the poet worked, was in a fine house on a fashionable street, and I noticed the place bore every mark of elegant bachelor ease and convenience that good taste could dictate. The best "Songs From Vagabondia," I am told, are written in comfortable apartments, where there are a bath and a Whitely Exerciser; but patient, persistent effort and work overtime are necessary to lick the lines into shape so they will live. Good poets run their machinery in

49

double shifts. ¶ " Go away! " cried Bliss Carman, when
he had opened the door in reply to my sprightly knock.
" Go away! I am giving to airy nothings a local habita-
tion and a name. This is my busy night—do you not
see ? " And fully understanding the conditions, for I am
a poet myself, I went away and left the author to his
labors ⚒ ⚒

It is a mistake to assume that genius is the capacity for
evading hard work. " La Vie de Boheme " is a beautiful
myth that was first worked out with consummate labor
by a man of imagination named Murger, and told again
with variations by Balzac and Du Maurier. Boheme is
not down on the map, because it is not a money-order
post-office. It is only a Queen Mab fairy fabric of a
warm, transient desire; its walls being constructed of the
stuff that dreams are made of, and its little life is rounded
with a pipe and tabor, two empties and a brass tray.
Yet the semblance of the thing is there and this often
deceives the very elect. Around every art studio are
found the young men in velveteen who smoke infinite
cigarettes, and throw off opinions about this great man
and that, and prate prosaically in blase monotone of the
Beautiful. Sometimes these young persons give lectures
on "Art as I Have Found It "; but do not be deceived
by this—the art that lives is probably being produced
by small, shy, red-headed men who work on a top floor,
and whom you can only find with the help of a search-
warrant. One sort talks of art, the other kind produces

PAGANINI

---

it. One tells of truth, the other is living it. ¶ Edgar
Allan Poe wrote the most gruesome stories that have
ever been told, just to prove that life is a tragedy and
not worth living. But who ever lived fuller and applied
himself to hard work more conscientiously in order to
make his point? Poe wrote and rewrote, and changed
and added and interlined and balanced it all on his
actor's tongue, and read it aloud before the glass. Poe
shortened his days and flung away a valuable fag-end
of his life, trying to show that life is not worth living,
and thus proved it is. Gray spent thirteen years writing
his " Elegy," and so made clear the point that the man
who does good work does not at the last lay him down
and rest his head upon the lap of earth, a youth to
fortune and to fame unknown. Gray secured both fame
and fortune. He was so successful that he declined the
Laureateship, and had the felicity to die of gout. Gray's
immortality is based upon the fact that his life gave the
lie to his logic. The man who thinks out what he wants
to do, and then works and works hard, will win, and no
others do, or ever have, or can—God will not have it so.

PAGANINI

S a violinist Paganini far surpassed all other players who ever lived; and when one follows the story of his life, the fact is apparent that he succeeded because he worked.

And yet behold the paradox! The idea existed in his own day, and is abroad yet, that " the devil guided his hand," for the thought that the devil is more powerful than God has ever been held by the majority of men—more especially if a fiddle is concerned.

Such patience, such persistency, such painstaking effort as the man put forth for a score of years would have made him master at anything. The public knows nothing of these long years of labor and preparation—it sees only the result, and this result shows such consummate ease and naturalness—all done without effort— that it exclaims, "A genius—the devil guides his hand! " The remark was made of Titian and his wonderful color effects, and then again of Rembrandt with his mysterious limpid shadows—their competitors could not understand it! And so they disposed of the subject by attributing it to a supernatural agency.

Things all men can do and explain are natural; things we can not explain are " supernatural." Progress consists in taking things out of the supernatural pigeonhole and placing them in the natural. As soon as we comprehend the supernatural, we are a bit surprised to find it is perfectly natural.

But the limitations of great men are seen in that when

they have acquired the skill to do a difficult thing well, and the public cries, " Genius! " why the genius humors the superstition and begins to allow the impression to get out mysteriously that he " never had a lesson in his life." ❧ ❧

Any man who caters to the public is to a great degree spoiled by the public. Actors act off the stage as well as on, falling victims to their trade: their lives are stained by pretense and affectation, just as the dyer's hand is subdued to the medium in which it works. The man of talent who is much before the public poses because his audience wishes him to; one step more and the pose becomes natural—he can not divest himself of it. Paganini by hard work became a consummate player; and then so the dear public should receive its money's worth, he evolved into a consummate poseur—but he was still the Artist.

PAGANINI

LARGE number of writers have described the appearance and playing of Niccolo Paganini, but none ever did the assignment with the creepy vividness of Heinrich Heine. The rest of this chapter is Heine's. I make the explanation because the passage is so well known that it would be both indiscreet and inexpedient for me to bring my literary jimmy to bear and claim it as my own—much as I would like to.

Says Heinrich Heine:

I believe that only one man has succeeded in putting Paganini's true physiognomy upon paper—a deaf painter, Lyser by name, who, in a frenzy full of genius, has with a few strokes of chalk so well hit the great violinist's head that one is at the same time amused and terrified at the truth of the drawing. " The devil guided my hand," the deaf painter said to me, chuckling mysteriously, and nodding his head with a good-natured irony in the way he generally accompanied his genial witticisms. This painter was, however, a wonderful old fellow; in spite of his deafness he was enthusiastically fond of music, and he knew how, when near enough to the orchestra, to read the music in the musicians' faces, and to judge the more or less skilful execution by the movements of their fingers; indeed, he wrote critiques on the opera for an excellent journal at Hamburg. And yet is that peculiarly wonderful? In the visible symbols of the performance the deaf painter could see the sounds. There are men to whom the sounds themselves are invisible symbols in which they hear

PAGANINI

colors and forms. ¶ I am sorry that I no longer possess Lyser's little drawing; it would perhaps have given you an idea of Paganini's outward appearance. Only with black and glaring strokes could those mysterious features be seized, features which seemed to belong more to the sulphurous kingdom of shades than to the sunny world of life. " Indeed, the devil guided my hand," the deaf painter assured me, as we stood before the pavilion at Hamburg on the day when Paganini gave his first concert there. " Yes, my friend, it is true that he has sold himself to the devil, body and soul, in order to become the best violinist, to fiddle millions of money, and principally to escape the damnable galley where he had already languished many years. For, you see, my friend, when he was chapel-master at Lucca he fell in love with a princess of the theater, was jealous of some little abbate, was perhaps deceived by the faithless amata, stabbed her in approved Italian fashion, came in the galley to Genoa, and as I said, sold himself to the devil to escape from it, became the best violin-player, and imposed upon us this evening a contribution of two thalers each. But, you see, all good spirits praise God! There in the avenue he comes himself, with his suspicious impresario."

It was Paganini himself whom I then saw for the first time. He wore a dark gray overcoat, which reached to his heels, and made his figure seem very tall. His long black hair fell in neglected curls on his shoulders, and formed a dark frame round the pale, cadaverous face, on which sorrow, genius and hell had engraved their lines. Near him danced along a little pleasing figure, elegantly prosaic—with rosy, wrinkled face, bright gray

55

PAGANINI

little coat with steel buttons, distributing greetings on all sides in an insupportably friendly way, leering up, nevertheless, with apprehensive air at the gloomy figure who walked earnest and thoughtful at his side. It reminded one of Retzsch's presentation of " Faust " and Wagner walking before the gates of Leipzig. The deaf painter made comments to me in his mad way, and bade me observe especially the broad, measured walk of Paganini. " Does it not seem," said he, " as if he had the iron cross-pole still between his legs? He has accustomed himself to that walk forever. See, too, in what a contemptuous, ironical way he sometimes looks at his guide when the latter wearies him with his prosaic questions. But he can not separate himself from him; a bloody contract binds him to that companion, who is no other than Satan. The ignorant multitude, indeed, believe that this guide is the writer of comedies and anecdotes, Harris from Hanover, whom Paganini has taken with him to manage the financial business of his concerts. But they do not know that the devil has only borrowed Herr George Harris' form, and that meanwhile the poor soul of this poor man is shut up with other rubbish in a trunk at Hanover, until the devil returns its flesh-envelope, while he perhaps will guide his master through the world in a worthier form—namely as a black poodle."

But if Paganini seemed mysterious and strange enough when I saw him walking in bright midday under the green trees of the Hamburg Jungfernstieg, how his awful bizarre appearance startled me at the concert in the evening! The Hamburg Opera House was the scene of this concert, and the art-loving public had flocked there so early, and in such numbers, that I only just succeeded in obtaining a little place in the orchestra. Although it was post-day, I saw in the first row of boxes the whole educated commercial world, a whole Olympus of bankers and other millionaires, the gods of coffee and sugar by the side of their fat goddesses, Junos of Wandrahm and Aphrodites of Dreckwall. A religious silence reigned through the assembly. Every eye was directed towards the stage. Every ear was making ready to listen. My neighbor, an old furrier, took the dirty cotton out of his ears in order to drink in better the costly sounds for which he had paid his two thalers At last a dark figure, which seemed to have arisen from the underworld, appeared upon the stage. It was Paganini in his black costume—the black dress-coat and the black waistcoat of a horrible cut, such as is prescribed by infernal etiquette at the court of Proserpine. The black trousers hung anxiously around the thin legs. The long arms appeared to grow still longer, as, holding the violin in one hand and the bow in the other, he almost touched the floor with them, while displaying to the public his unprecedented obeisances. In the angular curves of his body there was a horrible woodenness, and also something absurdly animal-like, that during these bows one could not help feeling a strange desire to laugh. But his face, that appeared still more cadaverously pale in the glare of the orchestra lights, had about it something so imploring, so simply humble, that a sorrowful compassion repressed one's desire to smile. Had he learnt these complimentary bows from an automaton, or a dog? Is that the entreating gaze of one sick unto death, or is there lurking behind it

the mockery of a crafty miser? Is that a man brought
into the arena at the moment of death, like a dying
gladiator, to delight the public with his convulsions?
Or is it one risen from the dead, a vampire with a violin,
who, if not the blood out of our hearts, at any rate sucks
the gold out of our pockets?

Such questions crossed our minds while Paganini was
performing his strange bows, but all those thoughts
were at once still when the wonderful master placed his
violin under his chin and began to play.

As for me, you already know my musical second-sight,
my gift of seeing at each tone a figure equivalent to the
sound, and so Paganini with each stroke of his bow
brought visible forms and situations before my eyes;
he told me in melodious hieroglyphics all kinds of
brilliant tales; he, as it were, made a magic lantern play
its colored antics before me, he himself being chief
actor. At the first stroke of his bow the stage scenery
around him had changed; he suddenly stood with his
music-desk in a cheerful room, decorated in a gay,
irregular way after the Pompadour style; everywhere
little mirrors, gilded Cupids, Chinese porcelain, a
delightful chaos of ribbons, garlands of flowers, white
gloves, torn lace, false pearls, powder-puffs, diamonds
of gold-leaf and spangles—such tinsel as one finds in the
room of a prima donna. Paganini's outward appearance
had also changed, and certainly most advantageously;
he wore short breeches of lily-colored satin, a white
waistcoat embroidered with silver, and a coat of bright
blue velvet with gold buttons; the hair in little carefully
curled locks bordered his face, which was young and
rosy, and gleamed with sweet tenderness as he ogled the

pretty young lady who stood near him at the music-desk, while he played the violin.

Yes, I saw at his side a pretty young creature, dressed in antique costume, the white satin swelled out above the waist, making the figure still more charmingly slender; the high raised hair was powdered and curled, and the pretty round face shone out all the more openly with its glancing eyes, its little rouged cheeks, its tiny beauty-patches, and the sweet, impertinent little nose. In her hand was a roll of white paper, and by the movements of her lips as well as by the coquettish waving to and fro of her little upper lip she seemed to be singing; but none of her trills was audible to me, and only from the violin with which young Paganini led the lovely child could I discover what she sang, and what he himself during her song felt in his soul.

Oh, what melodies were those! Like the nightingale's notes, when the fragrance of the rose intoxicates her yearning young heart with desire, they floated in the twilight. Oh, what melting, languid delight was that! The sounds kissed each other, then fled away pouting, and then, laughing, clasped each other and became one, and died away in intoxicating harmony. Yes, the sounds carried on their merry game like butterflies, when one, in playful provocation, will escape from another, hide behind a flower, be overtaken at last, and then, wantonly joying with the other, fly away into the golden sunlight. But a spider, a spider can prepare a sudden tragical fate for such enamored butterflies!

Did the young heart anticipate this? A melancholy sighing tone, a sad foreboding of some slowly approaching misfortune, glided softly through the enrapturing

59

PAGANINI

melodies that were streaming from Paganini's violin.
His eyes became moist. Adoringly he knelt down before
his amata. But, alas! as he bowed down to kiss her feet,
he saw under the sofa a little abbate! I do not know
what he had against the poor man, but the Genoese
became pale as death. He seized the little fellow with
furious hands, drew a stiletto from its sheath, and
buried it in the young rogue's breast.

At this moment, however, a shout of "Bravo! Bravo!"
broke out from all sides. Hamburg's enthusiastic sons
and daughters were paying the tribute of their uproarious applause to the great artist, who had just ended the
first of his concert, and was now bowing with even more
angles and contortions than before. And on his face the
abject humility seems to me to have become more
intense. From his eyes stared a sorrowful anxiety like
that of a poor malefactor. "Divine!" cried my neighbor, the furrier, as he scratched his ears; "that piece
alone was worth two thalers."

When Paganini began to play again a gloom came before
my eyes. The sounds were not transformed into bright
forms and colors; the master's form was clothed in
gloomy shades, out of the darkness of which his music
moaned in the most piercing tones of lamentation.

Only at times, when a little lamp that hung above cast
its sorrowful light over him, could I catch a glimpse of
his pale countenance, on which the youth was not yet
extinguished. His costume was singular, in two colors,
yellow and red. Heavy chains weighed upon his feet.
Behind him moved a face whose physiognomy indicated
a lusty goat-nature. And I saw at times long, hairy
hands seize assistingly the strings of the violin on which

PAGANINI

Paganini was playing. They often guided the hand which held the bow, and then a bleat-laugh of applause accompanied the melody, which gushed from the violin ever more full of sorrow and anguish. They were melodies which were like the song of the fallen angels who had loved the daughters of earth, and being exiled from the kingdom of the blessed, sank into the underworld with faces red with shame. They were melodies in whose bottomless depths glimmered neither consolation nor hope. When the saints in heaven hear such melodies, the praise of God dies upon their paled lips, and they cover their heads weeping. At times when the obligato goat's laugh bleated in among the melodious pangs, I caught a glimpse in the background of a crowd of small women-figures who nodded their odious heads with wicked wantonness. Then a rush of agonizing sounds came from the violin, and a fearful groan and a sob, such as was never heard upon earth before, nor will be perhaps heard upon earth again, unless in the valley of Jehoshaphat, when the colossal trumpets of doom shall ring out, and the naked corpses shall crawl forth from the grave to abide their fate. But the agonized violinist suddenly made one stroke of the bow, such a mad, despairing stroke, that his chains fell rattling from him, and his mysterious assistant and the other foul, mocking forms vanished.

At this moment my neighbor, the furrier, said, "A pity, a pity! a string has snapped—that comes from constant pizzicato."

Had a string of the violin really snapped? I do not know. I only observed the alternation in the sounds, and Paganini and his surroundings seemed to me again

PAGANINI

suddenly changed. I could scarcely recognize him in the monk's brown dress, which concealed rather than clothed him. With savage countenance half-hid by the cowl, waist girt with a cord, and bare feet, Paganini stood, a solitary defiant figure, on a rocky prominence by the sea, and played his violin. But the sea became red and redder, and the sky grew paler, till at last the surging water looked like bright, scarlet blood, and the sky above became of a ghastly corpse-like pallor, and the stars came out large and threatening; and those stars were black—black as glooming coal. But the tones of the violin grew ever more stormy and defiant, and the eyes of the terrible player sparkled with such a scornful lust of destruction, and his thin lips moved with such a horrible haste, that it seemed as if he murmured some old accursed charms to conjure the storm and loose the evil spirits that lie imprisoned in the abysses of the sea. Often, when he stretched his long, thin arm from the broad monk's sleeve, and swept the air with his bow, he seemed like some sorcerer who commands the elements with his magic wand; and then there was a wild wailing from the depth of the sea, and the horrible waves of blood sprang up so fiercely that they almost besprinkled the pale sky and the black stars with their red foam. There was a wailing and a shrieking and a crashing, as if the world was falling into fragments, and ever more stubbornly the monk played his violin. He seemed as if by the power of violent will he wished to break the seven seals where-with Solomon sealed the iron vessels in which he had shut up the vanquished demons. The wise king sank those vessels in the sea and I seemed to hear the voices of the imprisoned spirits while Paganini's violin growled its most wrathful bass.

But at last I thought I heard the jubilee of deliverance, and out of the red billows of blood emerged the heads of the fettered demons: monsters of legendary horror, crocodiles with bats' wings, snakes with stags' horns, monkeys with shells on their heads, seals with long patriarchal beards, women's faces with one eye, green camels' heads, all staring with cold, crafty eyes, and long, fin-like claws grasping at the fiddling monk. From the latter, however, in the furious zeal of his conjuration, the cowl fell back and the curly hair, fluttering in the wind, fell round his head in ringlets, like black snakes ﳥ ﳥ

So maddening was this vision that to keep my senses I closed my ears and shut my eyes. When I again looked up the specter had vanished, and I saw the poor Genoese in his ordinary form, making his ordinary bows, while the public applauded in the most rapturous manner ﳥ " That is the famous performance upon G," remarked my neighbor. " I myself play the violin, and I know what it is to master the instrument." Fortunately, the pause was not considerable, or else the musical furrier would certainly have engaged me in a long conversation upon art. Paganini again quietly set his violin to his chin, and with the first stroke of his bow the wonderful transformation of melodies again began.

They no longer fashioned themselves so brightly and corporeally. The melody gently developed itself, majestically billowing and swelling like an organ chorale in a cathedral, and everything around, stretching larger and higher, had extended into a colossal space which, not

PAGANINI

the bodily eye, but only the eye of the spirit could seize.
In the midst of this space hovered a shining sphere,
upon which, gigantic and sublimely haughty, stood a
man who played the violin. Was that sphere the sun?
I do not know. But in the man's features I recognized
Paganini, only ideally lovely, divinely glorious, with a
reconciling smile. His body was in the bloom of powerful
manhood, a bright blue garment enclosed his noble
limbs, his shoulders were covered by gleaming locks of
black hair; and as he stood there, sure and secure, a
sublime divinity, and played the violin, it seemed as if
the whole creation obeyed his melodies. He was the
man-planet about which the universe moved with
measured solemnity and ringing out beatific rhythms.
Those great lights, which so quietly gleaming swept
around, were they stars of heaven, and that melodious
harmony which arose from their movements, was it the
song of the spheres, of which poets and seers have
reported so many ravishing things? At times, when I
endeavored to gaze out into the misty distance, I
thought I saw pure white garments floating around, in
which colossal pilgrims passed muffled along with white
staves in their hands, and singular to relate, the golden
knob of each staff was even one of those great lights
which I had taken for stars. These pilgrims moved in a
large orbit around the great performer, the golden
knobs of their staves shone even brighter at the tones
of the violin, and the chorale which resounded from
their lips, and which I had taken for the song of the
spheres, was only the dying echo of those violin tones.
A holy, ineffable ardor dwelt in those sounds, which
often trembled scarce audibly, in mysterious whisper

64

on the water, then swelled out again with a shuddering sweetness, like a bugle's notes heard by moonlight, and then finally poured forth in unrestrained jubilee, as if a thousand bards had struck their harps and raised their voices in a song of victory.

PAGANINI

N Seventeen Hundred Eighty-four, Niccolo Paganini was born at Genoa. His father was a street-porter who eked out the scanty exchequer by playing a violin at occasional dances or concerts. That his playing was indifferent is evident from the fact that he was very poor—his services were not in demand.

The poverty of the family and the failure of the father fired the ambition of the boy to do something worthy. When he was ten years old he could play as well as his father, and a year or so thereafter could play better. The lad was tall, slender, delicate and dreamy-eyed. But he had will plus, and his desire was to sound the possibilities of the violin. And this reminds me that Hugh Pentecost says there is no such thing as will— it is all desire: when we desire a thing strongly enough, we have the will to secure it—but no matter!

Young Niccolo Paganini practised on his father's violin for six hours a day; and now when the customers who used to hire his father to play came, they would say, " We just as lief have Niccolo."

Soon after this they said, " We prefer to have Niccolo." And a little later they said, " We must have Niccolo." Some one has written a book to show that playing second fiddle is just as worthy an office as playing first. This doubtless is true, but there are so many more men who can play second, that it behooves every player to relieve the stress by playing first if he can.

PAGANINI

Niccolo played first and then was called upon to play solos. He was making twice as much money as his father ever had, but the father took all the boy's earnings, as was his legal right. The father's pride in the success of the son, the young man always said, was because he was proving a good financial investment. It does not always pay to raise children—this time it did. It was finally decided to take the boy to the celebrated musician, Rolla, for advice as to what was best to do about his education. Rolla was sick abed at the time the boy called and could not see him; but while waiting in the entry the lad took up a violin and began to play. The invalid raised himself on one elbow and pantingly inquired who the great master was that had thus favored him with a visit.

" It 's the lad who wants you to give him lessons," answered the attendant.

" Impossible! no lad could play like that—I can teach that player nothing! "

Next the musician Paer was visited, and he passed the boy along to Giretta, who gave him three lessons a week in harmony and counterpoint. The boy had abrupt mannerisms and tricks of his own in bringing out expressions, and these were such a puzzle to the teacher that he soon refused to go on.

Niccolo possessed a sort of haughty self-confidence that aggravated the master; he believed in himself and was fond of showing that he could play in a way no one else

could. Adolescence had turned his desire to play into a
fury of passion for his art: he practised on single passages for ten or twelve hours a day, and would often
sink in a swoon from sheer exhaustion. This deep,
torpor-like sleep saved him from complete collapse, just
as it saved Mendelssohn, and he would arise to go on
with his work.

Paganini's wisdom was shown at this early age in that
he limited his work to a few compositions, and these he
made the most of, just as they say Bossuet secured his
reputation as the greatest preacher of his time by a
single sermon that he had polished to the point of perfection ✄ ✄

When fifteen years old Paganini contrived to escape
from his father and went to a musical festival at Lucca.
He managed to get a hearing, was engaged at once as
a soloist, and soon after gave a concert on his own
account. In a month he had accumulated a thousand
pounds in cash.

Very naturally, such a success turned the head of this
lad who never before had had the handling of money.
He began to gamble, and became the dupe of rogues—
male and female—who plunged him into an abyss of
wrong. He even gambled away the " Stradivarius "
that had been presented to him, and when his money,
watch and jewels were gone, his new-found friends of
course decamped, and this gave the young man time to
ponder on the vanities of life.

PAGANINI

When he played again it was on a borrowed "Guarnerius," and after the rich owner, himself a violinist,
had heard him play, he said, " No fingers but yours shall
ever play that violin again! "
Paganini accepted the gift, and this was the violin he
played for full forty years, and which, on his death, was
willed to his native city of Genoa. There it can be seen
in its sealed-up glass case.
Up to his thirtieth year Paganini continued his severe
work of subduing the violin. By that time he had
sounded its possibilities, and thereafter no one heard
him play except in concert. It is told that one man,
anxious to know the secrets of Paganini's power,
followed him from city to city, watching him at his
concerts, dogging him through the streets, spying upon
him at hotels. At one inn this man of curiosity had the
felicity to secure a room next to the one occupied by
Paganini; and one morning as he watched through the
keyhole, he was rewarded by seeing the master open the
case where reposed the precious " Guarnerius." Paganini lifted the instrument, held it under his chin, took
up the bow and made a few passes in the air—not a
sound was heard. Then he kissed the back of the violin,
muttered a prayer, and locked the instrument in its
case ॐ ॐ
At concert rehearsals he always played a mute instrument; and Harris, his manager, records that for the
many years he was with Paganini he never heard him

69

PAGANINI

play a single note except before an audience. ¶ I have a full-length daguerreotype of Paganini taken when he was forty years of age. No one ever asked this man, " Kind sir, are you anybody in particular ? "

Paganini was tall and wofully slim. His hands and feet were large and bony, his arms long, his form bowed and lacking in all that we call symmetry. But the long face with its look of abject melancholy, the curved nose, the thin lips and the sharp, protruding chin, made a combination that Fate has never duplicated. You could easily believe that this man knew all the secrets of the Nether World, and had tasted the joys of Paradise as well. Women pitied and loved him, men feared him, and none understood him. He lived in the midst of throngs and multitudes—the loneliest man known in the history of art ✲ ✲

Paganini, when he had reached his height, played only his own music; he played divinely and incomprehensibly; next to his passion for music was his greed for gold. These three facts sum up all we really know about the master—the rest fades off into mist—mystery, fable and legend. We do know, however, that he composed several pieces of music so difficult that he could not play them himself, and of course no one else can. Imagination can always outrun performance. Paganini had no close friends; no confidants: he never mingled in society, and he never married.

At times he would disappear from the public gaze for

70

PAGANINI

several months, and not even his business associates
knew where he was. On one such occasion a traveler
discovered him in a monastic retreat in the Swiss
Mountains, wearing a horsehair robe and a rope girdle;
others saw him disguised as a mendicant; and still
another tells of finding him working as a day-laborer
with obscure and ignorant peasants. Then there are
tales told of how he was taken captive by a titled lady
of great wealth and beauty, who carried him away to
her bower, where he eschewed the violin and tinkled
only the guitar the livelong day.

Everywhere the report was current that Paganini had
killed a man, and been sentenced to prison for life. The
story ran that in prison he found an old violin, three
strings of which were broken, and so he played on one
string, producing such ravishing music that the keepers
feared he was "possessed." They decided they must
get rid of him, and so contrived to have him thrown
overboard from a galley; but he swam ashore, and
although he was everywhere known, no man dared
place a hand on him.

A late writer in a London magazine, however, has given
evidence of being a psychologist and man of sense; he
says, and produces proof, that after the concert season
was over Paganini withdrew to a monastery in the
mountains of Switzerland, and there the monks who
loved him well, guarded his retreat. There he found the
rest for which his soul craved, and there he practised on

71

PAGANINI
--

his violin hour after hour, day after day. All this is
better understood when we remember that after each
retreat, Paganini appeared with brand-new effects
which electrified his hearers—" effects taught him by
the devil."

Constant appearing before vast multitudes and ceaseless
travel create a depletion that demands rest. Paganini
held the balance true by fleeing to the mountains; there
he worked and prayed. That Paganini had a soft heart,
in spite of the silent, cold and melancholy mood that
usually possessed him, is shown in his treatment of his
father and mother, who lived to know the greatness of
their son. He wrote his mother kind and affectionate
letters, some of which we have, and provided lavishly
for every want of both his parents. At times he gave
concerts for charity, and on these occasions vast sums
were realized.

Paganini died in Eighteen Hundred Forty, aged fifty-
six years. His will provided for legacies to various men
and women who had befriended him, and he also gave
to others with whom he had quarreled, thus proving he
was not all clay.

The bulk of his fortune, equal to half a million dollars,
was bequeathed to his son, Baron Achille Paganini.
And as if mystery should still enshroud his memory and
this, true to his nature, should be carried out in his last
will, there are those who maintain that Achille Paganini
was not his son at all—only a waif he had adopted. Yet

72

PAGANINI

Achille always stoutly maintained the distinction—but what boots it, since he could not play his father's violin? ✄ ✄

Yet this we know—Paganini, the man of mystery and moods, once lived and produced music that, Orpheus-like, transfixed the world. We are better for his having been and this world is a nobler place in that he lived and played, for listen closely and you can hear, even now, the sweet, sad echoes of those vibrant strings, touched by the hand of him who loved them well.

And when we remember the prodigious amount of practise that Paganini schooled himself to in youth; and join this to the recently discovered record of his long monastic retreats, when for months he worked and played and prayed, we can guess the secret of his power. If you wish me to present you a recipe for doing a deathless performance, I would give you this: Work, travel, solitude, prayer, and yet again—work.

FREDERIC CHOPIN

CHOPIN

Nature does not design like art, however realistic she may be. She has caprices, inconsequences, probably not real, but very mysterious. Art only rectifies these inconsequences, because it is too limited to reproduce them. Chopin was a resume of these inconsequences which God alone can allow Himself to create, and which have their particular logic. He was modest on principle, gentle by habit, but he was imperious by instinct and full of a legitimate pride which was unconscious of itself. Hence arose sufferings which he did not reason and which did not fix themselves on a determined object.

—*George Sand in " The Story of My Life"*

FREDERIC CHOPIN

AYBE I am all wrong about it, yet I can not help believing that the spirit of man will live again somewhere in a better world than ours. Fenelon says, "Justice demands another life in order to make good the inequalities of this." Astronomers prophesy the existence of stars long before they can see them. They know where they ought to be, and training their telescopes in that direction they wait, knowing they will find.

Materially, no one can imagine anything more beautiful than this earth, for the simple reason that we can not imagine anything we have not seen; we may make new combinations, but the whole is all made up of parts of things with which we are familiar. This great green earth out of which we have sprung, of which we are a part, that supports our bodies, and to which our bodies must return to repay the loan, is very, very beautiful.

¶ But the spirit of man is not fully at home here; as we grow in soul and intellect, we hear, and hear again, a voice which says, "Arise and get thee hence, for this is not thy rest." And the greater and nobler and more sublime the spirit, the more constant the discontent. Discontent may come from various causes, so it will not do to assume that the discontented are always the pure in heart, but it is a fact that the wise and excellent have all known the meaning of world-weariness. The more you study and appreciate this life, the more sure you are that this is not all. You pillow your head upon Mother Earth, listen to her heart-throb, and even as your spirit is filled with the love of her, your gladness is half-pain and there comes to you a joy that hurts.

To look upon the most exalted forms of beauty, such as a sunset at sea, the coming of a storm on the prairie, the shadowy silence of the desert, or the sublime majesty of the mountains, begets a sense of sadness, an increasing loneliness.

It is not enough to say that man encroaches on man so that we are really deprived of our freedom, that civilization is caused by a bacillus, and that from a natural condition we have gotten into a hurly-burly where rivalry is rife—all this may be true, but beyond and outside of all this there is no physical environment in way of plenty which earth can supply, that will give the tired soul peace. They are the happiest who have the least; and the fable of the stricken king and the shirtless beggar contains the germ of truth. The wise hold all earthly ties very lightly—they are stripping for eternity.

World-weariness is only a desire for a better spiritual condition. There is more to be written on this subject of world-pain—to exhaust the theme would require a book. And certain it is that I have no wish to

FREDERIC CHOPIN

say the final word on any topic. The gentle reader has certain rights, and among these is the privilege of summing up the case. But the fact holds that world-pain is a form of desire. All desires are just, proper and right; and their gratification is the means by which Nature supplies us that which we need. Desire not only causes us to seek that which we need, but is a form of attraction by which the good is brought to us, just as the ameba creates a swirl in the waters that brings its food within reach. Every desire in Nature has a fixed, definite purpose in the Divine Economy, and every desire has its proper gratification. If we desire the friendship of a certain person, it is because that person has certain soul-qualities that we do not possess, and which complement our own. Through desire do we come into possession of our own; by submitting to its beckonings we add cubits to our stature; and we also give out to others our own attributes, without becoming poorer, for soul is not limited.

All Nature is a symbol of spirit, so I believe that somewhere there must be a proper gratification for this mysterious nostalgia of the soul. The Eternal Unities require a condition where men and women will live to love, and not to sorrow; where the tyranny of things hated shall not ever prevail, nor that for which the heart yearns turn to ashes at our touch.

FREDERIC CHOPIN

I BELIEVE Stevie is not quite at home here—
he'll not remain so very long," said a woman
to me in Eighteen Hundred Ninety-five.
Five years have gone by, and recently the
cable flashed the news that Stephen Crane was dead ॐ
Dead at twenty-nine, with ten books to his credit, two
of them good, which is two good books more than most
of us scribblers will ever write. Yes, Stephen Crane
wrote two things that are immortal. " The Red Badge
of Courage " is the strongest, most vivid work of
imagination ever fished from an ink-pot by an American.
¶ " Men who write from the imagination are helpless
when in presence of the fact," said James Russell Lowell.
In answer to which I 'll point you "The Open Boat,"
the sternest, creepiest bit of realism ever penned, and
Stevie was in the boat.
American critics honored Stephen Crane with more
ridicule, abuse and unkind comment than was bestowed
on any other writer of his time. Possibly the vagueness,
and the loose, unsleeked quality of his work invited the
gibes, jeers, and the loud laughter that tokens the vacant
mind; yet as half-apology for the critics we might say
that scathing criticism never killed good work; and this
is true, but it sometimes has killed the man.
Stephen Crane never answered back, nor made explanation, but that he was stung by the continued efforts of
the press to laugh him down, I am very sure.
The lack of appreciation at home caused him to shake

FREDERIC CHOPIN

the dust of America from his feet and take up his abode across the sea, where his genius was being recognized, and where strong men stretched out sinewy hands of welcome, and words of appreciation were heard, instead of silly, insulting parody. In passing, it is well to note that the five strongest writers of America had their passports to greatness viséed in England before they were granted recognition at home. I refer to Walt Whitman, Thoreau, Emerson, Poe and Stephen Crane.

Stevie did not know he cared for approbation, but his constant refusal to read what the newspapers said about him was proof that he did. He boycotted the tribe of Romeike, because he knew that nine clippings out of every ten would be unkind, and his sensitive soul shrank from the pin-pricks.

Contemporary estimates are usually wrong, and Crane is only another of the long list of men of genius to whom Fame brings a wreath and finds her poet dead.

Stephen Crane was a reincarnation of Frederic Chopin. Both were small in stature, slight, fair-haired, and of that sensitive, acute, receptive temperament—capable of highest joy and keyed for exquisite pain. Haunted with the prophetic vision of quick-coming death, and with the hectic desire to get their work done, they often toiled the night away and were surprised by the rays of the rising sun. Both were shrinking yet proud, shy but bold, with a tenderness and a feminine longing for love that earth could not requite. At times mad gaiety, that

81

FREDERIC CHOPIN

ill-masked a breaking heart, took the reins, and the spirits of children just out of school seemed to hold the road. At other times—and this was the prevailing mood—the manner was one of placid, patient, calm and smooth, unruffled hope; but back and behind all was a dynamo of energy, a brooding melancholy of unrest, and the crouching world-sorrow that would not down.

Chopin reached sublimity through sweet sounds; Crane attained the same heights through the sense of sight and words that symboled color, shapes and scenes. In each the distinguishing feature is the intense imagination and active sympathy. Knowledge consists in a sense of values—of distinguishing this from that, for truth lies in the mass. The delicate nuances of Chopin's music have never been equaled by another composer; every note is cryptic, every sound a symbol. And yet it is dance-music, too, but still it tells its story of baffled hope and stifled desire—the tragedy of Poland in sweet sounds.

Stephen Crane was an artist in his ability to convey the feeling by just the right word, or a word misplaced, like a lady's dress in disarray, or a hat askew. This daring quality marks everything he wrote. The recognition that language is fluid, and at best only an expedient, flavors all his work. He makes no fetish of a grammar— if grammar gets in the way, so much the worse for the grammar. All is packed with color, and charged with feeling, yet the work is usually quiet in quality and

82

FREDERIC CHOPIN

modest in manner. ¶Art is born of heart, not head; and
so it seems to me that the work of these men whose
names I have somewhat arbitrarily linked, will live.
Each sowed in sorrow and reaped in grief. They were
tender, kind, gentle, with a capacity for love that passes
the love of woman. They were each indifferent to the
proprieties, very much as children are. They lived in
cloister-like retirement, hidden from the public gaze,
or wandered unnoticed and unknown. They founded
no schools, delivered no public addresses, and in their
own day made small impress on the times. Both were
sublimely indifferent to what had been said and done
—the term precedent not being found within the covers
of their bright lexicon of words. In the nature of each
was a goodly trace of peroxide of iron that often mani-
fested itself in the man's work,
The faults in each spring from an intense personality,
uncolored by the surroundings, and such faults in such
men are virtues.
They belong to that elect few who have built for the
centuries. The influence of Chopin, beyond that of other
composers, is alive today, and moves unconsciously, but
profoundly, every music-maker; the seemingly careless
style of Crane is really lapidaric, and is helping to file
the fetters from every writer who has ideas plus, and
thoughts that burn.
Mother Nature in giving out energy gives each man
about an equal portion. But that ability to throw the

83

FREDERIC CHOPIN

weight with the blow, to concentrate the soul in a
sonnet, to focus force in a single effort, is the possession
of God's Chosen Few. Chopin put his affection, his
patriotism, his wrath, his hope, and his heroism into his
music—as if the song of all the forest birds could be
secured, sealed and saved for us!

FREDERIC CHOPIN

HE father of Chopin was a Frenchman who went up to Poland seeking gain and adventure. He became a soldier under Kosciusko and arose to rank of Captain. He found such favor with the nobility by his gracious ways that he became a teacher of French in the family of Count Frederic Skarbek. In the family group was a fair young dependent of nervous temperament—slight, active, gentle and intelligent. She was descendent from a line of aristocrats, but in a country where revolutions have been known to begin and end before breakfast, titles stand for little.

Nicholas Chopin, ex-soldier, teacher of French and Deportment, married this fine young girl, and they lived in one of Count Skarbek's straw-thatched cottages at the little village of Zelazowa-Wola, twenty-nine miles from Warsaw. Here it was that Frederic Chopin was born, in Eighteen Hundred Nine—that memorable year when Destiny sent a flight of great souls to the planet Earth.

The country was bleak and battle-scarred; it had been drained of its men and treasure, and served as a dueling-ground and the place of skulls for kings and such riffraff who have polluted this fair world with their boastings of a divine power.

The struggle of Poland to free herself from the grip of the imperial succubi has generated an atmosphere of ultramarine, so we view the little land of patriots (and fanatics) through a mist of melancholy. The history of Poland is written in blood and tears.

Go ask John Sobieski, who saw his father hanged by order of Ferdinand Maximilian, and child though he was, realized that banishment was the fate of himself and mother; and then ten years after, himself, stood death-guard over this same Maximilian in Mexico, and told that tyrant the story of his life, and shook hands with him, calling it quits, ere the bandage was tied over the eyes of the ex-dictator and the sunlight shut out forever ❧ ❧

Go ask John Sobieski!

The woes of Poland have produced strange men. Under such rule as she has known relentless hate springs up in otherwise gracious hearts from the scattered dragons' teeth; and in other natures, where there is not quite so much of the motive temperament, a deep strain of sorrow and religious melancholy finds expression. The exquisite sensibility, delicate insight, proud reserve and brooding world-sorrow of Frederic Chopin were the inheritance of mother to son. This mother's mind was saturated with the wrongs her people had endured: she herself had suffered every contumely, for where chance had caused fact to falter, imagination had filled the void ❧ ❧

It is easy to say that Chopin's was an abnormal nature, and of course it was, but when disease divides this world from another only by the thinnest veil, the mind has

FREDERIC CHOPIN

been known to see things with a clearness and vividness never before attained. With Chopin the strands of life were often taut to the breaking-point, but ere they snapped, their vibration gave forth to us some exquisite harmonies ✙ ✙

Curiously enough, this power to see and do is often the possession of dying men. The life flares up in a flame before it goes out forever. The passion of the consumptive Camille, as portrayed by Dumas, is typical—no healthy woman ever loved with that same intense, eager and almost vindictive desire. It was a race with Death ✙ ✙

Perfect health brings unconsciousness of body, and disease that almost relieves the spirit of this weight of flesh produces the same results. Again we have the Law of Antithesis.

That such a youth as Frederic Chopin should seek in music a surcease from his world-sorrow is very natural. A stricken people turns to music; it forms a necessary part of all religious observance, and the dirge of mourners, the wail of the " keener," and the songs of the banshee evolve naturally into being wherever the heart is sore oppressed. It was the slave-songs that made slavery bearable; and in the long ago, exiles in Babylon found a solemn joy by singing the songs of Zion. Chopin drank in the songs of Poland with his mother's milk, and while yet a child began to give them voice in his own way.

FREDERIC CHOPIN

In the meantime his father's fortunes had mended a bit, and the family had moved to Warsaw, where Nicholas Chopin was Professor of Languages at the Lyceum. The title of the office fills the mouth in a very satisfying way, but the emoluments attached hardly afforded such a gratification ⚜ ⚜

In Warsaw there was much misery, for the plunderer had worked conscription and seizure to its furthest limit. Want and destitution were on every hand, but still this brave people maintained their University and clung to its traditions. The family of the Professor of Languages consisted of himself, wife, three daughters and the son Frederic. Their income for several years was not over fifteen dollars a month, but still they managed to maintain an appearance of decency, and by the help of the public library, the free museum and the open-air concerts, they kept abreast of the times in literature, art and music.

There was absolute economy required, every particle of food was saved, and when cast-off dresses were sent from the home of the Count it was a godsend for the mother and girls, who measured and patched and pieced, making garments for themselves, and for Frederic as well; so while their raiment was not gaudy nor expressed in fancy, it served.

Chopin once said to George Sand, " I never can think of my mother without her knitting-needles!" And George Sand has recorded, " Frederic never had but

FREDERIC CHOPIN

one passion and that was his mother." ¶ Into all of her knitting this mother's flying needles worked much love. The entire household was one of mutual service, and gentle, trusting affection. The weekly letters of Chopin to his mother from Paris, and the cold sweat on his forehead at the thought of his parents knowing of his relationship with George Sand, are credit-marks to his character. There is a sweet recompense in mutual deprivation where trials and difficulties only serve to cement the affections; and who shall say how much the wondrous blending of strength and delicacy in the music of Chopin is due to the memory of those early days of toil and trial, of strength and forbearance, of hope and love? ✄ ✄

To be born into such a family is a great blessing. The value of the environment is shown in that all three of the sisters became distinguished in literature. Two of them married men of intellect, wealth and worth, and through the collaboration of these sisters, books were produced that did for the plain people of Poland what Harriet Martineau's books on sociology did for the people of England. Frederic played and practised at the Lyceum where his father taught, and the ambition of his parents was that he should grow up and take the place of Professor of Music in the Lyceum. Adalbert Zevyny, one of the leading pianists in the city, became attracted to the boy and took him as a pupil, without pay ✄ ✄

FREDERIC CHOPIN

The teacher soon became a little boastful of his precocious pupil, and when there came a public concert for the benefit of the poor, we find reference made to Chopin thus, "A child not yet eight years of age played, and connoisseurs say he promises to replace Mozart." In reality the boy was nearer twelve than eight, but his size and looks suggested to the management the idea of plagiarizing, in advance, our honored countryman, Phineas T. Barnum. Hence the announcement on the programs.

But now the nobility of the neighborhood began to send carriages for the fair-haired lad, so he could play for their invited guests. Then came snug little honorariums that soon replaced his patched-up wardrobe for something more fashionable.

Frederic took all the applause quite as a matter of course, and on one occasion, after he had played divinely, he asked a proud lady this question, " How do you like my new collar? "

He was to the manner born, and the gentle blood of his mother formed him as a fit companion for aristocrats.

These occasional musicales at the houses of the great made money matters easier, and Frederic began to take lessons from Joseph Elsner, who taught him the science of composition, and introduced him into the deeper mysteries of music-making. Elsner, it was, more than any other man, who forced the truth upon Chopin that he must play to satisfy himself, and in composition be

90

his own most exacting critic. In other words, Elsner developed and strengthened in Chopin the artistic conscience—that impulse which causes an artist to scorn doing anything save his best.

From little excursions to neighboring towns and country houses about Warsaw, Chopin now ventured farther away from home, chaperoned by his friend, Prince Radziwill. He visited Berlin, Venice, Prague, Heidelberg, and mingled on an absolute equality with the nobility. If they had titles, he had talents. And his talents often made their decorations sing small.

His modesty was witching, and while in public concerts his playing was not pronounced enough to capture the gallery, yet in small gatherings he won all hearts, and the fact that he played his own compositions made him an added object of enthusiasm to the elect. Chopin arrived in Paris when he was twenty-two years of age. It was not his intention to remain more than a few weeks, but Paris was to be his home for eighteen years— and then Pere la Chaise.

FREDERIC CHOPIN

WOMAN who beholds her thirtieth birthday in sight, and girlhood gone, is approaching a climacteric in her career. Flaubert has named twenty-nine as the eventful year in the life of woman, and thirty-three for men. Every normal woman craves love and tenderness—these are her God-given right. If they have not come to her by the time the bloom is fading from her cheeks, there is danger of her reaching out and clutching for them. The strongest instinct in young girls is self-protection—they fight on the defensive. But at thirty, women have been known to grow a trifle anxious, just as did the Sabine women who dispatched a messenger to the Romans asking this question, " How soon does the program begin ? "

And thus are conditions reversed, for it is the youth of twenty or so who seeks conquest with fiery soul. Alexander was only nineteen when he sighed for more worlds to conquer. He did n't have to wait long before he found that this one had conquered him. Youth considers itself immortal, and its powers without limit, but as a man approaches thirty he grows economical of his resources and parsimonious of his emotions. Men of thirty, or so, are apt to be coy.

And so one might say that it is around thirty that for the first time the man and the woman meet on an equality, without sham, shame or pretense. Before that time the average woman abounds in affectation and untruth; the man is absurdly aggressive and full of foolish flattery.

92

FREDERIC CHOPIN

¶ As to the question, " Should women propose? " the
answer is, " Yes, certainly, and they do when they are
twenty-nine."
Aurore Dudevant saw her thirtieth birthday looming on
the horizon of her life. Nine years before she had been
married to an ex-army-officer, who dyed his whiskers
purple. Aurore had been a dutiful wife, intent for the
first few years on filling her husband's heart and home
with joy. She had failed in this, and the proof of failure
lay in that he much preferred his dogs, guns and horses
to her society. For days he would absent himself on his
hunting excursions, and at home he did not have the
tact to hide the fact that he was awfully bored.
Thackeray, once for all, has given us a picture of the
heavy dragoon with a soul for dogs—one to whom all
music, save the bay of a fox-hound, makes its appeal in
vain. Aurore detested dogs for dogs' sake, yet she
rode horses astride with a daring that made her husband's bloodshot eyes bulge in alarm. He did n't much
care how fast and hard she rode at the fences and over
the ditches, but he was supposed to follow her, and this
he did not care to do. He had reached an age when a
man is mindful of the lime in his bones, and his 'cross-
country riding was mostly a matter of memory and
imagination, and best done around the convivial table.
¶ Aurore was putting him to a test, that 's all. She was
proving to him that she could meet him on his own
preserve, give him choice of weapons, and make him

93

cry for mercy. ¶ Her bent was literature, with music, science and art as side-lines. She read Montaigne, Rochefoucald, Racine and Moliere, and a modern by the name of Alfred de Musset, and quoted her authors at inconvenient times. She flashed quotations and epigrams upon the doughty dragoon in a way he could neither fend nor parry. At other times she was deeply religious and tearfully penitent.

In fact, she was living on a skimped allowance of love, and had never received the attention that a good woman deserves. Her chains were galling her. She sighed for Paris—forty miles away—Paris and a career.

The epigrams were coming faster, shot in a sort of frenzy and fever. And when she asked her liege for leave to go to Paris, he granted her prayer, and agreed to give her ten dollars a week allowance.

She grabbed at the offer, and he bade her Godspeed and good riddance.

So leaving her two children behind, until such a time as she could provide a home for them, with scanty luggage and light heart and purse, she started away.

Other women have gone up to Paris from country towns, too, and the chances are as one to ten thousand that the maelstrom will sweep them into hades.

But Madame Dudevant was different—in two years she had won her way to literary fame, and was commanding the jealous admiration of the best writers of Paris. Her first work was a collaboration with Jules

FREDERIC CHOPIN

Sandeau in a novel. Every woman who ever wrote well began by collaborating with a man. Sandeau had formerly come from Nohant, and how much he had to do with Madame Dudevant's breaking loose from her homes-ties no one knows. Anyway, the second novel was written by the Madame alone, and as a tribute to her friend the name " George Sand " was placed upon the title-page as author. Jules Sandeau, all-'round hack-writer and critic, was greatly pleased by the compliment of having his name anglicized and printed on the title-page of " Indiana," but later he was not so proud of it. George Sand soon proved herself to be a bigger man than Sandeau.

She was not handsome, either in face or in form. She was inclined to be stout—was rather short—and her complexion olive. But she lured with her eyes—great sphinx-like eyes of hazel-brown—that looked men through and through. Liszt has told us that " she had eyes like a cow," which is not so bad as Thomas Carlyle's remark that George Eliot had a face like a horse. George Sand was silent when other women talked, and her look told in a half-proud, half-sad way that she knew all they knew, and all she herself knew beside. ¶ Without going into the issue as to what George Sand was not, let us frankly admit that pain, deprivation, misunderstanding and maternity had taught her many things not found in books, and that she looked at Fate out of her wide-open eyes with a gaze that did not blink.

95

She was wise beyond the lot of women. I was just going to say she was a genius, but I remember the remark of the De Goncourts to the effect that, "There are no women of genius—women of genius are men." Possibly the point could be covered by saying George Sand had a man's head and a woman's heart.

Women did not like her, yet what other woman was ever so honored by woman as was George Sand in those two matchless sonnets addressed to her by Elizabeth Barrett Browning?

The amazing energy of George Sand, her finely flowing sentences—all charged with daring satire and insight into the heart of things—made her work sought by readers and publishers. Her pen brought her all the money she needed; and she had secured a divorce from "That Man," and now had her two children with her in Paris. That she could do her literary work and still attend to her manifold social duties must ever mark her as a phenomenon. She was no mere adventuress. That she was systematic, orderly and abstemious in her habits must go without saying, otherwise her vitality would not have held out and allowed her to attend the funerals of nearly all her retainers.

In throwing overboard the Grub Street Sandeau for Franz Liszt, Madame Dudevant certainly showed discrimination; but in retaining the name of "Sand," she paid a delicate compliment to the man who first introduced her to the world of art. Liszt was too strong a man to remain long captive—he refused to supply the doglike and abject devotion which Aurore always demanded. Then came Michael de Bourges the learned counsel, Calmatto the mezzotinter, Delacroix the artist, De Musset the poet, and Chopin the musician.

It was in the year Eighteen Hundred Thirty-nine, that Chopin and Sand first met at a parlor musicale, where Chopin was taken by Liszt, half against his will, simply because George Sand was to be there.

Chopin did not want to meet her.

All Paris had rung with the story of how she and De Musset had gone together to Venice, and then in less than a year had quarreled and separated. Both made good copy of the " poetic interval," as George Sand called it. Chopin was not a stickler for conventionalities, but George Sand's history, for him, proved her to be coarse and devoid of all the finer feeling that we prize in women.

Chopin had no fear of her—not he—only he did not care to add to his circle of acquaintances one so lacking in inward grace and delicacy.

He played at the musicale—it was all very informal— and George Sand pushed her way up through the throng that stood about the piano and looked at the handsome boy as he played—she looked at him with her big, hazel, cow eyes, steadfastly, yearningly, and he glancing up, saw the eyes were filled with tears.

When the playing ceased, she still stood looking at the

FREDERIC CHOPIN

---

great musician, and then she leaned over the piano and whispered, " Your playing makes me live over again every pain that has ever wrung my heart; and every joy, too, that I have ever known is mine again." &

FREDERIC CHOPIN

FTER their first meeting, when Chopin played at a musicale, George Sand was apt to be there too—they often came together. She was five years older than he, and looked fifteen, for his slight figure and delicate, boyish face gave him the appearance of youth unto the very last. In letters to Madame Mariana, George Sand often refers to Chopin as "My Little One," and when some one spoke of him as "The Chopinetto," the name seemed to stick.

That she was the man in the partnership is very evident. He really needed some one to look after him, provide mustard-plasters and run for the camphor and hot-water bottle. He was the one who did the weeping and pouting, and had the "nerves" and made the scenes; while she, on such occasions, would viciously roll a cigarette, swear under her breath, console and pooh-pooh.

Liszt has told us how, on one occasion, she had gone out at night for a storm-walk, and Chopin, being too ill, or disinclined to go, remained at home. Upon her return she found him in a conniption, he having composed a prelude to ward off an attack of cold feet, and was now ready to scream through fear that something had happened to her. As she entered the door he arose, staggered and fell before her in a fainting fit.

A whole literature has grown up around the relations of Chopin and George Sand, and the lady in the case has, herself, set forth her brief with painstaking detail in her

FREDERIC CHOPIN

"Histoire de Ma Vie." With De Musset, George Sand had to reckon on dealing with a writing man, and his accounts of " The Little White Blackbird " had taught her caution. Thereafter she abjured the litterateurs, excepting when in her old age she allowed Gustave Flaubert to come within her sacred circle—but her friendship with Flaubert was placidly platonic, as all the world knows. And so were her relations with Chopin, provided we accept her version as gospel fact.

George Sand lacked the frankness of Rousseau; but I think we should be willing to accept the lady's statements, for she was present and really the only one in possession of the facts, excepting, of course, Chopin, and he was not a writer. He could express himself only at the keyboard, and the piano is no graphophone, for which let us all be duly thankful. So we are without Chopin's side of the story. We, however, have some vigorous writing by a man by the name of Hadow $\mathcal{S}$ Mr. Hadow enters the lists panoplied with facts, and declares that the friendship was strictly platonic, being on the woman's side of a purely maternal order. Chopin was sick and friendless, and Madame Dudevant, knowing his worth to the art world, succored him—nursing him as a Sister of Charity might, sacrificing herself, and even risking her reputation in order to restore him to life and health.

And this view of the case I am quite willing to accept. Mr. Hadow is no joker, like that man who has recently

100

---

written an appreciation of Xantippe, showing that the wife of Socrates was one of the most patient women who ever lived, and only at times resorted to heroic means in order to drive her husband out into the world of thought. She willingly sacrificed her own good name that another might have literary life.

Hadow has gotten all the facts together and then dispassionately drawn his conclusions; and these conclusions are eminently complimentary to all parties concerned 🙠 🙠

It was only a few months after Chopin met George Sand that he was attacked with a peculiar hacking cough. His friends were sure it was consumption, and a leading physician gave it as his opinion that if the patient spent the approaching Winter in Paris, it would be death in March 🙠 🙠

The facts being brought to the notice of George Sand, she had but one thought—to save the life of this young man. He was too ill to decide what was best to do, and was never able by temperament to take the initiative, anyway, so this strong and capable woman, forgetful of self and her own interests, made all the arrangements and took him to the Isle of Majorca in the Mediterranean Sea. There she cared for him alone as she might for a babe, for six long, weary months. They lived in the cells of an old monastery at Valdemosa, away up on the mountainside overlooking the sea. Here where the roses bloomed the whole year through, surrounded by groves of orange-trees, shut in by vines and flowers, with no society save that of the sacristan and an aged woman servant, she nursed the death-stricken man back to life and hope.

To better encourage him she sent for and surprised him with his piano, which had to be carried up the mountain on the backs of mules. In the quiet cloisters she cared for him with motherly tenderness, and there he learned again to awake the slumbering echoes with divine music. Several of his best pieces were composed at Majorca during his convalescence, where the soft semi-tropical breeze laved his cheek, the birds warbled him their sweetest carols, and away down below, the sea, mother of all, sang her ceaseless lullaby. When they returned to France the following Spring, M. Dudevant had accommodatingly vacated the family residence at Nohant in favor of his wife. It was here she took the convalescent Chopin. He was charmed with the rambling old house, its walled-in gardens with their arbors of clustering grapes, and the green meadows stretching down to the water's edge, where the little river ran its way to the ocean ❦ ❦

Back of the house was a great forest of mighty trees, beneath whose thick shade the sun's rays never entered, and a half-mile away arose the spire of the village church. There were no neighbors, save a cheery old priest, and the simple villagers who made respectful obeisance as they passed.

FREDERIC CHOPIN

Here it was that Matthew Arnold came to pay his tribute to genius, also Liszt and the fair Countess d'Agoult, Delacroix, Renan, Lamennais, Lamartine, and so many others of the great and excellent. Chopin was enchanted with the place, and refused to go back to Paris. Madame Dudevant insisted, and explained to him that she took him to Majorca to spend the Winter, but she had no intention or thought of caring for him longer than the few months that might be required to restore him to health. But he cried and clung to her with such half-childish fright that she had not the heart to send him away.

The summer months passed and the leaves began to turn scarlet and gold, and he only consented to return to Paris on her agreeing to go with him. So they returned together, and had rooms not so very far apart.

He went back sturdily to his music-teaching, with an occasional musicale, yet gave but one public concert in the space of ten years.

The exquisite quality of Chopin's playing appealed only to the sacred few, but his piano scores were slowly finding sale, through the advertisement they received by being played by Liszt, Tausig and others. Yet the critics almost uniformly condemned his work as bizarre and erratic.

Each Summer he spent at lovely Nohant, and there found the rest and quiet which got nerves back to the norm and allowed him to go on with his work. So passed

FREDERIC CHOPIN

the years away. Of this we are very sure—no taint
exists on the record of Chopin excepting possibly his
relationship with George Sand. That he endeavored to
win her full heart's love, for the purpose of honorable
marriage, Mr. Hadow is fully convinced. But when his
suit failed, after an eight years' courtship, and the
lover was discarded, he ceased to work. His heart was
broken; he lingered on for two years, and then death
claimed him at the early age of forty years.

FREDERIC CHOPIN

THERE is a tendency to judge a work of art by its size. Thus the sculptor who does a "heroic figure" is the man who looms large to the average visitor at the art-gallery ⚜ Chopin wrote no lengthy symphonies, oratorios or operas. His music is poetry set to exquisite sounds. Poetry is an ecstasy of the spirit, and ecstasies in their very nature are not sustained moods.

The poetic mood is transient. A composition by Chopin is a soul-ecstasy, like unto the singing of a lark.

No other man but Chopin should have been allowed to set the songs of Shelley to music. With such names as Shelley, Keats, Poe and Crane must Chopin's name be linked ⚜ ⚜

In Chopin's music there is much loose texture; there are wide-meshed chords, daring leaps and abrupt arpeggios. These have often been pointed out as faults, but such harmonious discords are now properly valued, and we see that Chopin's lapses all had meaning and purpose, in that they impart a feeling—making their appeal to souls that have suffered—souls that know.

More of Chopin's music is sold in America every year than was sold altogether during the lifetime of the composer. His name and fame grow with each year. Everywhere—wherever a piano is played—on concert platform, in studio or private parlor, there you will find the work of Frederic Chopin. That such a widespread distribution must have a potent and powerful effect

FREDERIC CHOPIN

---

upon the race goes without argument, although the furthest limit of that influence no man can mark. It is registered with Infinity alone. And thus does that modest, mild and gentle revolutionist Frederic Chopin live again in minds made better.

106

ROBERT SCHUMANN

SCHUMANN

Beneath these flowers I dream, a silent chord. I can not wake my own strings to music; but under the hands of those who comprehend me, I become an eloquent friend. Wanderer, ere thou goest, try me! The more trouble thou takest with me, the more lovely will be the tones with which I shall reward thee.

—*Robert Schumann*

ROBERT SCHUMANN

HAT any man should ever write his thoughts for other men to read, seems the very height of egoism ✵ Literature never dies, and so the person who writes constitutes himself a rival of Shakespeare and seeks to lure us from Montaigne, Milton, Emerson and Carlyle. To write nothing better than grammatical English, to punctuate properly, and repeat thoughts in the same sequence that have been repeated a thousand times, is to do something icily regular, splendidly null.

To down the demons of syntax and epithet is not enough. To compose blameless sonatas and produce symphonies in the accepted style, is not adding an iota to the world's worth.

The individual who tries to compose either ideas or harmonious sounds, and hopes for success, must compose because he can not help it. He must place the thing in a way it has never before been placed; on the subject he must throw a new light; he must carry the standard forward, and plant it one degree nearer the uncaptured citadel of the Ideal. And he must remember this: the very prominence of his position will cause him to be the target of contumely, abuse and much stupid misunderstanding. If he complains of these things (as he probably will), he reveals a rift in the lute and proves that he is only a half-god, after all.

Men of the highest type of culture—those of masterly talent—are not gregarious in their nature. The " jiner " instinct goes with a man who is a little doubtful, and so he attaches himself to this society, club or church. ¶ The very tendency to " jine " is an admission of weakness—it is a getting under cover, a combining against the supposed enemy. The " jiner " is an ameba that clings to flotsam, instead of floating free in the great ocean of life. The lion loves his mate, but prefers to flock by himself.

The pioneer in art, as in any other field, must be willing to face deprivations and loneliness and heart-hunger. He must find companionship with birds and animals, and be brother to the trees and swift-flying clouds. When men meet on the desert or in the forest wilds, how grateful and how gracious is their hand-clasp! When love and understanding come to those who live on the border-land of two worlds, how precious and priceless the boon!

ROBERT SCHUMANN

ROBERT SCHUMANN was the son of a book-publisher of Zwickau. He was a handsome lad with the flash of genius in his luminous eyes, and an independence like that of an Alpine goat. When very young they say he used to have tantrums. If your child has a tantrum, it is bad policy for you to imitate him and have one, too.

A tantrum is only one of the little whirlwinds of God—it is misdirected energy, power not yet controlled. When Robert had a tantrum, his father would shake him violently to improve his temper, or fall upon him with a strap that hung handy behind the kitchen-door. Then the mother, when the father was out of the way, would take the lad and cry over him, and coddle him, and undo the discipline.

The best treatment for tantrums is—nothing. The more you let a nervous, impressionable child alone, the better.
¶ When the lad was fourteen years old, we find him setting type in his father's printery. He was working on a book called, " The World's Celebrities," and his share of the work dealt with Jean Paul Richter. He grew interested in the copy and stopped setting type and read ahead, as printers sometimes will. The more he read, the more he was fascinated. He fell under the spell of Jean Paul the Only.

Jean Paul, inspired by Jean Jacques, was the inspirer of the whole brood of young writers of his time. To him they looked as to a Deliverer.

ROBERT SCHUMANN

Jean Paul the Only! The largest, gentlest, most generous heart in all literature! The peculiar mark of Richter's style is analogy and comparison; everything he saw reminded him of something else, and then he tells you of things of which both remind him. He leads and lures you on, and takes you far from home, but always brings you safely back. Yet comparison proves us false when we deal with Richter himself. He stands alone, like Adam's recollection of his fall, which according to Jean Paul was the one sweet, unforgetable thing in all the life of the First Citizen of his time.

Jean Paul seems to have combined in that mighty brain all feminine as well as masculine attributes. The soul in which the feminine does not mingle is ripe for wrong, strife and unreason. " It was mother-love, carried one step further, that enabled the Savior to embrace a world," says Carlyle.

The sweep of tender emotion that murmurs and rustles through the writing of Jean Paul is like the echo of a lullaby heard in a dream. Perhaps it came from that long partnership when mother and son held the siege against poverty, and the kitchen-table served them as a writing-desk, and the patient old mother was his sole reviewer, critic, reader and public.

For shams, hypocrisy and pretense Jean Paul had a cyclone of sarcasm, and the blows he struck were such as only a son of Anak could give; but in his heart there was no hate. He could despise a man's bad habits and still love the man behind the veneer of folly. So his arms seem ever extended, welcoming the wanderer home ✂

Dear Jean Paul, big and homely, what an insight you had into the heart of things, and what a flying-machine your imagination was! Room for many passengers? Yes, and children especially, for these you loved most of all, because you were ever only just a big overgrown boy yourself. You cried your eyes out before your hair grew white, and then a child or a woman led you about; and thus did you supply Victor Hugo a saying that can not die: "To be blind and to be loved—what happier fate!" ✂ ✂

Yes, Jean Paul used to cry at his work when he wrote well, and I do, too. I always know when I write particularly well, for at such times I mop furiously. However, I seldom mop.

Robert Schumann began to write little essays, and the essays were as near like Jean Paul's as he could make them. He read them to his mother, just as Jean Paul used to write for his mother and call her " my Gentle Reader "—he had but one.

Robert's mother believed in her boy—what mother does not? But her love was not tempered by reason, and in it there was a sentimental flavor akin to the maudlin ✂

The father wanted the lad to take up his own business, as German fathers do, but the mother filled the lad's head with the thought that he was fit for something higher and better. She was not willing to let the seed

ROBERT SCHUMANN

ripen in Nature's way—she thought hothouse methods
were an improvement.

Such a mother's ambition centers in her son. She wants
him to do the thing she has never been able to do. She
thirsts for honors, applause, publicity, and all those
things that bring trouble and distress and make men old
before their time.

So we find the boy at eighteen packed off to Heidelberg
to study law, with no special preparation in knowledge
of the world, of men or books. But old father antic, the
law, was not to his taste. Robert liked music and poetry
better. His fine, sensitive, emotional spirit found its
best exercise in music; and at the house of Professor
Carus he used to sing with the professor's wife. This
Professor Carus, by the way, is, I believe, directly related
to our own Doctor Paul Carus, of whom all thinking
people in America have reason to be proud. I am told
that when a boy of eighteen or nineteen mingles his
voice several evenings a week with that of a married
lady aged, say, thirty-five, and they also play "four
hands" an hour or so a day, that the boy is apt to
surprise the married lady by falling very much in love
with her. Boys are quite given to this thing, anyway, of
falling in love with women old enough to be their
mothers—I don't know why it is. Sometimes I am rather
inclined to commend the scheme, since it often brings
good results. The fact that the woman's emotions are
well tempered with a sort of maternal regard for her

114

charge holds folly in check, dispels that tired feeling, promotes digestion, and stimulates the action of the ganglionic cells.

It was surely so in this instance, for Madame Carus taught the youth how to compose, and fired his mind to excel as a pianist. He wrote and dedicated small songs to her, and their relationship added cubits to the boy's stature ☙ ☙

From a boy he became a man at a bound. Just as one single April day, with its showers and sunshine, will transform the seemingly lifeless twigs into leafy branches, so did this young man's intellect ripen in the sunshine of love.

As for Professor Carus, he was too busy with his theorems and biological experiments to trouble himself about so trivial a matter as a youngster falling in love with his accomplished wife—here the Professor's good sense was shown.

Jean Paul Richter lighted his torch at the flame of Jean Jacques Rousseau. In a letter to Agnes Carus, Schumann has acknowledged his obligation to Richter, in a style that is truly Richteresque.

Says Robert:

Dear Lady:—I read from Jean Paul last night until I fell asleep and then I dreamed of you. It was at the torch of Jean Paul that I lighted my tallow dip, and now he is dead and these eyes shall never look into his, nor will his voice fall upon my ears. I cry salt tears to

ROBERT SCHUMANN

think that Jean Paul never knew you. If I could only have brought you two together and then looked upon you, realizing, as I would, that you had both come from High Olympus! Blissful are the days since I knew you, for you have brought within my range of vision new constellations, and into my soul has come the clear, white light of peace and truth. With you I am purified, freed from sin, and harmony fills my tired heart. Without you—why, really I have never dared think about it, for fear that reason would topple, and my mind forget its 'customed way—let 's talk of music * * *

Professor Carus kept his ear close to the ground for a higher call, and when the call came from Leipzig, he moved there with his family.

It was not many weeks before Robert was writing home, explaining that lawyers were men who get good people into trouble, and bad folks out; and as for himself he had decided to cut the business and fling himself into the arms of the Muse.

This letter brought his mother down upon him with tears and pleadings that he would not fail to redeem the Schumanns by becoming a Great Man. Poetry was foolishness and all musicians were poor—there were a hundred of them in Zwickau who lived on rye-bread and wienerwurst 🦢 🦢

The boy promised and the mother went home pacified. But not many weeks had passed before Robert set out on a pilgrimage to Bayreuth, to visit the scene of Jean Paul's romances. On this same tour he went to Munich,

and there met Heinrich Heine, who was from that day
to enter into his heart and jostle Jean Paul for first
place. He was accompanied on this memorable trip by
Gisbert Rosen, who proved his lifelong friend and
confidant. Very naturally Leipzig was the ardently
desired goal of his wanderings. At once on arriving
there, he sought out the home of Professor and Madame
Carus. That his greeting (and mayhap hers) did not
contain all the warmth the boy lover had anticipated is
shown in a letter to Rosen, wherein he says: " This world
is only a huge graveyard of buried dreams, a garden of
cypress and weeping willows, a silent peep-show with
tearful puppets. Alas for our high faith—I wonder if
Jean Paul was n't right when he said that love lessens
woman's delicacy, and time and distance dissipate it
like morning dew? "

Yet Madame Carus was kind, for Robert played at
little informal concerts at her house, and she urged him
to abandon law for music; and he refers the matter to
Rosen, asking Rosen's advice and explaining how he
wants to be advised, just as we usually do. Rosen tells
him that no man can succeed at an undertaking unless
his heart is in the work, and so he shifts the responsibility
of deciding on Professor Carus, whom Robert "respects,"
but does not exactly admire enough to follow his advice.
¶ Robert does not consider the Professor a practical
man, and so leaves the matter to his wife. In the meantime songs are written similar to Heine's, and essays

117

turned off, pinned with the precise synonym, the phrase exquisite, just like Jean Paul's. Progress in piano-playing goes steadily forward, with practise on the violin, all under the tutelage of Madame Carus, who one fine day takes the young man to play for Frederick Wieck, the best music-teacher in Leipzig.

ROBERT SCHUMANN

USICIANS?" said Wieck, "I raise them!"
¶ And so he did. He proved the value of his
theories by making great performers of Maria
and Clara, his daughters—two sisters more
gifted in a musical way have never been born. Germany
excels in philosophy and music—a seeming paradox.
Music is supposed to be a compound of the stuff that
dreams are made of—hazy, misty, dim, intangible feelings set to sounds—we close our eyes and they take us
captive and carry us away on the wings of melody. And
so it may be true that music is born of moonshine, and
fragrant memories, and hopes too great for earth, and
loves unrealized; yet its expression is the most exacting
of sciences. A Great Musician has not only to be a poet
and a dreamer, but he must also be a mathematician,
cold as chilled steel, and a philosopher who can follow a
reason to its lair and grapple it to the death. And that
is why Great Musicians are so rare, and that is also why,
perhaps, there are no great women composers. " Women
of genius are men," said the De Goncourts. A Great
Musician is a paradox, a miracle, a multiple-sided man
—stern, firm, selfish, proud and unyielding; yet sen-
suous as the ether, tender as a woman, innocent as a
child, and as plastic as potters' clay. And with most of
them, let us frankly admit it, the hand of the Potter
shook. When people write about musicians, they seldom
write moderately. The man is either a selfish rogue or an
angel of light—it all depends upon your point of view.

ROBERT SCHUMANN

And the curious part is, both sides are right. ¶ Wieck
was very fond of his daughters, and like good house-
wives who are proud of their biscuit, he apologized for
them. " He never quite forgave our mother because we
were girls," said Clara once, to Kalkbrenner. Wieck,
the good man, was a philosopher, and he had a notion
that the blood of woman is thinner than that of man—
that it contains more white serum and fewer red
corpuscles, and that Nature has designed the body of a
woman to nourish her offspring, but that man's energy
goes to feed his brain. Yet his girls were so much beyond
average mortals that they would set men a pace in spite
of the handicap.

Fortunate it is for me that I do not have to act as the
court of last appeal on this genius business. The man
who decides against woman will forfeit his popularity,
have his reputation ripped into carpet-rags, and his
good name worked up into crazy-quilts by a thousand
Woman's Clubs.

But certain it is that women are the inspirers of music.
As critics they are more judicial and more appreciative.
Without women there would be no Symphony Concerts,
any more than there would be churches.

Women take men to the Grand Opera and to Musical
Festivals—and I am glad.

120

ROBERT SCHUMANN

CLARA WIECK was only ten years old, with dresses that came to her knees, when Robert Schumann first began to take lessons of her father. She was tall for her age, and had a habit of brushing her hair from her eyes as she played, that impressed the young man as very funny. She could not remember a time when she did not play: and she showed such ease and abandon that her father used to call her in and have her illustrate his ideas on the keyboard ⚜ ⚜

Robert did n't like the child—she was needlessly talented. She could do, just as a matter of course, the things that he could scarcely accomplish with great effort. He did n't like her.

Already Clara had played in various concerts, and was a great favorite with the local public. Soon her father planned little tours, when he gave performances assisted by his two daughters, who could play both violin and piano. Their fame grew and fortune smiled. Wieck took a larger house and raised his prices for pupils.

Robert Schumann wandered over to Zwickau to visit his folks, then went on down the Rhine to Heidelberg to see Rosen. It was nearly a year before he got back to Leipzig, resolved to continue his music studies. Wieck had a front room vacant, and so the young man took lodgings with his teacher.

It was not so very long before Clara was wearing her dresses a little longer. She now dressed her hair in two

121

braids instead of one, and these braids were tied with ribbons instead of a shoe-string. More concerts were being arranged, and the attendance was larger—people were saying that Clara Wieck was an Infant Phenomenon ✣ ✣

Robert was progressing, but not so rapidly as he wished. To aid matters a bit, he invented a brace and extension to his middle finger. It gave him a farther reach and a stronger stroke, he thought. In secret he practised for hours with this "corset" on his finger; he did n't know that a corset means weakness, not strength. After three straight hours of practise one day, he took the machine from his hand and was astonished to see the finger curl up like a pretzel. He hurried to a physician and was told that the member was paralyzed. Various forms of treatment were tried, but the tendons were injured, and at last the doctors told him his brain could never again telegraph to that hand so it would perfectly obey orders. He begged that they would cut the finger off, but this they refused to do, claiming that, even though the finger was in the way, piano-playing in any event was not the chief end of man—he might try a pick and shovel ✣ ✣

Clara, who now wore her dress to her shoe-tops, sympathized with the young man in his distress. She said, "Never mind, I will play for you—you write the music and I will play it!"

Gradually he became resigned to this, and spent much

ROBERT SCHUMANN

of his time composing music for Heine's songs and his own. Wieck did n't much like these songs, and forbade his daughter playing such trashy things—only a paraphrase of Schubert's work, anyway, goodness me! The girl pouted and rebelled, and erelong Robert Schumann was requested to take lodgings elsewhere. Moodily he obeyed, but he managed to keep up a secret correspondence with Clara, through the help of her sister. Whenever Clara played in public, Robert was sure to be there, even though the distance were a hundred miles. He had given up playing, and now swung between composing and literature, having assumed the editorship of a musical magazine.

When Clara now played in concert, she wore a train, and her hair was done up on the top of her head.

Schumann's musical magazine was winning its way—the young man had a literary style. Mendelssohn commended the magazine, and its editor in turn commended Mendelssohn. A new star had been discovered on the horizon—a Pole, Chopin by name. And whenever Clara Wieck appeared, there were extended notices, lavish in praise, profuse in prophecy.

Herz had written an article for a rival journal about Clara Wieck, wherein the statement was made that no woman trained on, that her playing was intuitive, and the limit quickly reached—marriage was death to a woman's art, etc.

To this Schumann replied with needless heat, and his

123

friends began to joke him about his "disinterested-ness." He was getting moody, and there were times when he was silent for days. His passion for Clara Wieck was consuming his life. He resolved to go direct to Frederick Wieck and have it out.

ROBERT SCHUMANN

HEY are always called " the Schumanns "— Robert and Clara. You can not separate them, any more than you can separate the great Robert Browning and Elizabeth Barrett. " Whomsoever God hath joined together, let no man put asunder," seems rather a needless injunction, since we know that man's efforts in the line of separation have ever but one result: opposition fans the flame ⚜ Just as Elizabeth Barrett's father forcibly opposed the mating of his daughter, so did Frederick Wieck oppose the love of his daughter Clara for Robert Schumann ⚜ And one can not blame the man so very much—he knew the young man and he knew the girl; and deducting fifty per cent for paternal pride, he saw that the girl was much the stronger character of the two. Clara had already a recognized reputation as a performer; her playing had made her father rich, and he was sure that greater things were to come. Beside that, she was only seventeen years old—a mere child.

Robert was twenty-six, with most of his future before him—he was advised to win a name and place for himself before aspiring to the hand of a great artist: and so he was bowed out.

He took the matter into the courts, and the decision was that, as she was now eighteen years old, she had the right to wed, if she were so minded.

And so they were married; but Frederick Wieck was not present at the ceremony to give the bride away.

ROBERT SCHUMANN

CHUMANN was essentially feminine in many ways, as the best men always are. In spite of his mental independence, he did his best work when shielded in the shadow of a stronger personality. Without Clara, Robert would probably be unknown to us. She gave him the courage and the confidence that he lacked; and she it was who interpreted his work to the world.

Heine characterized Meyerbeer's " Les Huguenots " as " like a Gothic cathedral whose heaven-soaring spire and colossal cupolas seem to have been planted there by the sure hand of a giant; whereas the innumerable features, the rosettes and arabesques that are spread over it everywhere like a lacework of stone, witness to the indefatigable patience of a dwarf."

Very different is the work of Robert Schumann, who, like his master Schubert, knew little of the architectonics of the Art Divine. But Schubert seems to have been the first to give us the " lyric cry "—the prayer of a heart bowed down, or the ecstasy of a soul enrapt.

Schumann built on Schubert. Music was to Schumann the expression of an emotion. He saw in pictures, then he told in tones, what his inward eye beheld. He even went so far as to give the names of persons, their peculiarities and experiences on the keyboard. It is needless to say that the tension of mind in such experiments is apt to reach the breaking strain. We are under bonds for the moderate use of every faculty, and he who

ROBERT SCHUMANN

misuses any of God's gifts may not hope to go unscathed.
¶ The exquisite quality of Robert Schumann's imagination served to make him shun the society of vulgar
people. The inability to grasp things intuitively harassed
him, and he acquired a habit of keeping silence, except
with the elect. He lived within himself, unless Clara
were by, and then he leaned on her.

And what a strong, brave and beautiful soul she was!
In a sense she sacrificed her own career for the man she
loved. And by giving all, she won all.

Most descriptions of women begin by telling how the
individual looked and what she wore. No pen-portraits
of Clara Schumann have come down to us, for the
reason that she was too great, too elusive in spirit, for
any snapshot artist to attempt her. She never looked
twice the same. In feature she was commonplace, her
form lacked the classic touch, and her raiment was as
plain as the plumage of a brown thrush in an autumn
hedgerow. She was as homely as George Eliot, Mary
Wollstonecraft, Rosa Bonheur, George Sand, or Madame
De Stael. No two of the women named looked alike, but
I once saw a composite photograph of their portraits
and the picture sent no thrills along my keel. Their
splendor was a matter of spirit. Have you ever seen the
Duse?—there is but one. In repose this woman's face
is absolute nullity. She starts with a blank—you would
never take a second glance at her at a pink tea. Her
dress is bargain day, her form so-so, her features clay.

ROBERT SCHUMANN

¶ But mayhap she will lift her hand and resting her chin upon it will look at you out of half-closed eyes that never are twice alike. If you are speaking you will suddenly become aware that she is listening, and then you will become uncomfortable and try to stop, but can not; for you will realize that you have been talking at random, and you want to redeem yourself.

The presence of this plain woman is a challenge—she knows! Yet she never contradicts, and when she wills it, she will lead you out of the maze and make you at peace with yourself; for our quarrel with the world is only a quarrel with self. When we are at peace with self we are at peace with God.

The Duse is a surprise, in that her homeliness of face masks an intellect that is a revelation. Her body is an exasperation to the tribe of Worth, but it houses a soul that has lived every life, died every death, known every sorrow, tasted every joy, and been one with the outcast, the despised, the forsaken; and has stood, too, clothed in shining raiment by the side of the great, the noble, the powerful. Knowing all, she forgives all. And across the face and out of the eyes, and even from her silence, come messages of sympathy—messages of strength, messages of a faith that is dauntless. Great people are simply those who have sympathy plus. Clara Schumann knew the excellence of her chosen mate, and through her sympathy made it possible for him to express himself at his highest and best. She also guessed his limitations and sought to hold him 'gainst the calamity she saw looming on the horizon, no bigger than a man's hand.⚜ When he was moody and there came times of melancholy, she invited young people to the house; and so Robert mingled his life with theirs, and in their aspirations he shook off the demons of doubt.

It was in this way that he became interested in various rising stars, and although in some instances we are aware that his prophecies went astray, we know that he hailed Chopin and Brahms long before they had come within the ken of the musical world, that so often looks through the large end of the telescope. And this kindly encouragement, this fostering welcome that the Schumanns gave to all aspiring young artists, is not the least of their virtues. We love them because they were kind.

ROBERT SCHUMANN

CLARA SCHUMANN was wise beyond the lot of woman. She knew this fact which very few mortals ever realize: The triumphs of yesterday belong to yesterday, with all of yesterday's defeats and sorrows—the day is Here, the time is Now. She did not drag her troubles behind her with a rope, nor wax vain over achievements done. When the light of her husband's intellect went out in darkness and he lived for a space a lingering death, she faced the dawn each morning, resolved to do her work and do it the best she could.

When death came to Robert's relief, her one ambition, like that of Mary Shelley, was to write her husband's name indelibly on history's page.

The professedly and professionally cheerful person is very depressing. The pessimist always has wit, for wit reveals itself in the knowledge of values. And the individual who accepts what Fate sends, and undoes Calamity by drinking all of it, is sure to have a place in our calendar of saints.

Clara Schumann, a widow at thirty-seven, with a goodly brood of babies, and no income to speak of, lived one day at a time, did her work as well as she could, and always had a little time and energy over to use for others less fortunate.

Such fortitude is sure to bear fruit, and friends flocked to her as never before. The way to secure friends is to be one ⚜ ⚜

ROBERT SCHUMANN

Madame Schumann made concert tours throughout the
Continent and England, meeting on absolute equality
the music-loving people, as well as the Kings of Art. She
played her husband's pieces with such a wealth of
expression that folks wondered why they had never
heard of them. And so today, wherever hearts are sad,
or glad, and songs are sung, and strings vibrate, and
keys respond to love's caress, there is in hearts that
know and feel, a shrine; and on this shrine in letters
of gold two words are carved, and they are these:
THE SCHUMANNS.

SEBASTIAN BACH

BACH

The name of Bach would have been famous in musical history without Johann Sebastian, but with his name added it becomes the most illustrious that the world has ever known. Bach had many pupils, but none surpassed his own sons, six of whom became great musicians, but with these the musical faculty died.

—*Sir Hubert Parry*

SEBASTIAN BACH

HE art of today is imitative. Once men had convictions, but we have only opinions, and these are usually borrowed. The artificiality of life, and the rush and the worry afford no time for great desires to possess our souls.

We average well, but no Colossus looms large above the crowd and goes his solitary way unmindful of the throng: we look alike, act alike, think alike, and in order that the likeness may be complete, we dress alike.

To wear a hat of your own selection or voice thoughts of your own thinking is to invite unseemly mirth, and finally scorn and contumely.

The great creators were solitary, rural in their instincts, ignorant and heedless of what the world was saying and doing. They were men of deep convictions and enthusiasms, unmindful of laughter or ridicule, caring little even for approbation.

No "boom town" can possibly produce a genius: it only fosters sundry small Napoleons of finance. America is a nation of boomers—financial, political, social and theological 🦋 🦋

We have sarcasm and cynicism, and we possess much that is clever, all produced by snatches of success, well

135

mixed with disappointment and the bitterness which much contact with the world is sure to evolve. Our age that goes everywhere, knows everybody's business, and religiously reads only " the last edition," produces a Bill Nye, a Sam Jones, a Teddy Roosevelt, a DeWitt Talmage, a Hopkinson Smith, a Sam Walter Foss, a Victor Herbert; but it is not at all likely to produce a Praxiteles, a Michelangelo, a Rembrandt, an Immanuel Kant or a Johann Sebastian Bach.

SEBASTIAN BACH

HAT Shakespeare is to literature, Michelangelo to sculpture, and Rembrandt to portrait-painting, Johann Sebastian Bach is to organ-music. He was the greatest organist of his time, and his equal has not yet been produced, though nearly three hundred years have passed since his death. " The organ reached perfection at the hands of Bach," says Haweis. As a composer for the organ, Bach stands secure—his position is at the head, and is absolutely unassailable.

In point of temperament and disposition Bach bears a closer resemblance to Michelangelo than to either of the others whose names I have mentioned. He was stern, strong, self-contained, and so deeply religious that he was not only a Christian but a good deal of a pagan as well. A homely man was Bach—quiet, simple in tastes and blunt in speech.

The earnest way in which this plain, unpretentious man focused upon his life-work and raised organ-music to the highest point of art must command the sincere admiration of every lover of honest endeavor.

Bach was so great that he had no artistic jealousy, no whim, and when harshly and unjustly criticized he did not concern himself enough with the quibblers to reply. He made neither apologies nor explanations. The man who thus allows his life to justify itself, and lets his work speak, and who, when reviled, reviles not again, must be a very great and lofty soul.

137

SEBASTIAN BACH

Bach was a villager and a rustic, and, like Jean Francois Millet, used to hoe in his garden, trim the vines, play with his children, putting them to bed at night, or in the day cease from his work to cut slices of brown bread which he spread with honey for the heedless little importuner, who had interrupted him in the making of a chorale that was to charm the centuries. At times he would leave his composing to help his wife with her household duties—to wash dishes, sweep the room or care for a peevish, fretful child. After the evening prayer, like Millet, again, when his household were all abed, he would often walk out into the night alone, and traverse his solitary way along a wintry road, through the woods or by the winding river, a dim, misty, shadowy figure, spectral as the " Sower," lonely as the " Fagot-Gatherer," talking to himself, mayhap, and communing with his Maker.

In his later years, when he traveled from one village or city to another to attend musical gatherings, he was always accompanied by one or more of his sons. His ambition was centered on his children, and his hope was in them. Yet nothing has been added to either organ-building, organ-playing or composition for the organ since his time.

He never knew, any more than Shakespeare knew, that he had set a pace that would never be equaled. He would have stood aghast with incredulity had he been told that centuries would come and go and his name be

138

acclaimed as Master. ¶ Such was Sebastian Bach—simple, polite, modest, unaffected, generous, almost shy—doing his work and doing it as well as he could, living one day at a time, loving his friends, forgetting his enemies. His heart was filled with such melodies that their echo is a blessing and a benediction to us yet. Art lives! ✄ ✄

SEBASTIAN BACH

EREDITY is that law of our being which provides that a man shall resemble his grandfather—or not. The Bach family has supplied the believers in heredity more good raw material in way of argument than any dozen other families known to history, combined.

The Herschels with three eminent astronomers to their credit, or the Beechers with half a dozen great preachers, are scarcely worth mentioning when we remember the Bachs, who for two hundred fifty years sounded the "A" for nearly all Germany.

The earliest known member of this musical family was Vert Bach, who was born about Fifteen Hundred Fifty. He was a miller and baker by trade, but devoted so much time to playing at dances, rehearsing at church festivals, and attending gipsy musical performances, that in his milling business he never prospered and nobody called him " Pillsbury."

This man had a son by the name of Hans, a weaver and a right merry wight, who traveled over the country attending weddings, christenings and such like festivals, playing upon a fiddle of his own construction. So famous was Hans Bach that his name lives in legend and folklore, wherein it is related that often betimes when he arrived at a village, the word would be passed and the whole population would quit work and caper on the green. So luring was his fiddle, and so potent his voice in song and story, that in a few instances preachers with long faces warned their flocks against him; and once we find a country Dogberry had his minions lay the innocent Hans by the heels and give him a taste of the stocks, simply because he seduced a party of hay-makers into following him off to a dance at a tavern, and in the meantime a storm coming up, the hay got wet. Poor Hans protested that he had nothing to do with the storm, but his excuses were construed as proof of guilt and went for naught.

At last in his wanderings, Hans found a buxom lass who was willing to take him for better or worse.

And they were married and lived happily ever after, or fairly so.

This marriage quite sobered the fun-loving fiddler, so that he settled down and worked at his weaving; and at odd hours made himself a bass viol that looked to be father of all the fiddles. In Eisenach I was told that this viol was ten feet high. Hans used to play this instrument at the village church, and his playing drew such crowds that the preacher had just cause for jealousy, and improved the opportunity, yet stifling his rage he ordered the verger to lock the doors and allow no one to depart until after the sermon and collection.

A goodly family was born to Hans and his worthy wife, and all were trained in music, so that an orchestra was formed, made up of the father, mother, and boys and girls. All the instruments used were made by Hans, and these included marvelous fiddles, some with one string and others with twenty; wooden wind-instruments like flutes, and drums to match the players, some of whom were wee toddlers. It is said that the music this orchestra made was more or less unique.

The best part of all this musical exploitation of Hans was that one of his boys, Heinrich by name, applied himself so diligently to the art that he became the organist in the village church, and then he was called to play the great organ at Arnstadt. Heinrich was not a roisterer like his father: he was a man of education and dignity. He composed many pieces, and trained his choruses so well that his fame went abroad as the chief musician of all Thuringia. He held his position at Arnstadt for fifty years, and died in Sixteen Hundred Ninety-two, at which time Johann Sebastian Bach, his nephew, was seven years old.

In his day Heinrich Bach was known as the " Great Bach," and he had two sons who were nearly as famous as himself, and would have been quite so, were it not for the fact that they had a cousin by the name of Johann Sebastian.

Johann Sebastian was a son of Johann Ambrosius, a brother of Heinrich, and Johann Ambrosius, of course, a son of the merry Hans. Johann Ambrosius was a musician, too, but did not distinguish himself especially in this line. His distinction lies in the fact that he was the father of Johann Sebastian, and this is quite enough for any one man, even if Gail Hamilton did once protest that the office of male parent was insignificant and devoid of honor.

Johann Ambrosius was a shiftless kind of fellow who drank much beer out of an earthen pot, and whittled out fiddles, sitting on a bench in the sun. He sort of let his family shift for themselves. Heinrich Bach, his brother, used to speak of him as one of his " poor relations," but at the annual Bach family festival, when a full hundred Bachs gathered to sing and play, Johann Ambrosius would attend and play on a flute or fiddle and prove that he was worthy of the name.

On one such annual reunion he took his little boy, Johann Sebastian, eight years old. The boy's mother had died a year or so before, and after the mother's death the father seemed to think more of his children than ever before—which is often the case, I 'm told ⚞ They walked the distance, about forty miles, in two days, to where the festival occurred. It was one of the white milestones in the boy's life—that trip with its revelation of sleeping in barns, singing, and playing on many instruments, dining by the wayside, all winding up with a solemn service at a great stone church, where the preacher gave them his benediction, and the great company separated with handshakings, embracings and tears, to meet again in a year. Johann Ambrosius did not attend the next reunion. Before the Spring had come and birds sang blithely, a band composed of twenty-five played funeral-dirges at his grave—and little Johann

SEBASTIAN BACH

Sebastian was an orphan. ¶ Johann Sebastian's elder brother, Christoph, who had married a few years before and moved away, attended the funeral, and when he went back home he took little Johann Sebastian with him—there was no other place to go. The lad was allowed to take one thing with him as a remembrance of the home that he was now leaving forever—his father's violin in a green bag, with a leathern drawstring. On the bag were his father's initials, woven into the cloth by the boy's mother—a present from sweetheart to lover before their marriage.

Christoph was a musician, too, and a prosperous fellow —quite the antithesis of his father. It takes a lot of love to bring up a child, and the miracle of mother-love is a constant wonder to every thinking person. Without mother-love how would the cross-grained, perverse little tyrant ever survive the buffets which the world is sure to give? It is love that makes existence possible.

Christoph wished to be kind to his little brother, but it was a kindness of the head and not of the heart. Only an hour a day was allowed the boy for playing on the violin he had brought in the green bag, because Christoph and his wife " did not want to hear the noise." Then when the boy stole off to the forest and played there, he was waylaid on the way home and well cuffed for disobeying orders. All this seems very much like the Goneril and Cordelia business, or the history of Cinderella, but as Johann Sebastian told it himself in the after-years, we have reason to believe it was not fiction. ¶ Little Johann Sebastian had been his father's favorite, and this fact perhaps made Christoph fear the boy was going to tread in his father's lazy footsteps. So he set about to discipline the lad.

It must be admitted that Johann Ambrosius Bach, who whittled out fiddles in the sun, and who drank much beer out of an earthen pot, was shiftless, but it further seems that he was tender-hearted and kind and took much interest in teaching Sebastian to play the violin, even while the child wore dresses. And sometimes I think it is really better, if you have to choose, to drink beer out of an earthen pot and be kind and gentle, than to have a sharp nose for other folks' faults and be continually trying to pinch and prod the old world into the straight and narrow path of virtue. Yet there is wisdom in all folly, and I can see that the prohibition concerning little Sebastian's playing the violin only an hour a day— mind you! was not without its benefits. Surely it would often be a wise bit of diplomacy on the part of the teacher to order the pupil not to study his arithmetic lesson but an hour a day, on penalty. Of course it might happen occasionally that the pupil in an earnest desire to please, might not study at all, yet there are exceptions to all rules, and we must remember that when Tom Sawyer forbade the boys using his whitewash-brush, the scheme worked well.

One instance, however, might be cited where the law

of compensation seems really to have stood no chance. Christoph had a goodly musical library and a collection of the best organ-music that had been produced up to that time. He kept this music in a case, and carried the key to the case in his pocket. On rare occasions he had shown bits of this music to Sebastian, who read music like print when it is easy. The boy devoured all the music he could lay his hands on, and hummed it over to himself until every note and accent was fixed in his memory. He dearly wanted to examine that music in the locked-up case, but his brother declared his ambition nonsense—he was too young. But the boy contrived a way to pick the lock—for a music-lover laughs at lock-smiths—and at night when all the household were safely in bed, he would steal downstairs in his bare feet and get a sheet of the music and copy it off by moonlight, sitting in the deep ledge of the window. Thus did he work for six months, whenever the moon shone bright enough to read the lines and signs and marks. But alas! one day the elder brother was rummaging around the boy's room in search of things contraband and he pounced upon the portfolio of copied music. He summoned the offender into his presence. The facts were admitted, and Johann Sebastian had his bare legs well tingled with an apple-sprout. Then the portfolio was confiscated and carried away, despite pleadings, promises and tears. And the question still remains whether "discipline" is not a matter of gratification to the

146

person in power rather than a sincere and honest attempt to benefit the person disciplined.

Nevertheless, Johann Sebastian Bach was working out his own education: he belonged to the boys' chorus at Ohrdruf, as all boys in the vicinity did. Music in every German village was an important item, and the best singers and best behaved members of the village choir were set apart as a sort of select choir—a choir within a choir—and were often gathered together to sing on special occasions at weddings and festivals. Johann Sebastian had a sweet, well-modulated voice, and whenever he was to sing, he carried his violin in the green bag, so he could play, too, if needed. Thus he played and sang at serenades, just as did Martin Luther, many years before, in Johann Sebastian's own native town of Eisenach ✄ ✄

Johann Sebastian's fame grew until it reached to Luneburg, twelve miles away, and he was invited there to sing in the choir of Saint Michael's. The pay he received was very slight, but that was not to be considered. An occasional bowl of soup and piece of rye-bread, and the privilege of sleeping in the organ-loft, all combined with freedom, made his paradise complete. He played on the harpsichord in the pastor's study sometimes; and occasionally the organist, who could not help loving such a music-loving boy, would allow him to try the big organ, and at every service he was present to play his violin, or if any of the other players were absent he

147

SEBASTIAN BACH

would just fill in and play any instrument desired.
¶ Then we hear of him trudging off to Hamburg, a
hundred miles away, with only a few coppers in his
pocket, to hear the great organist Reinke. He slept in
cattle-sheds by the way, played his violin at taverns for
something to eat, or plainly stated his case to sympathetic cooks at backdoors. One instance he has recorded
when all the world seemed to frown. He had trudged all
day, with nothing to eat, and at evening had sat down
near the open window of an inn, from which came
savory smells of supper. As he sat there, suddenly there
were thrown out a couple of small dried herrings. The
hungry boy eagerly seized upon them, just as a dog
would. But what was his surprise to find, as he gnawed,
in the mouth of each fish a piece of silver! Some one had
read the story of Saint Peter to a purpose. Young Bach
looked in vain for a person to thank, but perceiving no
one he took it as the act of God and an omen that his
pilgrimage to hear the great organist should not be in
vain ❧ ❧

The wonders of Reinke's playing and the marvel of the
mighty music filled his soul with awe, and fired his
ambition to do a like performance.

Did the great Reinke know as he played that bright
Sabbath morning, filling the cathedral with thunders of
echoing bass, or sounds of sweet, subtle melody—did he
know that away back in the throng stood a dusty,
tawny-haired boy who had tramped a hundred miles

148

just for this event? And did the organist guess as he played that he was inspiring a human soul to do a grand and wondrous work, and live a life whose influence should be deathless? Probably not—few men indeed know when virtue has gone out of them.

Perhaps Reinke was playing just to suit himself, and had purposely put the unappreciative, lazy, sleepy occupants of the pews out of his thought, all unmindful that there was one among a thousand, back behind a pillar, dusty and worn, but now unconsciously refreshed and oblivious to all save the playing of the great organ. There stood the boy bathed in sweet sounds, with streaming eyes and responsive heart.

His inward emotions supplemented the outward melody, for music demands a listener, and at the last is a matter of soul, not sound: its appeal being a harmony that dwells within. So played Reinke, and back by the door, peering from behind a pillar, stood the boy.

SEBASTIAN BACH

SEBASTIAN BACH was such a useful member of the choir at Luneburg that the town musician from Weimar, who happened to be going that way, induced him to go home with him as assistant organist.

This was a definite move in the direction of fame and fortune. Men who can make themselves useful are needed—there is ever a search for such. They wanted Bach at Weimar. Johann Sebastian Bach, aged eighteen, was wanted because he did his work well.

After three or four months at Weimar he made a visit to Arnstadt, where his uncle had so long been organist. His name at Arnstadt was a name to conjure with, and in fact throughout all that part of the country, whenever a man proved to be a musician of worth and power the people out of compliment called him a " Bach."

Johann Sebastian was invited to play for the people, and all were so delighted that they insisted he should come and fill the place made vacant by the death of the " Great Bach."

So he came and was duly installed.

And the young man drilled his chorus, wrote cantatas, and arranged chants and hymns. But he was far from contented. He was being pushed on by a noble unrest. It was not so very long before we find him packing off to Denmark, with little ceremony, to listen to the playing of Buxtehude, the greatest player of his age.

Bach had been quite content to tiptoe into the church

when Reinke played, grateful for the privilege of listening, half-expecting to be thrust out as an interloper. He had gained confidence since then, and now introduced himself to Buxtehude and was greeted by the octogenarian as a brother and an equal, although sixty years divided them. His visit extended itself from one week to two, and then to a month or more, and a message came from his employers that if he expected to hold his place he had better return.

Bach's visit to Buxtehude formed another white milestone in his career. He came back filled with enthusiasm and overflowing with ideas and plans that a single lifetime could not materialize. Those who have analyzed the work of Buxtehude and Bach tell us that there is a richness of counterpoint, a vigor of style, a fulness of harmony, and a strong, glowing, daring quality that in some pieces is identical with both composers. In other words, Bach admired Buxtehude so much that for a time he wrote and played just like him, very much as Turner began by painting as near like Claude Lorraine as he possibly could. Genius has its prototype, and in all art there is to be found this apostolic succession. Bach first built on Reinke; next he transferred his allegiance to Buxtehude; from this he gradually developed courage and self-reliance until he fearlessly trusted himself in deep water, heedless of danger. And it is this fearless, self-reliant and self-sufficient quality that marks the work of every exceptional man in every line of art.

151

SEBASTIAN BACH

"Here's to the man who dares," said Disraeli. All strong men begin by worshiping at a shrine, and if they continue to grow they shift their allegiance until they know only one altar and that is the Ideal which dwells in their own heart.

SEBASTIAN BACH

ND now behold how Heinrich Bach had educated his people into the belief that there was only one way to play, and that was as he did it. It is not at all probable that Heinrich put forward any claims of perfection, but the people regarded his playing as high-water mark, and any variation from his standards was considered fantastic and absurd.

In all of the old German Protestant churches are records kept giving the exact history of the church. You can tell for two hundred years back just when an organist was hired or dismissed; when a preacher came and when he went away, with minute mention as to reasons.

And so we find in the records of the Church at Arnstadt that the organist, Johann Sebastian Bach, took a vacation without leave in the year Seventeen Hundred Five, and further, when he returned his playing was "fantastical."

With the young man's compositions the Consistory expressed echoing groans of dissatisfaction. A list of charges was drawn up against him, one of which runs as follows: "We charge him with a habit of making surprising variations in the chorales, and intermixing divers strange sounds, so that thereby the congregation was confounded."

Bach's answers are filed with the original charges, and are all very brief and submissive. In some instances he pleads guilty, not thinking it worth his while, strong

153

man that he was, to either apologize or explain. ¶ But the most damning count brought against him was this: " We further charge him with introducing into the choir-loft a Stranger Maiden, who made music." To this, young Bach makes no reply. Brave boy!

The sequel is shown that in a few weeks he was married to this " Stranger Maiden," who was his cousin. She was a Bach, too, a descendant of the merry Hans, and she, also, played the organ. But great was the horror of the Arnstadites that a woman should play a church organ. Mein Gott im Himmel—a woman might be occupying the pulpit next!

Johann Sebastian's indifference to criticism is partially explained by the fact that he was in correspondence with the Consistory at Mulhausen, and also with the Duke Wilhelm Ernest, of Saxe-Weimar. Both Mulhausen and Weimar wanted his services. Under such conditions men have ever been known to invite a rupture—let us hope that Johann Sebastian Bach was not quite so human.

SEBASTIAN BACH

ICHELANGELO never married, but Bach held the average good by marrying twice ❧ He was the father of just twenty children. His first wife was a woman with well-defined musical tastes, as was meet in one with such an illustrious musical pedigree. It was n't fashion then to educate women, and one biographer expresses a doubt as to whether Bach's first wife was able to read and write. To read and write are rather cheap accomplishments, though. Last year I met several excellent specimens of manhood in the Tennessee Mountains who could do neither, yet these men had a goodly hold on the eternal verities ❧ ❧

We know that Bach's wife had a thorough sympathy with his work, and that he used to sing or play his compositions to her, and when the children got big enough, they tried the new-made hymn tunes, too. These children sang before they could talk plain, and the result was that the two elder sons, Wilhelm Friedemann and Phillip Emmanuel, became musicians of marked ability. Half a dozen other sons became musicians also, but the two named above made some valuable additions to the music fund of the world. Haydn has paid personal tribute to Emmanuel Bach, acknowledging his obligation, and expressing to him the belief that he was a greater man than his father.

The nine years Bach spent at Weimar, under the patronage of the Duke Wilhelm Ernest, were years rich in results. His office was that of Concert Master, and Leader of the Choir at Ducal Chapel. The duties not being very exacting, he had plenty of time to foster his bent. Freed from all apprehension along the line of the bread-and-butter question he devoted himself untiringly to his work. It was here he developed that style of fingering that was to be followed by the players on the harpsichord, and which further serves as the basis for our present manner of piano-playing. Bach was the first man to make use of the thumb in organ-playing, and I believe it was James Huneker who once said that " Bach discovered the human hand."

Bach made a complete study of the mechanism of the organ, invented various arrangements for the better use of the pedals, and gave his ideas without stint to the makers, who, it seems, were glad to profit by them. Even then Weimar was a place of pilgrimage, although Goethe had not yet come to illumine it with his presence. But the traditions of Weimar have been musical and artistic for four hundred years, and this had its weight with Goethe when he decided to make it his home ✠ In Bach's day, pilgrims from afar used to come to attend the musical festivals given by the Duke of Saxe-Weimar; and these pilgrims would go home and spread the name of Johann Sebastian Bach. Many invitations used to come for him to go and play at the installation of a new organ, or to superintend the construction of an organ, or to lead a chorus. Gradually his fame grew, and although

SEBASTIAN BACH

he might have lived his life and ended his days there in the rural and peaceful quiet of Weimar, yet he harkened to the voice and arose and went forth with his family into a place that afforded a wider scope for his powers.
¶ As Kapellmeister to the Court at Kothen he had the direction of a large orchestra, and it seems also supervised a school of music.

When the Court moved about from place to place it was the custom to take the orchestra, too, in order to reveal to the natives along the way what good music really was. This was all quite on the order of the Duke of Mantua, who used to travel with a retinue of two hundred servants and attendants.

On one such occasion the Kothen Court went to Carlsbad. The visit extended itself to six months, when Bach became impatient to return to his family, and was allowed to go in advance of the rest of the company. On reaching home he found his wife had died and been buried several weeks before.

It was a severe shock to the poor man, but fortunately there was more philosophy to his nature than romance, which is a marked trait in the German character. All this is plainly evidenced by the fact that in many German churches when a good wife dies, the pastor, at the funeral, as the best friend of the stricken husband, casts his eyes over the congregation for a suitable successor to the deceased. And very often the funeral baked meats do coldly furnish forth the marriage feast.

157

SEBASTIAN BACH

Man is made to mourn, but most widowers say but a year ⚜ ⚜

The prompt second marriage of Bach was certainly a compliment to the memory of his first wife, who was a most amiable helpmeet and friend. No soft sentiment disturbed the deep immersement of this man in his work. He was as businesslike a man as Ralph Waldo Emerson, who arranged his second marriage by correspondence, and then drove over in a buggy one afternoon to bring home the promised bride, making notes by the way on the Over-Soul and man's place in the Universal Cosmos ⚜ ⚜

Events proved the wisdom of Johann Sebastian Bach's choice. His first wife filled his heart, but this one was not only to do as much, but often to guide his hand and brain. He was thirty-eight with a brood of nine. Anna Magdalena was twenty-three, strong, fancy-free, and by a dozen, lacking one, was to increase the limit.

As the years went by, Bach occasionally would arise in public places, and with uncovered head thank God for the blessings He had bestowed upon him, especially in sending him such a wife.

Anna Magdalena Wulken was a singer of merit, a player on the harp, and a person of education. She certainly had no seraglio notions of wanting to be petted and pampered and taken care of, or she would not have assumed the office of stepmother to that big family and married a poor man. Bach never had time to make money. Very soon after their marriage Bach began to dictate music to his wife. A great many pieces can be seen in Leipzig and Berlin copied out in her fine, painstaking hand, with an occasional interlining by the Master. Other pieces written by him are amended by her, showing plainly that they worked together.

As proof that this was no honeymoon whim, the collaboration continued for over a score of years, in spite of increasing domestic responsibilities.

From Kothen, Bach was called to Leipzig and elected by the municipal authorities the Musical Director and Cantor of the Thomas School. For twenty-seven years he labored here, doing the work he liked best, and doing it in his own way. He escaped the pitfalls of petty jealousies, into which most men of artistic natures fall, by rising above them all. He accepted no insults; he had no grievances against either man or fate; earnest, religious, simple—he filled the days with useful effort. ¶ He was so well poised that when summoned by Frederick the Great to come and play before him, he took a year to finish certain work he had on hand before he went. Then he would have forgotten the engagement, had not his son, who was Chamber Musician to the King, insisted that he come. In the presence of Frederick it was the King who was abashed, not he. He knew his kinship to Divinity so well that he did not even think to assert it. And surely he was one fit to stand in the presence of kings.

159

SEBASTIAN BACH

For number, variety and excellence, only two men can be named as his competitors: these are Mozart and Handel. But in point of performance, simplicity and sterling manhood, Bach stands alone.

FELIX MENDELSSOHN

FELIX MENDELSSOHN

The correspondence of Goethe and Zelter displeases me. I always feel out of sorts when I have been reading it. Do you know that I am making great strides in water-colors? Schirmer comes to me every Saturday at eleven, and paints for two hours at a landscape, which he is going to make me a present of, because the subject occurred to him whilst I was playing the little " Rivulet " (which you know). It represents a fellow who saunters out of a dark forest into a sunny little nook; trees all about, with stems thick and thin; one has fallen across the rivulet; the ground is carpeted with soft, deep moss, full of ferns; there are stones garlanded with blackberry-bushes; it is fine warm weather; the whole will be charming.

—Mendelssohn to Devrient

FELIX MENDELSSOHN

HIRTY-EIGHT years is not a long life, but still it is long enough to do great things. Felix Mendelssohn-Bartholdy was born in the year Eighteen Hundred Nine, at Hamburg, and died at Leipzig in the year Eighteen Hundred Forty-seven. His career was a triumphal march. The road to success with him was no zigzag journey—from the first he went straight to the front. Whether as a baby he crowed in key, and cried to a one-two-three melody, as his old nurse used to aver, is a little doubtful, possibly. But all agree that he was the most precocious musical genius that ever lived, excepting Mozart; and Goethe, who knew them both, declared that Mendelssohn's music bore the same relationship to Mozart's as the talk of a grown-up cultured person to the prattle of a child &x &x

But then Goethe was not a musician, and sixty years had passed from the time Goethe saw Mozart before he met Mendelssohn. Goethe loved the brown-curled Jewish boy at sight; and whether on meeting Mozart he ever recovered from the taint of prejudice that most people feel when a prodigy is introduced, is a question. ¶ But who can wonder that the old poet's heart went out to the youthful Mendelssohn as soon as he saw him!

163

FELIX MENDELSSOHN

He was a being to fill a poet's dream—such a youth as
the Old Masters used to picture as the Christ when He
confounded the wise men. And then the painters posed
this same type of boy as Daniel in the lions' den; and
back in the days of Pericles, the Greeks were fond of
showing the beautiful youth, just approaching adolescence, in the nude, as the god of Love. When the face
has all the soft beauty of a woman, and the figure, slight,
slender, lithe and graceful, carries only a suggestion of
the masculine strength to come—then beauty is at
perihelion. The "Eros" of Phidias was not the helpless,
dumpy cherub "Cupid"—he was a slender-limbed boy
of twelve years who showed collar-bone and revealed
every rib.

Beauty and strength of the highest type are never
complete—their lure lies in a certain reserve, and
behind all is a suggestion of unfoldment. Maturity is not
the acme of beauty, because in maturity there is nothing
more to hope for—only the uncompleted fills the heart,
for from it we construct the Ideal.

Goethe looked out of his window and seeing Felix
Mendelssohn playing with the children, exclaimed to
Zelter, "He is a Greek god in the germ, and I here
solemnly protest against his wearing clothes."

The words sound singularly like the remark of Doctor
Schneider, made ten years later, when Herr Doctor
removed the sheet that covered the dead body of
Goethe, and gazing upon the full-rounded limbs, the

164

FELIX MENDELSSOHN

mighty chest, the columnar neck and the Jove-like head,
exclaimed, " It is the body of a Greek god! " And the
surgeons stood there in silent awe, forgetful of their
task ✣ ✣

Zelter, who introduced Mendelssohn to Goethe, was a
fine old character, nearly as fine a type as Goethe himself. Heine once said, " Musicians constitute a third
sex." And that there have been some unsexed, or at
least unmanly men, who were great musicians, need not
be denied. The art of music borders more closely upon
the dim and mystic realms of the inspirational than any
of the other arts. Music refuses to give up its secrets in a
formula and at last eludes the sciolist with his ever-
ready theorem. But still, all musicians are not dreamers.
Zelter, for instance, was a most hard-headed, practical
man: a positivist and mathematician with a turn for
economics, and a Gradgrind for facts. He was a stone-
mason, and worked at his trade at odd times all
through his life, just because he felt it was every man's
duty to work with his hands. Imagine Tolstoy playing
the piano and composing instead of making shoes, and
you have Zelter.

This curious character was bound to the Mendelssohn
family by his love for Moses Mendelssohn, the grandfather of Felix. Moses Mendel added the " sohn " in
loving recognition of his father, just as " Bartholdy "
was added by the father of Felix in loving token to his
wife. It was the grandfather of Felix who first gave

165

FELIX MENDELSSOHN

glory to the name. We sometimes forget that Moses
Mendelssohn was one of the greatest thinkers Germany
has produced—the man who summed up in his own
head all the philosophy of the time and gave Spinoza to
the world. This was the man to whom the erratic Zelter
was bound in admiration, and when it was suggested
that he teach musical composition to the grandchild of
his idol, he accepted the post with zest.

But there came a shade of disappointment to the grim
and bearded Zelter when he failed to find a trace of
resemblance between the child and the child's grandfather. The boy was sprightly, emotional, loving; and
could play the piano from his tenth year better than
Zelter himself. When Goethe teasingly suggested this
fact, Zelter replied, "You mean he plays different, not
better." Goethe apologized.

Yet the boy was not a philosopher, and this grieved
Zelter, who wanted him to be the grandson of his grandfather, and a musician besides.

The lad's skill in composition, however, soon turned the
old teacher's fears into joy. Such a pupil he had never
had before! And he did not reason it out that no one
else had ever had, either. The child, like Chopin, read
music before he read print, and improvised, merging one
tune with another, bringing harmony out of hopeless
chaos. Zelter followed, fearing success would turn the
boy's head—berating, scolding, chiding, encouraging—
and all the time admiring and loving. The pretty boy

166

was not much frightened by the old man's rough ways, but seized upon such of the instruction as he needed and filled in the rest with his own peerless soul.

The parents were astounded at such progress. At first they had wished merely to round out the boy's education with a proper amount of musical instruction, and now they reluctantly allowed the old teacher to have his way—the lad must make his career a musical one. The boy composed a cantata, which was given in the parlors of his parents' home, with an orchestra secured for the occasion. Felix stood on a chair and led his band of musicians with that solemn dignity which was his through life. Zelter grumbled, ridiculed and criticized—that was the way he showed his interest. The old musician declared they were making a " Miss Nancy " of his pupil—saturating him with flattery, and he threatened to resign his office—most certainly not intending to do so.

It was about this time that Zelter threw out the hint that he was going down to Weimar to see his friend Goethe—would Felix like to go? Felix would be delighted, and when the boy's father and mother were interviewed, they were pleased, too, at the prospect of their boy's making the acquaintance of the greatest poet of Germany. Felix was duly cautioned about how he should conduct himself. He promised, of course, and also agreed to write a letter home every day, recording the exact language that the author of " Werther " used in his presence. ¶ Goethe and the Carlylian Zelter had been cronies for many years. The poet delighted in the company of the gruff old stone-mason musician, and together they laughed at the world over their pipes and mugs. And sometimes, alas, they hotly argued and raised their voices in donner-und-blitzen style, as Germans have been known to do. Yet they were friends, and the honest Zelter's yearly visits were as a godsend to the old poet, who was often pestered to distraction by visitors who only voiced the conventional, the inconsequential and absurd. Here was a man who tried his steel. ¶ Now, Zelter had his theories about teaching harmony —theories too finely spun for any one but himself to grasp. Possibly he himself did not seize them very firmly, but only argued them in a vain attempt to clear the matter up in his own mind. The things we are not quite sure of are those upon which we insist.

Goethe had pooh-poohed and smitten the table with his " stein " in denial.

And now Zelter, the frank and bold, stealthily and by concocted plot and plan took his pupil, Felix Mendelssohn, with him on a visit to Weimar. He wanted to confound his antagonist and to reveal by actual proof the success that could be achieved where correct methods of instruction were followed.

Jean Jacques had written a novel showing what right theories, properly followed up, could do for his hero. Zelter had done better—he exhibited the youth.

168

FELIX MENDELSSOHN

"A girl in boy's clothes, I do believe," said Goethe, with his usual banter, in the evening when a little company had gathered in the parlors. Felix sat on his teacher's knee, with his arms around the old man's neck, girl-like. "Does he play?" continued Goethe, going over and opening the piano.

"Oh, a little!" answered Zelter indifferently.

The ladies insisted—they always had music when Zelter made them a visit.

"Come, make some noise and awaken the spirits that have so long lain slumbering!" ordered the old poet ⚶ Zelter advanced to the piano and played a stiff, formal little tune of his own.

He arose and motioned to Felix.

"Play that!" said the teacher.

The child sat down, and with an impatient little gesture and half-smile at the audience, played the piece exactly as Zelter had played it, with a certain drawling style that was all Zelter's own. It was so funny that the listeners burst into shouts of laughter. But the boy instantly restored order by striking the bass a strong stroke with both hands, running the scale, and weaving that simple little air into the most curious variations ⚶ For ten minutes he played, bringing in Zelter's little tune again and again, and then Zelter in a voice of pretended wrath cried, "Cease that tin-pan drumming and play something worth while."

Goethe arose, stroked the boy's pretty brown curls,

169

kissed him on the forehead and said: "Yes, play something worth while. I know you two rogues—you have
been practising on that piece for a year or more, and now
you pretend to be improvising—I'll see whether you
can play!"

And going to a portfolio he took out a manuscript piece
of music written out in the fine, delicate hand of
Mozart, and placed it on the music-rack of the piano.
Felix played the piece as if it were his own; and then
laying it aside, went back and played it through from
memory ❧ ❧

Then piece after piece was brought out for him to play,
and Zelter leaned back and by his manner said, " Oh,
it is nothing!"

And certainly it was nothing to the boy—he played with
such ease that his talent was quite unknown to himself.
He had not yet discovered that every one could not
produce music just as they could talk.

Goethe's admiration for the boy was unbounded. The
two weeks of Mendelssohn's prescribed visit had expired
and Goethe begged for an extension of two weeks more.
Every evening there was the little impromptu concert.
After that Felix paid various visits to Weimar. Goethe's
house was his home, and the affection between the old
poet and the young musician was very gentle and very
firm. "All souls are of one age," says Swedenborg.
Goethe was seventy-three and Mendelssohn thirteen
when they first met, but very soon they were as equals—

170

boys together. ¶ Goethe was a learner to the day of his passing: he wanted to know. In the presence of those who had followed certain themes further than he had, he was as an eager, curious child. When Goethe was seventy-eight and Mendelssohn eighteen, they spent another month together; and a regular program of instruction was laid out. Each morning at precisely nine, they met for the poet's " music lesson," as Goethe called it, and the boy would play from some certain composer, showing the man's peculiar style, and the features that differentiated him from others. Goethe himself has recorded in his correspondence that it was Felix Mendelssohn who taught him of Hengstenberg and Spontini, introduced him to Hegel's "Æsthetics," and revealed to him for the first time the wonders of Beethoven ✠ Can you not close your eyes and see them—the mighty giant of fourscore, with his whitened locks, and the slight, slender, handsome boy?

The old man is seated in his armchair near the window that opens on the garden. The youth is at the piano and plays from time to time to illustrate his thought, then turns and talks, and the old man nods in recognition. The boy sings and the old man chords in with a deep, mellow bass which the years have not subdued.

When there are others present these two may romp, joke and talk much—masking their hearts by frivolity— but together they sit in silence, or speak only in lowered voices as all true lovers always do. Their conversation is

FELIX MENDELSSOHN

sparse and to the point; each is mindful of the dignity
and worth that the other possesses: each recognizes the
respect that is due to the mind that knows and the
heart that feels. "All souls are of one age."

FELIX MENDELSSOHN

WITH one exception, Felix Mendelssohn was unlike all the great composers who lived before him—he was born in affluence; during his life all the money he could use was his. No struggle for recognition marked his growth. He never knew the pang of being misunderstood by the public he sought to serve. Whether these things were to his lasting disadvantage, as many aver, will forever remain a question of opinion.

Felix Mendelssohn was the culminating flower of a long line of exquisite culture. He was an orchid that does not reproduce itself. With him died the race. All that beauty of soul, vivacity, candor and sparkling gaiety, with the nerved-up capacity for work, were but the flaring up of life ere it goes out in the night of death. Such men never found either a race or a school. They are the comets that dash across the plane of our vision, obeying no orbit, leaving behind only a memory of blinding light.

The character of Mendelssohn was distinctly feminine, and it follows that his music should be played by men and not by women, otherwise we get a suggestion of softness and tameness that is apt to pall. Man, like Deity, creates in his own image.

Sorrow had never pierced the heart of this prosperous and very respectable person.

He was never guilty of indiscretion or excess, and no demon of discontent haunted his dreams.

173

FELIX MENDELSSOHN

In Mendelssohn's music we get no sense of Titanic power such as we feel when " Wagner " is being played; no world problems vex us. The delicate, plaintive, spiritual seductions of Chopin, who swept the keys with an insinuating gossamer touch, are not there. The brilliant extravaganzas of Liszt—passages illumined by living lightning—are wholly wanting. But in it all you feel the deep, measured pulse of a religious conviction that never halts nor doubts. There are grace, ease, beauty, sweetness and exquisite harmony everywhere. In the " Saint Paul," as in his other oratorios, are such arias for the contralto as, " But the Lord is mindful of His own "; for the bass, " God have mercy upon us," and for the tenor, " Be thou faithful unto death." These reveal pure and exalted melody of highest type. It uplifts but does not intoxicate. Spontaneity is sacrificed to perfection, and the lack of self-assertion allows us to keep our wits and admire sanely.

Heinrich Heine, the pagan Jew, once taunted Mendelssohn with being a Jew and yet conducting a " Passion Play." The gibe was a home-thrust and a cruel one, since Mendelssohn had neither the wit nor the mental acuteness to avoid the pink of the man who was hated by Jew and Christian alike. Towards the exiled Heine, Mendelssohn had only a patronizing pity—" Why should any man offend the people in power? " he once asked ⚜ ⚜

Only the exiled can sympathize with the exile—only

FELIX MENDELSSOHN

the downtrodden and the sore-oppressed understand the
outcast. Golgotha never came to Mendelssohn, and this
was at once his blessing and his misfortune.

And the grim fact still remains that world-poets have
never been " respectable," and that the saviors of the
world are usually crucified between thieves.

In life Mendelssohn received every token of approbation that men can pay to other men. For him wealth
waited, kings uncovered, laurel bloomed and blossomed,
and love crowned all. His popularity was greater than
that of any other man of his time. He had no enemies,
no detractors, no rivals—his pathway was literally and
poetically strewn with roses. What more can any man
desire? Lasting fame and a name that never dies?
Avaunt! but first know this, that immortality is reserved
alone for those who have been despised and rejected of
men.

FELIX MENDELSSOHN

AINTSHIP is the exclusive possession of those who have either worn out, or never had, the capacity to sin.

Fortunately for Felix Mendelssohn he never had it—he was ever the bright, joyous, gracious, beautiful being that all his friends describe, and every one who met him was his friend thereafter. The character of "Seraphael" in the novel of "Charles Auchester," by Miss Sheppard, portrays Mendelssohn in a glowing, seraphic light. The book reveals the emotional qualities of a woman given over to her idol, and yet the man is Mendelssohn —he was equal to the best that could be said of him ✄ The weakness of Miss Sheppard's book lies in the fact that she is so true to life that we tire of the goodness and beauty, and long for a rogue to keep us company and break the pall of a sweetness that cloys.

The bitterest thing Mendelssohn ever said of a public performer was to describe a certain prima donna as acting like an " arrogant cook." All the good orchestra leaders are supposed to have fine fits of frenzy when they tear their hair in wrath at the discordant braying of careless players. But Mendelssohn never lost his temper. When his men played well, as soon as the piece was done he went among them shaking hands, congratulating and thanking them. This would have been a great stroke of policy in the eyes of a groundling, for the action never failed to catch the audience, and then the applause was uproarious. At such times Mendelssohn seemed to fail

176

in knowing the applause was for him, and appeared as one half-dazed or embarrassed, when suddenly remembering where he was, he would seize the nearest 'cello, violin or oboe, and drag the astonished man to the front to share the honors and bouquets. If this was artistry it was of a high order and should be ranked as art.

I once heard Henry Irving make a speech at Harvard University, and shall never forget the tremor in his voice and the half-embarrassment of his manner. What could have been more complimentary to college striplings? And then, as usual, he looked helplessly about for Ellen Terry, and having located her, held out his hand toward her and led her to the front to receive the homage. ¶ Tears filled my eyes. Was Irving's action art? Odsbodkins! I never thought of it: I was hypnotized and all swallowed up in loving admiration for Sir Henry and the beautiful Lady Ellen.

Felix Mendelssohn was beloved by his players. First, because he never wrote parts that only seraphs of light could play. In this he was unlike Wagner, who could think such music as no brass, no wood nor strings could perform, and so was ever in torments of doubt and disappointment. Second, he was always grateful when his players did the best they could. Third, he was graciously polite, even at rehearsals. The extent of his inclination to rebuke was shown once when he abruptly rapped for silence, and when quiet came said to his orchestra: " I am sure that any one of the gentlemen present could write a symphony. I think, too, that you can all improve on the music of the past—even that of Beethoven. But this afternoon we are playing Beethoven's music—will you oblige me? " And every man awoke to the necessity of putting the sweet, subtile, strong quality of the master into the work, instead of absent-mindedly sounding the note, fighting bluebottles, and taking care merely not to get off the key too much ⚶ At the great Birmingham Festival several hundred ladies in the audience contrived at a given signal to shower the great conductor with bouquets. And Mendelssohn, entering into the spirit of the fun, dexterously caught the blossoms and tossed them to his players, not even forgetting the triangles and the boys who played the kettledrums.

Bayard Taylor has described the lustrous brown eyes of Mendelssohn, that seemed to send rays of light into your own: " Such eyes are the possession of men who have seen heavenly visions. Genius shows itself in the eye. Those who looked into the eyes of Sir Walter Scott, Robert Burns or Lord Byron, always came away and told of it as an epoch in their lives. This was what I thought when I sat vis-a-vis with Felix Mendelssohn and looked into his eyes. I did not hear his voice, for I was too intent on gazing into the fathomless depths of those splendid eyes—eyes that mirrored infinity, eyes that had beheld celestial glory. Little did I think then that in two years those eyes would close forever." ⚶

FELIX MENDELSSOHN

I N a letter to Hensel, Felix Mendelssohn's sex-
quality is finely revealed, when he says that
his friends are advising him to marry, and he
is on the lookout for a wife.
Ye gods! there is something strangely creepy about the
thought of a man going out in cold blood to seek a wife.
Only two kinds of men search for a wife; one is the Turk,
and the other is his antithesis, who is advised to marry
for hygienic, prudential or sociologic reasons. John
Ruskin was "advised" to marry and the matter was
duly arranged for him. In a week he awoke to the
hideousness of the condition. Six years elapsed before
John Millais and Chief Justice Coleridge collaborated to
set him free, but the cicatrix remained.
The great books are those the authors had to write to
get rid of; the only immortal songs are those sung
because the singers could not help it. The best-loved
wife is the woman who married because her lover
had to marry her to get rid of her; the children that
are born because they had to be are the ones that stock
the race; and the love that can not help itself is the only
love that uplifts and inspires.
Felix Mendelssohn, the slight, joyous, girlish youth,
should have preserved his Cecilia-like virginity. He
should have left marriage to those who were capable of
nothing else; this would not have meant that he turn
ascetic, for the ascetic is a voluptuary in disguise. He
should simply have been married to his work. The

179

FELIX MENDELSSOHN

wonder is, though, that once the thought of marriage was forced upon him, he did not marry a Hittite who delighted in pork-chops and tomato-sauce, ordered Guinness Stout in public places, and disciplined him as a genius should be disciplined.

Fate was kind, however, and the lady of his choice was nearly as esthetic in face and form, as gentle and spirituelle as himself. She never humiliated him by cackle, nor led him a merry chase after society's baubles. Her only wish was to please him and to do her wifely duty. They pooled their weaknesses, and it need not be stated that this, the only love in the life of Mendelssohn, made not the slightest impress on his art, save to subdue it. The passing years brought domestic responsibilities, and the every-day trials of life chafed his soul, until the wasted body, grown tired before its time, refused to go on, and death set the spirit free.

FELIX MENDELSSOHN

ENDELSSOHN made five visits to England, where his success was even greater than it was at home. He learned to express himself well in English, but always spoke with the precision and care that marks the educated foreigner. So the result was that he spoke really better " English " than the English. The ease with which the Hebrew learns a language has often been noted and commented upon. Mendelssohn preferred German, but was not at a loss to carry on a conversation in French, Italian or English. ¶ His nature was especially cosmopolitan, and like the true aristocrat that he was, he was also a democrat, and at home in any society.

When he was invited by the Queen to call upon her at Buckingham Palace, he went alone, in his afternoon dress, and sent in his card as every gentleman does when he calls upon a lady. Her Majesty greeted him at the door of her sitting-room, and dismissed the servants. They met as equals. In compliment to her guest Victoria spoke only in German. The Queen, seeing the music-rack was not in order, apologized, womanlike, for the appearance of the room and began to dust things in the usual housewifely fashion.

Mendelssohn, with that fine grace which never forsook him, assisted her in putting things to rights, and when the piano was opened, he proceeded to carry out two pet parrots, laughingly explaining that if they were to have music, it was well to insure against competition.

FELIX MENDELSSOHN

He sat down at the piano and played, without being asked, and sang a little song in English in graceful but unobtrusive compliment to the hostess. Then the Queen sang in German, he playing the accompaniment. And in his letter to his sister Fanny, telling her of all this, in his easy, gossipy, brotherly way, Felix adds that the Queen has a charming soprano voice, that only needs a little cultivation and practise to make her fit to take the leading part in " Elijah."

This was no joke to Felix—he only regretted that Queen Victoria's official position was such that she could not spare enough time for music.

Albert did not appear upon the scene until Mendelssohn had extended his call to an hour, and was just ready to leave. The Prince Consort was too perfect a gentleman to ever obtrude when his wife was entertaining callers, but now he apologized for not knowing the Meister had honored them—which we hope was a white lie. But, anyway, Felix consented to remain and play a few bars of the oratorio they had heard him conduct the night before. Then Albert sang a little, and Victoria insisted on making a cup of tea for the guest before they parted. When he went away, Albert and Victoria both walked with him down the hall, and as he bade them good-by, Victoria spoke the kindly "Auf wiedersehen."
¶ In the story of her life, Victoria has in spirit corroborated this account of her meeting with Mendelssohn. She refers to him as her dear friend and the friend of her

husband, and pays incidentally a gentle tribute to his memory ❧ ❧

The universal quality of Mendelssohn's knowledge, his fine forbearance and diplomatic skill in leading a conversation into safe and peaceful waters, were very marked. He was recognized by the King of Saxony as a king of art, and so was received into the household as an equal; and surely no man ever had a more kingly countenance. His body, however, seemed to lag behind, and was no match for his sublime spirit. But when fired by his position as Conductor, or when at the piano, the slender body was nerved to a point where it seemed all suppleness and sinewy strength.

In his " Songs Without Words," the spirit of the Master is best shown. There the grace, the gentleness and the sublimity of his soul are best mirrored. And if at twilight you should hear his " On the Wings of Song," played by one who understands, perhaps you will feel his spirit near, and divine the purity, kindliness and excellence of Felix Mendelssohn-Bartholdy.

FRANZ LISZT

FRANZ LISZT

Were I to tell you what my feelings were on carefully perusing and reperusing this essay, I could hardly find terms to express myself. Let this suffice: I feel more than fully rewarded for my trials, my sacrifices and artistic struggles, on noting the impression I have made on you in particular. To be thus completely understood was my only ambition; and to have been understood is the most ravishing gratification of my longing.

—Liszt in a Letter to Wagner

FRANZ LISZT

IN writing of Liszt there is a strong temptation to work the superlative to its limit. In this instance it is well to overcome temptation by succumbing to it.

That word "genius" is much bandied, and often used without warrant; but for those rare beings who leap from the brain of Jove, full-armed, it is the only appellation. No finespun theory of pedagogics or heredity can account for the marvelous talent of Franz Liszt—he was one sent from God.

Yet we find a few fortuitous circumstances that favored his evolution. Possibly, on the other hand, there are those who might say the boy attracted to himself the human elements that he required, and thus worked out his freedom, acquiring that wondrous ability to express his inmost emotions. Art is the beautiful way of doing things. All art is the expression of sublime emotions; and there seems a strong necessity in every soul to impart the joy and the aspiration that it feels. And further, art is for the artist first, just as work is for the worker—it is all just a matter of self-development. And how blessed is it to think that every soul that works out its own freedom gives freedom to others! Liszt is the inspirer of musicians, just as Shakespeare is the inspirer of writers.

187

FRANZ LISZT

Strong men make it possible for others to be strong. No man of the century gave the science of music such an impulse for good as this man. To go no further in way of proof, let the truth be stated yet once again, that it was Franz Liszt who threw a rope to the drowning Wagner. ¶ On October Twenty-second, in the year Eighteen Hundred Eleven, when a man-child was born at the village of Raiding, Hungary, the heavens gave no sign, and no signal-flags nor couriers proclaimed the event, all as had been done a week before when a babe was born to the Prince and Princess Esterhazy at the same place. Now the child born last was the son of obscure parents, the father being an underling secretary of the Prince, known as Liszt. The child was very weak and frail, and for some months it was thought hardly possible it could live; but Destiny decreed that the boy should not perish ❧ ❧

The first recollections of Liszt take in, in a happy view, four men playing cards at a square table. One of these men was the boy's father, another was Mein Herr Joseph Haydn, and the other two players are lost in the fog of obscurity. Did they ever know what a wonderful game they played, as little Franz Liszt, sitting on a corner of the table, listened to their talk and admired the buttons on the coat of the Kappellmeister? After the card-game Haydn sat at the piano and played, and the boy, just three years old, thought he could do that, too. Then there was another Kappellmeister in the employ of

FRANZ LISZT

Prince Nicholas Esterhazy at Eisenstadt, and his name was Hummel. He was a pupil of Mozart, and used to tell of it quite often when he came up to Raiding on little visits, after the wine had been sampled. Liszt the Elder used to help Hummel straighten out his accounts, and where went Liszt the Elder, there, too, went little Franz Liszt, who was n't very strong and banked on it, and had to be babied. And so little Franz became acquainted with Hummel and used to sit on his knee at the piano, and together they played funny duets that set the company in a roar—two tunes at a time, harmonious discords and counterpoint, such as no one ever heard before, or since.

At this time there was no piano at the Liszt cottage, but the boy learned to play at the neighbors', and practised at the palace of the Prince. His father and mother once took him there to hear Hummel. On this occasion Hummel played the Concerto by Reis in C minor. At the close of the performance, little Franz climbed up on the piano-stool and very solemnly played the same thing himself, to the immense delight of the listeners.

The father of Liszt has recorded that at this time the child was but three years old, but after taking off the proper per cent for the pride of a fond parent, the probabilities are the boy was five. This is the better attested when we remember that it was only a few weeks later that, on the request of Prince Esterhazy, the boy played at a concert in Oedenburg.

This launched the boy on that public career which was to continue for just seventy years. There is good evidence that the boy could read music before he could read writing, and that he threw into his playing such feeling and expression as Ferdinand Reis, who merely imitated his master, Beethoven, had never anticipated. That is to say, when he played " Reis," he improved on him, with variations all his own—attempts often made with the work of great composers, but which incur risks not advised ❧ ❧

It will be seen that Liszt, although born in poverty, was from the very first in a distinctly musical environment. He could not remember a time when he did not attend the band-concerts—his parents wanted to go, and took the baby because there were no servants to take charge of him at home. Music was in the air, and everybody discussed it, just as in Italy you may hear the beggars in the streets criticizing art.

The delightful insouciance of this child-pianist won the heart of every hearer, and his success quite turned the head of his father, the worthy bookkeeper.

To give the child the advantages of an education was now his parents' one ambition. Having no money of his own, the father importuned his employer, the Prince, who rather smiled at the thought of spending time and money on such an elfin-like child. His playing was, of course, phenomenal, unaccountable, a sort of bursting out of the sun's rays, and, like the rainbow, a thing not to be seized upon and kept. It was mere precocity, and precocity is a rareripe fruit, with a worm at the core. This discouragement of the over-ambitious father was probably wise, for it gave the boy a chance to play I-Spy and leapfrog in the streets of the village, and to roam the fields. The lad became strong and well, and when ten years of age he had grown into a handsome youngster with already those marks of will and purpose on his beautiful face that were to be his credentials to place and power.

He had often played at concerts in the towns and villages about, and when there were visitors at the palace this fine, slim son of the bookkeeper was sent for to entertain them.

This attention kept ambition alive in the hearts of his parents, and after many misgivings they decided to hazard all and move to Vienna to give their boy the opportunities they felt he deserved.

The entire household effects being sold, the bookkeeper found he had nearly six hundred francs—one hundred fifty dollars. To this amount Prince Esterhazy added fifty dollars, and Hummel gave his mite, and with tears of regret at breaking up the home-nest, but with high hope, flavored by chill intervals of fear, the father, mother and boy started for Vienna.

Arriving in that city the distinguished Carl Czerny, pupil of Beethoven, was importuned to take the lad. Only the letter from Hummel secured the boy an audience, for Czerny was already overburdened with pupils. But when he had listened to the lad's playing, he consented to take him as a pupil, merely saying that he showed a certain degree of promise. It is sternly true that Czerny did not fully come into the Liszt faith until after that concert of April Thirteenth, Eighteen Hundred Twenty-three, when Beethoven, ripe with years, crowded his way to the front and kissed the player on both cheeks, calling him " my son." Such a greeting from the great Master spoke volumes when we consider the lifelong aversion that Beethoven held toward " prodigies," and his disinclination to attend all concerts but his own.

And thus did Franz Liszt begin his professional pilgrimage, consecrated by the kiss of the Master.

Paris was the next step—to Paris, the musical and artistic center of the world. To win in Paris meant fame and fortune wherever he wished to exhibit his powers. The way the name of Franz Liszt swept through the fashionable salons of Paris is too well known to recount. Scarcely thirteen years of age, he played the most difficult pieces with peculiar precision and power. And his simple, boyish, unaffected manner—his total lack of self-consciousness—won him the affection of every mother-heart. He was fondled, feted, caressed, and took it all as a matter of course. He had not yet reached the age of indiscretion.

FRANZ LISZT

USIC is a secondary sexual manifestation, just as are the songs of birds, their gay and gaudy plumage, the color and perfume of flowers that so delight us, and the luscious fruits that nourish us—all is sex. And then, do you not remember that expression of Renan's, "The unconscious coquetry of the flowers"? Without love there would be no poetry and no music. All the manifest beauty of earth is only Nature's nuptial decoration.

James Huneker, not always judicious, but a trifle more judicial than others that might be named, declares that two women, making a simultaneous attack upon the great composer, caused him to cut for sanctuary, and hence we have the Abbe Liszt, thus proving again that love and religion are twin sisters.

The old-time biographers can easily be placed in two classes: those who sought to pillory their man, and those who sought to protect him. Neither one told the truth; but each gave a picture, more or less blurred, of a being conjured forth from their own inner consciousness. Franz Liszt was naturalized in the Faubourg Saint Germain. It was here that he was first hailed as the infant prodigy, and proud ladies, at his performances, pressed to the front and struggled for the privilege of imprinting on his fair forehead a chaste and motherly kiss ❧ ❧

FRANZ LISZT

IGHT years had passed: years of work and travel and constant growing fame. The youth had grown into a man, and his return to the scene of his former triumphs was the signal for a regathering of the clans to note his progress—or decline. The verdict was that from "Le Petit Prodige," he had evolved into something far more interesting—"Le Grand Prodige." Tall, handsome, strong, and with a becoming diffidence and a half-shy manner, his name went abroad, and he became the rage of the salons. His marvelous playing told of his hopes, longings, fears and aspirations—proud, melancholy, imploring, sad, sullen —his tones told all.

Fair votaries followed him from one performance to another. Leaving out of the equation such mild incidents as the friendship for George Sand, which began with a brave avowal of platonics, and speedily drifted into something more complex; also the equally interesting incident of his being invited to visit the Chateau of the lovely Adele Laprunarede, and the Alpine winter catching the couple and holding them willing captives for three months, blocked there in a castle, with nothing worse than a conscience and an elderly husband to appease, we reach the one, supreme love-passion in the life of Liszt. The Countess d'Agoult is worthy of much more than a passing note.

At twenty years of age she had been married to a man twenty-one years her senior. It was a " mariage de

194

convenance "—arranged by her parents and a notary
in a powdered wig. It is somewhat curious to find how
many great women have contracted just such mar-
riages. Grim disillusionment following, true love holding
nothing in store for them, they turn to books, politics
or art, and endeavor to stifle their woman's nature with
the husks of philosophy.

Count d'Agoult was a hard-headed man of affairs—
stern, sensible and reasonably amiable—that is to say,
he never smashed the furniture, nor beat his wife. She
submitted to his will, and all the fine, girlish, bubbling
qualities of her mind and soul were soon held in check
through that law of self-protection which causes a
woman to give herself unreservedly only to the One who
Understands. Yet the Countess was not miserable—only
at rare intervals did there come moods of a sort of
dread longing, homesickness and unrest; but calm
philosophy soon put these moods to rout. She had
focused her mind on sociology and had written a short
history of the Revolution, a volume that yet commands
the respect of students. At intervals she read her
essays aloud to invited guests. She studied art, delved
a little in music, became acquainted with the leading
thinking men and women of her time, and opened
her salon for their entertainment.

Three children had been born to her in six years.
Maternity is a very necessary part of every good
woman's education—" this woman's flesh demands its

natural pains," says a great writer in a certain play. A staid, sensible woman was the Countess d'Agoult—tall, handsome, graceful, and with a flavor of melancholy, reserve and disinterestedness in her make-up that made her friendship sought by men of maturity. She talked but little, and won through the fine art of listening ✄ She was neither happy nor unhappy, and if the gaiety of girlhood had given way to subdued philosophy, there were still wit, smiles and gentle irony to take the place of laughter. "Life," she said, "consists in molting one's illusions." ✄ ✄

The Countess was twenty-nine years of age when " Le Grand Prodige," aged twenty-three, arrived in Paris, She had known him when he was " Le Petit Prodige "—when she was a girl with dreams and he but a child. She wished to see how he had changed, and so went to hear him play. He was insincere, affected and artificial, she said—his mannerisms absurd and his playing acrobatic. At the next concert where he played she sought him out and half-laughingly told him her opinion of his work. He gravely thanked her, with his hand upon his heart, and said that such honesty and frankness were refreshing. After the concert Liszt remembered this woman—she was the only one he did remember—she had made her impression ✄ ✄

He did not like her.

Soon Liszt was invited to the salon of the Countess d'Agoult, and he, the plebeian, proudly repulsed the fair aristocrat when her attentions took on the note of patronage. They mildly tiffed—a very good way to begin a friendship, once said Chateaubriand.

The feminine qualities in the heart of Liszt made a lure of the person who dared affront him. He needed the flint on which his mind could strike fire—nothing is so depressing as continual, mushy adulation. He sought out the Countess, and together they traversed the borderland of metaphysics, and surveyed, as the days passed, all that intellectual realm which the dawn of the Twentieth Century thinks it has just discovered.

She taunted him into a defense of George Sand, who had but recently returned from her escapade to Venice with Alfred de Musset. Liszt defended the author of "Leone Leoni," and read to the Countess from her books to prove his case.

When haughty, proud and religious ladies mix mentalities with sensitive youths of twenty-four, the danger-line is being approached. The Grand Passions that live in history, such as that of Abelard and Heloise, Petrarch and Laura, Dante and Beatrice, swing in their orbit around world-weariness. Love does not concern itself with this earth alone—it demands a universe for its free expression. And the only woman who is capable of the Grand Passion—who stakes all on one throw of the dice—is the melancholy woman, with this fine, religious reserve. No one suspected the Countess d'Agoult of indiscretion—she was too cold and self-contained for that!

197

FRANZ LISZT

And so is the world deceived by the Eternal Paradox of things—that law of antithesis which makes opposites look alike. Beneath the calm dignity of matronly demeanor the fires of love were banked. Probably even the Countess herself did not know of the volcano that was smoldering in her heart. But there came a day when the flames burst forth, and all the reserve, poise, quiet dignity, caution and discretion were dissolved into nothingness in love's alembic.

Poor Franz Liszt!

Poor Countess d'Agoult!

They were powerless in the coils of such a passion. It was a mad tumult of wild intoxication, of delicious pain, of burning fears, and vain, tossing unrest. The woman's nature, stifled by its six years of coaxing marital repression, was asserting itself. Liszt did not know that a woman could love like this—neither did the woman. Once they parted, after talking the matter over solemnly and deciding on what was best for both—they parted coldly—with a mere touching of the lips in a last good-by ❦ ❦

The next week they were together again.

Then Liszt fled to the Abbe Lamennais, and in tears sought, at the confessional and in dim retirement, a surcease from the passion that was devouring him. Here was a pivotal point in the life of Liszt, and the Church came near then, claiming him for her own. And such would have been the case, were it not for the fact that

FRANZ LISZT

one of the children of the Countess d'Agoult was sick unto death. He knew of the sleepless vigils—the weary watching of the fond mother.

The child died, and Franz Liszt went to the parent in her bereavement, to offer the solace of religion and bid her a decent, respectful farewell, ere he left Paris forever. He thought grief was a cure for passion, and that in the presence of death, love itself was dumb. How could he understand that, in most strong natures, tears and pain, and hope and love are kin, and that each is in turn the manifestation of a great and welling heart!

Liszt stood by the side of the Countess as the grave closed over the body of her firstborn child. And as they stood there, under the darkening sky, her hand went groping blindly for his. She wrote of this, years and years after, when seventy winters had silvered her hair and her steps were feeble—she wrote of this, in her book called, "Souvenirs," and tells how, in that moment of supreme grief, when her life was whitened and purified by the fires of pain, her hand sought his. The deep current of her love swept the ashes of grief away, and she reached blindly for the hands—those wonderful music-making hands of Liszt—that they might support her. And standing there, side by side, as the priest intoned the burial service, he whispered to her, "Death shall not divide us, nor is eternity long enough to separate thee from me!"

FRANZ LISZT

IT was only a few days after that Liszt left Paris—but not for a monastery. He journeyed to Switzerland, and stopping at Basle he was soon joined by the Countess, her two children, and her mother.

All Paris was set in an uproar by the " abduction." The George Sand school approved and loudly applauded the " eclat "; but it was condemned and execrated by the majority. As for the injured husband, it is said he gave a banquet in honor of the event; his feelings, no doubt, being eased by the fact that the goodly dot his wife had brought him at her marriage was now his exclusive possession. He had never gauged her character, anyway, and he inwardly acknowledged that her mind was of a sort with which he could not parry.

And now she had wronged him; yet in his grief he took much satisfaction, and in his martyrdom there was sweet solace.

The chief blame fell on Liszt, and the accusation that he had " broken up a happy home " came to his ears from many sources. " They blame you and you alone," a friend said to him.

" Good! good! " said Liszt, " I gladly bear it all."

George Sand, plain in feature, quiet in manner, soft and feminine when she wished to be, yet possessing the mind of a man, went to Switzerland to visit the runaway Liszt and the " Lady Arabella." At first thought, one might suppose that such a visit, after the former

200

relationship, might have been a trifle embarrassing for both. But the fact that in the interval George Sand had been crunching the soul of Chopin formed an estoppel on the memory of all the soft sentiment that had gone before. George Sand brought her two children, Maurice and Solange, and the " Lady Arabella " had two of her own to keep them company. A little family party was made up, and with a couple of servants and a guide, a little journey was taken through the mountain villages, all in genuine gipsy style. George Sand, who worked up all life, its sensations and emotions, into good copy, has given us an account of the trip, that throws some very interesting side-lights on the dramatis personæ.

The recounter and her children were all clothed in peasant costume—man-style, with blouses and trousers. Gipsy garbs were worn by the servants, and Liszt was arrayed like a mountaineer, and carried a reed pipe, upon which he, from time to time, awoke the echoes. When the dusty, unkempt crew arrived at a village inn, the landlord usually made hot haste to secrete his silverware. Once when a sudden rainstorm drove the wayfarers into a church, Liszt took his seat at the organ and played—played with such power and feeling that the village priest ran out and called for the neighbors to come quickly, as the Angel Gabriel, in the guise of a mountaineer, was playing the organ. Anthem, oratorio, and sweet, subtle, soulful improvisation followed, and the villagers knelt, and eyes were filled with tears.

FRANZ LISZT

George Sand records that she never heard such playing by the Master before; she herself wept, and yet through her tears she managed to see a few things, and here is one picture which she gives us: " The Lady Arabella sat on the balustrade, swinging one foot, and cast her proud and melancholy gaze over the lower nave, and waited in vain for the celestial voices that were supposed to vibrate in her bosom ❧ Her abundant light hair, disheveled by the wind and rain, fell in bewildering disorder, and her eyes, reflecting the finest hue of the firmament, seemed to be wandering over the realm of God's creation after each sigh of the huge organ, played by the divine Liszt.

" ' This is not what I expected,' said she to me languidly. ¶ " 'Ah, that is what you said of the mountain peaks and the glacier, yesterday,' said I."

It will be seen, by those who have read between the lines, that George Sand did not much like " the fair Lady Arabella of the wondrous length of limb." In passing, it is well to note, in way of apology for this allusion as to "length of limb," that George Sand was once spoken of by Heine as " a dumpy-duodecimo." It is to be regretted that we have no description of George Sand by the Lady Arabella.

Years passed in study and writing, with occasional concert tours, wherein the public flocked to hear the greatest pianist of his time. The power, grasp and insight of the man increased with the years, and

202

FRANZ LISZT

wherever he deigned to play, the public was not slow in giving him that approbation which his masterly work deserved. Liszt was one of the Elect Few who train on. On these short concert trips his wife (for such she must certainly be regarded) seldom accompanied him—this in deference to his wish, and this, it seems, was the first and last and only cause of dissension between them ⚘ The Countess was born for a career and her spirit chafed at the forced retirement in which she lived.

Ten years had gone by and three children had been born to her and Liszt. One of these, a boy, died in youth, but one of the daughters became, as we know, the wife of Richard Wagner, and the other daughter married Oliver Emile Ollivier, the eminent statesman and man of letters—member of the Cabinet in that memorable year, Eighteen Hundred Seventy, when France declared war on Germany. Both of these daughters of Liszt were women of rare mentality and splendid worth, true daughters of their father.

Position is a pillory; sometimes the populace will pelt you with rose-leaves—at others, with ancient vegetables. Liszt believed that for his wife's peace of mind, and his own, she should not crowd herself too much to the front—he feared what the mob might say or do. We can not say that she was jealous of his fame, nor he of hers. However, as a writer she was winning her way. But the fateful day came when the wife said, " From this day on I must everywhere stand by your side, your

wife and your equal, or we must part." ¶ They parted.
¶ Liszt made princely provision for her welfare, and the
support of their children, as well as those that had come
to her before they met.

She went south to Italy, and he began that most wonderful concert tour, where, in Saint Petersburg, sums equal
to ten thousand dollars were taken at the door for single
entertainments.

Countess d'Agoult was the respected friend of King
Emmanuel, and her salon at Turin was the meeting-
place of such men as Renan, Meyerbeer, Chopin,
Berlioz and Rossini. She carried on a correspondence
with Heinrich Heine, was the trusted friend of Prince
Jerome Bonaparte, Lamartine and Lamennais, and was
on a footing of equality with the greatest and best minds
of her age. She wrote several plays, one of which,
" Jeanne d'Arc," was presented at the Court Theater of
Turin, with the Royal Family present, and was a
marked success. Her criticism on the work of Ingres
made that artist's reputation, just as surely as Ruskin
made the fame of Turner. But one special reason why
Americans should remember this woman is because she
first translated Emerson's " Essays " and caused them
to be published in Italian and French.

I am not sure that Liszt ever quite forgave her for not
dying of broken heart, when they parted there at Lake
Maggiore. He thought she would take to opium or
strong drink, or both. She did neither, but proved, by

FRANZ LISZT

her after-life, that she was sufficient unto herself. She was worthy of the love of Liszt, because she was able to do without it, She was no parasitic, clinging vine that strangles the sturdy oak.

The Abbe Lamennais, the close friend of Liszt, once said, " Liszt is a great musician, the greatest the world has ever seen, but his wife can easily take a mental octave which he can not quite span."

The Countess d'Agoult died March Fifth, in Eighteen Hundred Seventy-six, at the age of seventy years. When tidings of her passing reached the Abbe Liszt, he caused all of his immediate engagements to be canceled and went into monastic retirement, wearing the robe of horsehair and a rope girdle at his waist. He filled the hours for the space of a month with silent reverie and prayer ⚜ ⚜

And even in that cloister-cell, with its stone floor and cold, bare walls, the leaden hours brought the soundless presence of a tall and stately woman. Through the desolate bastions of his brain she glided in sweet disarray, looked into his tear-dimmed eyes, smoothing softly the coarse pillow where rested that head with its lion's mane which we know so well—a head now whitened by the frost of years. No sound came to him there, save a soft voice which Fate refused to silence, and this voice whispered and whispered yet again to him: " Death shall not divide us, nor is eternity long enough to separate thee from me! "

FRANZ LISZT

ELIGION is not the cure of love. Perhaps religion is love and love is religion—anyway, we know that they are often fused. For a time after Liszt had parted from the Countess, fortune smiled. Then came various loans to friends, managerial experiments, the backing of an ill-starred opera, and a season of overwrought nerves.

Luck had turned against the supposed invincible Liszt. Then it was that the Princess Wittgenstein appears on the scene. This fine woman, earnest, strong in character, intellectual, had tried ten years of marital hard times and quit the partnership with a daughter and a goodly dot

The Princess had secretly loved Liszt from afar, and had followed him from town to town, glorying in his triumphs, feeding on his personality.

When trouble came she managed to have a message conveyed to him that an unknown woman would advance, without interest or security, enough money for him to pay all his debts and secure him two years of leisure in which he might regain his health and do such work as his taste might dictate.

Of course Liszt declined the offer, begging his unknown friend to divulge her identity that he might thank her for her disinterested faith in the cause of Art.

A meeting was brought about and the result was as usual. The Grand Duchess of Saxe-Weimar, in the face of scandal, took the Abbe and Princess under protection,

FRANZ LISZT

giving them the Chateau of Altenburg, near Weimar, for a retreat. There Liszt, guarded from all intrusion, composed the symphonies of " Dante " and " Faust," sonatas, masses and parts of " Saint Elizabeth." For thirteen years they lived an idyllic existence. Then, having married her daughter by her first husband to Prince Hohenlohe, the Princess set out for Rome to obtain a dispensation from the Pope, so she and the Abbe could be married. Her husband, who was a Prot- estant, had long before secured a divorce and married again. Pope Pius the Ninth granted her wish, and she hastened home and prepared for the wedding. It was said that flowers were already placed on the altar, the marriage feast was prepared, the guests invited, when news came that the Pope had changed his mind on the argument of one of the lady's kinsmen. We now have every reason to believe, though, that the Pope changed his mind on the earnest request of Liszt.

On the death of the Princess Wittgenstein, the Pope dispensed Liszt from his priestly ties, but he was called the Abbe until his death.

Whenever I find any one who can write better on a subject than I can, I refuse to go on.

There is a book called, " Music Study in Germany," written by my friend Amy Fay, and published by The Macmillan Company, from which I quote.

If Amy Fay had not chosen to be the superb pianist that she is, she might have struck thirteen in literature.

FRANZ LISZT

There are a dozen biographies of Liszt, but none of them has ever given us such a vivid picture of the man as has this American girl. The simple, unpretentious little touches that she introduces are art so subtle and true that it is the art which conceals art. The topmost turret of my ambition would be to have Amy Fay Boswellize my memory.

Says Amy Fay:

Liszt is the most interesting and striking-looking man imaginable, tall and slight, with deep-set eyes, long iron-gray hair, and shaggy eyebrows. His mouth turns up at the corners, which gives him a most crafty and Mephistophelian expression when he smiles, and his whole appearance and manner have a sort of Jesuitical elegance and ease. His hands are very narrow, with long and slender fingers that look as if they had twice as many joints as other people's. They are so flexible and supple that it makes you nervous to look at them. Anything like the polish of his manner I never saw. When he got up to leave the box, for instance, after his adieux to the ladies, he laid his hand on his heart and made his final bow—not with affection, or in mere gallantry, but with a quiet courtliness which made you feel that no other way of bowing to a lady was right or proper ⚜ But the most extraordinary thing about Liszt is his wonderful variety of expression and play of feature. One moment his face will look dreamy, shadowy, tragic; the next he will be insinuating, amiable, ironical, sardonic; but always the same captivating grace of manner. He is a perfect study. He is all spirit, but half the time, at least, a mocking spirit, I should say. All

FRANZ LISZT

Weimar adores him, and people say that women still go perfectly crazy over him. When he walks out, he bows to everybody just like a king! The Grand Duke has presented him with a beautiful house situated on the Park, and here he lives elegantly, free of expense.

Liszt gives no paid lessons whatever, as he is much too grand for that, but if one has talent enough, or pleases him, he lets one come to him and play to him. I go to him every other day, but I don't play more than twice a week, as I can not prepare so much, but I listen to others. Up to this point there have been only four in the class beside myself, and I am the only new one. From four to six o'clock in the afternoon is the time when he receives his scholars. The first time I went I did not play to him, but listened to the rest. Urspruch and Leitert, two young men whom I met the other night, have studied with Liszt a long time, and both play superbly. ¶ As I entered the salon, Urspruch was performing Schumann's " Symphonic Studies "—an immense composition, and one that it took at least half an hour to get through. He played so splendidly that my heart sank down into the very depths. I thought I should never get on there! Liszt came forward and greeted me in a very friendly manner as I entered. He was in a very good humor that day, and made some little witticisms. Urspruch asked him what title he should give to a piece he was composing. " Per aspera ad astra," said Liszt. This was such a good hit that I began to laugh, and he seemed to enjoy my appreciation of his little sarcasm. I did not play that time as my piano had only just come, and I was not prepared to do so, but I went home and practised tremendously for several days on Chopin's

209

FRANZ LISZT

"B minor sonata." It is a great composition and one of his last works. When I thought I could play it, I went to Liszt, though with a trembling heart. I can not tell you what it has cost me every time I have ascended his stairs. I can scarcely summon up courage to go there, and generally stand on the steps a few moments before I can make up my mind to open the door and go in ✄ ✄

Well, on this day the artists Leitert and Urspruch, and the young composer Metzdorf, were in the room when I came. They had probably been playing. At first Liszt took no notice of me beyond a greeting, till Metzdorf said to him, "Herr Doctor, Miss Fay has brought a sonata." "Ah, well, let us hear it," said Liszt. Just then he left the room for a minute, and I told the three gentlemen they ought to go away and let me play to Liszt alone, for I felt nervous about playing before them. They all laughed at me and said they would not budge an inch. When Liszt came back they said to him, "Only think, Herr Doctor, Miss Fay proposes to send us all home." I said I could not play before such artists. "Oh, that is healthy for you," said Liszt with a smile, and added, "you have a very choice audience now." I don't know whether he appreciated how nervous I was, but instead of walking up and down the room, as he often does, he sat down by me like any other teacher, and heard me play the first movement. It was frightfully hard, but I had studied it so much that I managed to get through with it pretty successfully. Nothing could exceed Liszt's amiability, or the trouble he gave himself, and instead of frightening me, he inspired me. Never was there such a delightful teacher! and he is the most sympathetic one I 've had. You feel so free with him, and he develops the very spirit of music in you. He does n't keep nagging at you all the time, but he leaves you your own conception. Now and then he will make a criticism or play a passage, and with a few words give you enough to think of all the rest of your life. There is a delicate point to everything he says as subtle as he is himself. He does n't tell you anything about the technique; that you must work out for yourself. When I had finished the first movement of the sonata, Liszt, as he always does, said "Bravo!" Taking my seat he made some little criticisms, and then he told me to go on and play the rest of it.

Now, I only half-knew the other movements, for the first one was so extremely difficult that it cost me all the labor I could give to prepare that. But playing to Liszt reminds me of trying to feed the elephant in the Zoölogical Garden with lumps of sugar. He disposes of whole movements as if they were nothing, and stretches out gravely for more! One of my fingers fortunately began to bleed, for I had practised the skin off, and that gave me a good excuse for stopping. Whether he was pleased at this proof of industry, I know not; but after looking at my finger and saying, " Oh! " very compassionately, he sat down and played the whole three last movements himself. That was a great deal and showed off his powers. It was the first time I had heard him, and I don't know which was the most extraordinary— the Scherzo, with its wonderful lightness and swiftness, the Adagio with its depth and pathos, or the last movement, where the whole keyboard seemed to " donnern und blitzen." There is such a vividness about everything

211

FRANZ LISZT

he plays that it does not seem as if it were mere music you are listening to, but it is as if he had called up a real, living form, and you saw it breathing before your face and eyes. It gives me almost a ghostly feeling to hear him, and it seems as if the air were peopled with spirits. Oh, he is a perfect wizard! It is as interesting to see him as it is to hear him, for his face changes with every modulation of the piece, and he looks exactly as he is playing. He has one element that is most captivating, and that is a sort of delicate and fitful mirth that keeps peering out at you here and there. It is most peculiar, and when he plays that way, the most bewitching expression comes over his face. It seems as if a little spirit of joy were playing hide-and-go-seek with you ॐ At home Liszt does n't wear his long Abbe's coat, but a short one, in which he looks much more artistic. His figure is remarkably slight, but his head is most imposing. It is so delicious in that room of his! It was all furnished and put in order for him by the Grand Duchess herself. The walls are pale gray, with a gilded border running round the room, or rather two rooms, which are divided, but not separated, by crimson curtains. The furniture is crimson, and everything is so comfortable—such a contrast to German bareness and stiffness generally. A splendid grand piano (he receives a new one every year,) stands in one window. The other window is always open and looks out on the park. There is a dovecote just opposite the window, and doves promenade up and down upon the roof of it, and fly about, and sometimes whirr down on the sill itself. That pleases Liszt. His writing-table is beautifully fitted up with things that match. Everything is in

212

bronze—inkstand, paper-weight, match-box, etc.—and there is always a lighted candle standing on it by which he and the gentlemen can light their cigars. There is a carpet on the floor, a rarity in Germany, and Liszt generally walks about and smokes and mutters, and calls upon one or the other of us to play. From time to time he will sit down and himself play where a passage does not suit him, and when he is in good spirits he makes little jests all the time. His playing was a complete revelation to me, and has given me an entirely new insight into music. You can not conceive, without hearing him, how poetic he is, or the thousand nuances that he can throw into the simplest thing, and he is equally great on all sides. From the zephyr to the tempest, the whole scale is equally at his command ✳

Liszt is not at all like a master, and can not be treated as one. He is a monarch, and when he extends his royal scepter you can sit down and play to him. You never can ask him to play anything for you, no matter how much you 're dying to hear it. If he is in the mood he will play; if not, you must content yourself with a few remarks. You can not even offer to play yourself.

You lay your notes on the table, so he can see that you want to play, and sit down. He takes a turn up and down the room, looks at the music, and if the piece interests him he will call upon you. We bring the same piece to him but once, and but once play it through ✳ Yesterday I had prepared for him his "Au Bord d'une Source." I was nervous and played badly. He was not to be put out, however, but acted as if he thought I had played charmingly, and then he sat down and played the whole thing himself, oh, so exquisitely! It made me feel like a wood-chopper. The notes just seemed to ripple off his fingers' ends with scarce any perceptible motion. As he neared the close I noticed that funny little expression come over his face, which he always has when he means to surprise you, and he then suddenly took an unexpected chord and extemporized a poetical little end, quite different from the written one. Do you wonder that people go distracted over him? ¶ One day this week, when we were with Liszt, he was in such high spirits that it was as if he had suddenly become twenty years younger. A student from the Stuttgart conservatory played a Liszt concerto. His name is V., and he is dreadfully nervous. Liszt kept up a running fire of satire all the time he was playing, but in a good-natured way. I should n't have minded it if it had been I. In fact, I think it would have inspired me; but poor V. hardly knew whether he was on his head or on his feet. It was too funny. Everything that Liszt says is so striking. For instance, in one place where V. was playing the melody rather feebly, Liszt suddenly took his seat at the piano and said, "When I play, I always play for the people in the gallery, so that those people who pay only five groschens for their seats also hear something." Then he began, and I wish you could have heard him! The sound did n't seem to be very loud, but it was penetrating and far-reaching. When he had finished, he raised one hand in the air, and you seemed to see all the people in the gallery drinking in the sound. That is the way Liszt teaches you. He presents an idea to you, and it takes fast hold of your mind and sticks there. Music is such a real, visible thing to him that he always has a symbol, instantly, in the

214

FRANZ LISZT

material world to express his idea. One day, when I was playing, I made too much movement with my hand in a rotary sort of a passage where it was difficult to avoid it. "Keep your hand still, Fraulein," said Liszt; "don't make omelet." I couldn't help laughing—it hit me on the head so nicely. He is far too sparing of his playing, unfortunately, and like Tausig, sits down and plays only a few bars at a time generally. It is dreadful when he stops, just as you are at the height of your enjoyment, but he is so thoroughly blase that he doesn't care to show off before people and doesn't like to have any one pay him a compliment about his playing. In Liszt I can at least say that my ideal in something has been realized. He goes far beyond all that I expected. Anything so perfectly beautiful as he looks when he sits at the piano I never saw, and yet he is almost an old man now. I enjoy him as I would an exquisite work of art. His personal magnetism is immense, and I can scarcely bear it when he plays. He can make me cry all he chooses, and that is saying a good deal, because I've heard so much music, and never have been affected by it. Even Joachim, whom I think divine, never moved me. When Liszt plays anything pathetic, it sounds as if he had been through everything, and opens all one's wounds afresh. All that one has ever suffered comes before one again. Who was it that I heard say once, that years ago he saw Clara Schumann sitting in tears near the platform during one of Liszt's performances? Liszt knows well the influence he has on people, for he always fixes his eyes on some one of us when he plays, and I believe he tries to wring our hearts. When he plays a passage and goes pearling down the keyboard, he often

215

looks over at me and smiles, to see whether I am appreciating it.

But I doubt if he feels any particular emotion himself when he is piercing you through with his rendering. He is simply hearing every tone, knowing exactly what effect he wishes to produce and just how to do it. In fact, he is practically two persons in one—the listener and the performer. But what immense self-command that implies! No matter how fast he plays you always feel that there is "plenty of time"—no need to be anxious! You might as well try to move one of the pyramids as fluster him. Tausig possessed this repose in a technical way, and his touch was marvelous; but he never drew the tears to your eyes. He could not wind himself through all the subtle labyrinths of the heart as Liszt does. Liszt does such bewitching little things! The other day, for instance, Fraulein Gaul was playing something to him, and in it were two runs, and after each run two staccato chords. She did them most beautifully and struck the chords immediately after. " No, no," said Liszt; " after you make a run you must wait a minute before you strike the chords, as if in admiration of your own performance. You must pause, as if to say, 'How nicely I did that!'" Then he sat down and made a run himself, waited a second, and then struck the two chords in the treble, saying as he did so, " Bravo! " and then he played again, struck the other chord and said again, " Bravo! " and positively, it was as if the piano had softly applauded.

Liszt hasn't the nervous irritability common to artists, but on the contrary his disposition is the most exquisite and tranquil in the world. We have been there incessantly

FRANZ LISZT

and I've never seen him ruffled except two or three times, and then he was tired and not himself, and it was a most transient thing. When I think what a little savage Tausig often was, and how cuttingly sarcastic Kullak could be at times, I am astonished that Liszt so rarely lost his temper. He has the power of turning the best side of every one outward, also the most marvelous and instant appreciation of what that side is. If there is anything in you, you may be sure that Liszt will know it. On Monday I had a most delightful tete-a-tete with Liszt, quite by chance. I had occasion to call upon him for something, and strange to say, he was alone, sitting by his table writing. Generally all sorts of people are up there. He insisted upon my staying for a while, and we had the most amusing and entertaining conversation imaginable. It was the first time I ever heard Liszt really talk, for he contents himself mostly with making little jests. He is full of esprit. Another evening I was there about twilight and Liszt sat at the piano looking through a new oratorio which had just come out in Paris, upon "Christus." He asked me to turn for him, and evidently was not interested, for he would skip whole pages and begin again, here and there. There was only a single lamp, and that a rather dim one, so that the room was all in shadow, and Liszt wore his Merlin-like aspect. I asked him to tell me how he produced a certain effect he makes in his arrangement of the ballad in Wagner's "Flying Dutchman." He looked very "fin" as the French say, but did not reply. He never gives a direct answer to a direct question. "Ah," said I, "you won't tell." He smiled and then immediately played the passage. It was a long arpeggio, and the effect he made was, as I had supposed, a pedal effect. He kept the pedal down throughout, and played the beginning of the passage in a grand sort of manner, and then all the rest of it with a very pianissimo touch, and so lightly, that the continuity of the arpeggios was destroyed, and the notes seemed to be just strewn in, as if you broke a wreath of flowers and scattered them according to your fancy. It is a most striking and beautiful effect, and I told him I did n't see how he ever thought of it. " Oh, I 've invented a great many things," said he, indifferently—" this, for instance"—and he began playing a double roll of octaves in chromatics in the bass of the piano. It was very grand and made the room reverberate. ¶ " Magnificent," said I.

" Did you ever hear me do a storm? " said he.

" No."

"Ah, you ought to hear me do a storm! Storms are my forte!" ✄ ✄

Then to himself between his teeth, while a weird look came into his eyes as if he could indeed rule the blast, " Then crash the trees! "

How ardently I wished that he would " play a storm," but of course he did n't, and he presently began to trifle over the keys in a blase style. I suppose he could n't quite work himself up to the effort, but that look and tone told how Liszt would do it. Alas, that we poor mortals here below should share so often the fate of Moses, and have only a glimpse of the Promised Land, and that without the consolation of being Moses! But perhaps, after all, the vision is better than the reality. We see the whole land, even if but from afar, instead

218

of being limited merely to the spot where our foot
treads ※ ※

Once again I saw Liszt in a similar mood, though his
expression was this time comfortably rather than wildly
destructive. It was when Fraulein Remmertz was
playing his "E flat concerto" to him. There were two
grand pianos in the room; she was sitting at one, and
he at the other, accompanying and interpolating as he
felt disposed. Finally they came to a place where there
was a series of passages beginning with both hands in
the middle of the piano, and going in opposite directions
to the ends of the keyboard, ending each time with a
short, sharp chord. "Pitch everything out of the
window!" cried he, and began playing these passages
and giving every chord a whack as if he were splitting
everything up and flinging it out, and that with such
enjoyment that you felt as if you'd like to bear a hand,
too, in the work of demolition! But I never shall forget
Liszt's look as he so lazily proposed to "pitch everything out of the window." It reminded me of the expression of a big tabby-cat as it sits by the fire and purrs
away, blinking its eyes and seemingly half-asleep, when
suddenly—!—! out it strikes with both its claws, and
woe to whatever is within its reach!

LUDWIG VAN BEETHOVEN

BEETHOVEN

Melody has by Beethoven been freed from the influence of Fashion and changing Taste, and raised to an ever-valid, purely human type. Beethoven's music will be understood to all time, while that of his predecessors will, for the most part, only remain intelligible to us through the medium of reflection on the history of Art.

—*Richard Wagner*

LUDWIG VAN BEETHOVEN

USIC is the youngest of the arts. Modern music dates back about four hundred years. It is not so old as the invention of printing. As an art it began with the work of the priests of the Roman Catholic Church in endeavoring to arrange a liturgy.

The medieval chant and the popular folk-song came together, and the science of music was born. Sculpture reached perfection in Greece, painting in Italy, portraiture in Holland; but Germany, the land of thought, has given us nearly all the great musicians and nine-tenths of all our valuable musical compositions.

Holland has taken a very important part in every line of art and handicraft, and in way of all-round development has set the pace for civilization.

Art follows in the wake of commerce, for without commerce there is neither surplus wealth nor leisure. The artist is paid from what is left after men have bought food and clothing; and the time to enjoy comes only after the struggle for existence.

When Venice was not only Queen of the Adriatic but of the maritime world as well, Art came and established there her Court of Beauty. It was Venice that mothered Giorgione, Titian, the Bellinis, and the men who wrought in iron and silver and gold, and those masterful bookmakers; it was beautiful Venice that gave sustenance and encouragement to Stradivari (who made violins as well as he could) up at Cremona, only a few miles away.

But there came a day when all those seventy bookmakers of Venice ceased to print, and the music of the anvils was stilled, and all the painters were dead, and Venice became but a monument of things that were, as she is today; for Commerce is King, and his capital has been moved far away.

So Venice sits sad and solitary—a pale and beautiful ruin, pathetic beyond speech, infested by noisy shopkeepers and petty pilferers, the degenerate sons of the robbers who once roamed the sea and enthroned her on her hundred isles.

All that Venice knew was absorbed by Holland. The Elzevirs and the Plantins took over the business of the seventy bookmakers, and the art-schools of Amsterdam, Leyden and Antwerp reproduced every picture of note that had been done in Venice. The great churches of Holland are replicas of the churches of Venice. And the Cathedral at Antwerp, where the sweet bells have chimed each quarter of an hour for three centuries, through peace and plenty, through lurid war and sudden death—there where hangs Rubens' masterpiece —that Cathedral is but an enlarged " Santa Maria de' Frari," where for two hundred years hung " The

LUDWIG VAN BEETHOVEN

Assumption," by Titian. ¶ In these churches of Holland were placed splendid organs, and the priests formed choirs, and offered prizes for the best singing and the best compositions. Music and painting developed hand in hand; for at the last, all of the arts are one—each being but a division of labor.

The world owes a great debt to the Dutch. It was Holland taught England how to paint and how to print, and England taught us: so our knowledge of printing and painting came to us by way of the apostolic succession of the Dutch.

The march of civilization follows a simple trail, well defined beyond dispute. Viewed in retrospect it begins in a hazy thread stretching from Assyria into Egypt, from Egypt into Greece, from Greece to Rome— widening throughout Italy and Spain, then centering in Venice, and tracing clear and deep to Amsterdam— widening again into Germany and across to England, thence carried in " Mayflowers " to America.

That remark of Charles Dudley Warner, once near neighbor to Mark Twain, that there is no culture west of Buffalo, was indelicate if not unkind; and residents of Omaha aver that it is open to argument. But the fact stands beyond cavil that what art we possess is traceable to our masters, the Dutch.

It must be admitted that the art of printing was first practised at Mayence on the Rhine, leaving the Chinese out of the equation; but it had to travel around down

225

through Italy before it reached perfection. And its universality and usefulness were not fully developed until it had swung around to Holland and was given by the Dutch back to Germany and the world. And as with printing, so with music. Germany has specialized on music. She has succeeded, but it is because Holland gave her lessons.

LUDWIG VAN BEETHOVEN

URING the fore part of the Seventeenth Century, there lived in Antwerp, Ludvig van Biethofen, grandfather of the genius known as Beethoven. A life-size portrait of him can be seen in the Plantin Musee, and if you did not know that the picture was painted before Beethoven was born, you would say at once, " Beethoven! " There is a look of stern endurance, as if the artist had admired Rembrandt's " Burgomaster " a little too well, yet that sturdiness belonged to the Master, too; and there are the abstracted far-away look, the touch of proud melancholy, and the becoming unkemptness that we know so well.

The child is grandfather to the man. Beethoven bore slight resemblance to his immediate parents, but in his talent, habits and all of his mental traits, he closely resembled this sturdy Dutchman who composed, sang, led the military band, and played the organ at the Church of Saint Jacques in Antwerp.

Being ambitious, Ludvig van Biethofen, while yet a young man, moved to Bonn, the home of Clement Augustus, Archbishop-Elector of Cologne.

The chief business of elector was, in case of necessity, to elect a King. America borrowed the elector idea from Germany. But our " electoral college " is a degenerate political appendicle that is continued, because, in borrowing plans of government, we took good and bad alike, not knowing there was a difference. The elector

LUDWIG VAN BEETHOVEN

scheme in the United States is occasionally valuable for defeating the will of the people in case of a popular majority ❧ ❧

In justice, however, let me say that the original argument of the Colonists was that the people should not vote directly for President, because the candidate might live a long way off, and the voter could not know whether he was fit or not. So they let the citizen vote for a wise and honest elector he knew.

The result is that we all now know the candidates for President, but we do not know the electors. The electoral college in America is just about as useful as the two buttons on the back of a man's coat, put there originally to support a sword-belt. We have discarded the sword, yet we cling to our buttons.

But the electors of Germany, in days agone, had a well-defined use. The people were not, at first, troubled to elect them—the King did that himself, and then as one good turn deserves another, the electors agreed to elect the successor the King designated, when death should compel him to abdicate. Then to fill in the time between elections, the electors did the business of the King. It will thus be seen that every elector was really a sort of King himself, governing his little State, amenable to no one but the King.

And so the chief business of the elector was to keep the people in his diocese loyal to the King.

There have always existed three ways of keeping the

228

people loving and loyal. One is to leave them alone, to trust them and not to interfere. This plan, however, has very seldom been practised, because the politicians regard the public as a cow to be milked, and something must be done to make it stand quiet.

So they try Plan Number Two, which consists in hypnotizing the public by means of shows, festivals, parades, prizes and many paid speeches, sermons and editorials, wherein and whereby the public is told how much is being done for it, and how fortunate it is in being protected and wisely cared for by its divinely appointed guardians. Then the band strikes up, the flags are waved, three passes are made, one to the right and two to the left; and we, being completely under the hypnosis, hurrah ourselves hoarse.

Plan Number Three is a very ancient one and is always held back to be used in case Number Two fails. It is for the benefit of the people who do not pass readily under hypnotic control. If there are too many of these, they have been known to pluck up courage and answer back to the speeches, sermons and editorials. Sometimes they refuse to hurrah when the bass-drum plays, in which case they have occasionally been arrested for contumacy and contravention by stocky men, in wide-awake hats, who lead the strenuous life. This Plan Number Three provides for an armed force that shall overawe, if necessary, all who are not hypnotized. The army is used for two purposes—to coerce disturbers at home, and to get up a war at a distance, and thus distract attention from the troubles near at hand. Napoleon used to say that the only sure cure for internal dissension was a foreign war: this would draw the disturbers away, on the plea of patriotism, so they would win enough outside loot to satisfy them, or else they would all get killed, it really did n't matter much; and as for loot, if it was taken from foreigners, there was no sin 🙙 🙙

A careful analyst might here say that Plan Number Three is only a variation of Plan Number Two—the end being gained by hypnotic effects in either event, for the army is conscripted from the people to use against the people, just as you turn steam from a boiler into the fire-box to increase the draft. Possibly this is true, but I have introduced this digression, anyway, only to show that the original office of elector was a wise and beneficent function of the Government, and could be revived with profit in America, to replace the outworn and useless vermiformis that we now possess in way of an electoral college.

LUDWIG VAN BEETHOVEN

HEN Kings allowed Church and State to separate they made a grave mistake. With the two united, as they were until a more recent time, they held a cinch on both the souls and the bodies of their subjects.

In the good old days in Germany the elector was always an archbishop. Our bishops now are a weakling lot. With no army to back their edicts the people smile at their proclamations, try on their shovel hats, and laugh at their gaiters. Or if they be Methodist bishops, who are only make-believe bishops, having slipped the cable that bound them to the past, we pound them familiarly on the back and address them as " Bish."

Clement Augustus, Elector of Cologne, maintained a court that vied with royalty itself. In his household were two hundred servants. He had coachmen, footmen, cooks, messengers, a bodyguard, musicians, poets and artists who hastened to do his bidding. He patronized all the arts, made a pet of science, offered a reward for the transmutation of metals, dabbled in astrology and practised palmistry.

Into this brilliant court came the strong and masterful Ludvig van Biethofen.

In a year his gracious presence, superb voice and rare skill as a musician, pushed him to the front and into favor with the powers, with a yearly salary of four hundred guilders. The history of this man is a deal better raw stock for a romance than the life of his grandson.

231

LUDWIG VAN BEETHOVEN

From Seventeen Hundred Thirty-two, when he entered the court as an unknown and ordinary musician with an acceptable tenor voice, to Seventeen Hundred Sixty-one, when he was Kapellmeister and a member of the private council of the Elector, his life was a steady march successward. Strong men were needed then as now, and his promotion was deserved. Various accounts and mention of this man are to be found, and one contemporary described him as he appeared at sixty. The only mark of age he carried was his flowing white hair. His smoothly shaven face showed the strong features of a man of thirty-five; and his carriage, actions and superb grace as an orchestra-leader made him a conspicuous figure in any company.

Ludvig van Biethofen had one son, Johann by name. This boy resembled his gifted father very little, and his training was such that he early fell a victim to arrested development ❈ ❈

If a parent does everything for a child, the child probably will never do anything for himself. It is Nature's plan—she seems to think that no one needs strength excepting the struggler, and being kind she comes to his rescue; but the man who puts forth no effort remains a weakling to the end.

Johann placed success beyond his reach very early in life by putting an enemy into his mouth to steal away his brains. His marriage to a daughter of a cook in Ehrenbreitstein Castle did not stop his waywardness, or give him decision as was hoped. Marriage as a scheme of reformation is not always a success, and women who lend themselves to it take great chances.

Mary Magdalena was a widow, and some say possessed of wiles. That she was beneath Johann in social station, but beyond him in actual worth, there is no doubt. And whether she snared the incautious man, or whether the marriage was arranged by the elder Biethofen as a diplomatic move in the interests of morality, matters little. The end justifies the means; and as a net result of this mating, without putting forward the circumstance as a precedent to be religiously followed, the world has Beethoven and his work.

LUDWIG VAN BEETHOVEN

PLATE affixed to Number Five Hundred Fifteen Bonngasse, Bonn, gives the birth of Ludwig van Beethoven as December Seventeenth, Seventeen Hundred Seventy. He was the second-born child of his mother, and after him came a goodly assortment of boys and girls. Two of his brothers lived to exercise a sinister influence over the life of the Master, and to darken days that should have been luminous with love. Little Ludwig was the pet and pride of the grandfather. The grandfather had even insisted that the baby should bear his name. Disappointment in his own child caused him to center his love in the grandchild. This instinct that makes men long to live again in the lives of their children—is it reaching out for immortality? And as the grandfather virtually supported the household, he was allowed to have his own way, and indeed that strong, yet cheery will was not to be opposed. The old man prophesied what the boy would do, just as love ever does, and has done, since the world began.

But only in his dreams was Ludvig van Biethofen to know of the success of his namesake. When the boy was scarce four years old, the old man passed away. The place in the orchestra that Johann held through favor was soon forfeited, and times of pinching poverty followed, and sorrows came like the gathering of a winter night.

Have you never shared the mocking shame and biting

LUDWIG VAN BEETHOVEN

pain of a drunkard's household? Then God grant you
never may. When the world withdraws its faith from a
man through his own imbecility, and employment is
denied; when promises are unkept; when order and
system are gone, and foresight fled, and loud accusation,
threat and contumely vary their strident tones with
maudlin protestations of affection, and vows made to be
broken, easily change to curses; when the fire dies on the
hearth, and children huddle in bed in the daytime for
warmth; when the scanty food that is found is eaten
ravenously, and blanching fear comes when a heavy
tread and fumbling at the lock are heard in the hall—
these things challenge language for fit expression and
cause words to falter.

The moody and dispirited Johann one day conceived a
bright thought—a thought so vivid that for the moment
it cleared the cobwebs from his mind and sobered his
boozy brain—the genius of his five-year-old boy should
be exploited to retrieve his battered fortunes!

The child was already showing signs of musical talent;
and diligent practise was now begun. Several chums at
the beer-gardens were interviewed and great plans
unfolded in beery enthusiasm. The services of several of
these men were secured as tutors, and one of them,
Pfeiffer, took lodgings with the Biethofens, and paid for
bed and board in music-lessons.

A new thought is purifying, ideas are hygienic; and
already things had begun to look brighter for the

household. It was n't exactly prosperity, but Johann had found a place in the band, and was earning as much as three dollars a week, which amount for two weeks running he brought home and placed in his wife's lap. ¶ But things were grievous for young Beethoven: he had two taskmasters, his father and Pfeiffer. One gave him lessons on the violin in the morning, and the other took him to a tavern where there was a clavichord and made him play all the afternoon.

Then occasionally Johann and Pfeiffer would come home at two o'clock in the morning from a concert where they had been playing and where the wine was red and also free, and they would drag the poor child from his bed to make him play. This was followed up until the boy's mother rebelled, and on one occasion Pfeiffer and Johann were sent to the military hospital and dry-docked for repairs.

On the whole, this man Pfeiffer was kindly and usually capable. In after-years Beethoven testified to the valuable assistance he had received from him; and when Pfeiffer had grown old and helpless, Beethoven sent funds to him by the publishers, Simrock.

Young Ludwig was a stocky, sturdy youth, decidedly Dutch in his characteristics, with no nerves to speak of, else he would have laid him down and died of heart-chill and neglect, as did four of his little brothers and sisters. But he stood the ordeals, and at parlor, tavern and beer-garden entertainments where he played, although his cheeks were often stained with tears, he took a sort of secret pride in being able to do things which even his father could not. And then he was always introduced as "Ludvig Biethofen, the grandchild of Ludvig van Biethofen," and this was no mean introduction. His appearance, even then, bore strong resemblance to the lost and lamented grandfather; and Van den Eeden, the Court Organist, in loving remembrance of his Antwerp friend, took the lad into his keeping and gave him lessons. When Van den Eeden retired, Neefe, his successor, took a kindly interest in the boy and even protected him from his father and the zealous Pfeiffer. So well was the boy thought of that when he was twelve years of age Neefe established him as his deputy at the chapel organ.

Shortly after this, the new Elector, Max Friedrich, bestowed on "Louis van Beethoven, my well-beloved player upon the organ and clavichord, a stipend of one hundred fifty florins a year, and if his talent doth increase with his years the amount is to be also increased." ৯ ৯

In token of the Elector's recognition Beethoven wrote three sonatas, the earliest of his compositions, and dedicated them to Max Friedrich in Seventeen Hundred Eighty-two.

In Seventeen Hundred Eighty-four, Elector Max Friedrich died, and Max Franz was appointed to take his place. His inauguration was the signal for a renewal of musical and artistic activity. Concerts, shows and

---

military pageants followed the installation. In a list of court appointments we find that Louis van Beethoven is put down as " second organist " with a salary of forty-five pounds a year. Below this is Johann Beethoven with a salary of thirty pounds a year. And in one of the court journals mention is made of Johann Beethoven with the added line, " father of Ludwig Beethoven," showing even then the man's source of distinction.

In Seventeen Hundred Eighty-seven, when in his eighteenth year, Beethoven made a visit to Vienna in company with several musicians from the Elector's court at Bonn. This visit was a memorable event in the life of the Master, every detail of which was deeply etched upon his memory, to be effaced only by death.
It was on this visit to Vienna that he met Mozart, and played for him. Mozart gave due attention, and when the player had ceased he turned to the company and said, " Keep your eye on this youth—he will yet make a noise in the world! "

The remark, if closely analyzed, reveals itself as non-committal; and although it has been bruited as praise the round world over, it was probably an electrotyped expression, used daily; for great musicians are called upon at every turn to listen to prodigies. I once attended " rhetoricals " where the Honorable Chauncey M. Depew was present. Being called upon to " make a few remarks," the Senator from New York arose and referred to one of the speeches given by a certain

238

sophomore as " unlike anything I ever heard before!"
Genius very seldom recognizes genius. ¶ Beethoven had
a self-sufficiency, even at that early time, that stood him
in good stead. He felt his power, and knew his worth.
That steadfast, obstinate quality in his make-up was
not in vain. He let others quote Mozart's remark; but
he had matched himself against the Master, and was not
abashed ⅜ ⅜

LUDWIG VAN BEETHOVEN

INSHIP is a question of spirit and not a matter of blood. How often do we find persons who, in feeling, are absolutely strangers to their own brothers and sisters! Occasionally even parents fail to understand their children. The child may hunger for sympathy and love that the mother knows nothing of, and cry itself to sleep for a tenderness withheld. Later this same child may evolve aspirations and ambitions that seem to the other members of the family mere whims and vagaries to be laughed down, or stoutly endured, as the mood prompts. ¶ Knowing these things, do we wonder at the question of long ago, " Who is my mother, and who are my brethren " ? Beethoven was a beautiful brown thrush in a nest of cuckoos. He could sing and sing divinely, and the members of his household were glad because it brought an income in which they all shared.

About the year Seventeen Hundred Ninety-five, Beethoven went to Vienna, and as he had been heralded by several persons of influence, his reception was gracious. Charity has its periods of evolving into a fad, and at this time the fashion was musical entertainments in aid of this or that. Slight suspicions exist that these numerous entertainments were devised by fledgling musicians for their own aggrandizement, and possibly patrons fanned the philanthropic flame to help on their proteges. Beethoven was of too simple and guileless a nature to aid his fortunes with the help of any social jimmy, but we see he was soon in the full tide of local popularity. His ability as a composer, his virile presence, and his skill as a player, made his company desired. From playing first for charity, then at the houses of nobility, and next as a professional musician, he gradually mounted to the place to which his genius entitled him.

Then we find his brothers, Carl and Johann, appearing on the scene, with a fussy yet earnest intent to take care of the business affairs of their eccentric and absent-minded brother. Ludwig let himself fall into their way of thinking—it was easier than to oppose them—and they began to drive bargains with publishers and managers. Their intent was to sell for cash and in the highest market; and their strenuous effort after the Main Chance put their gifted brother in a bad plight before the world of art. Beethoven's brothers seized his very early and immature compositions and sold them without his consent or knowledge. So humiliated was Beethoven by seeing these productions of his childhood hawked about that he even instituted lawsuits to get them back that he might destroy them. To boom a genius and cash his spiritual assets is a grave and delicate task—perhaps it is one of those things that should be left undone. Much anguish did these rapacious brothers cause the divinely gifted brown thrush, and when they began to quarrel over the receipts between themselves, he begged them to go away and leave him in peace. He finally had to adopt the ruse of going back to Bonn with them, where he got them established in the apothecary business, before he dared manage his own affairs. But they were bad angels, and the wind of their wings withered the great man as they hovered around him down to the day of his death.

LUDWIG VAN BEETHOVEN

HEN silence settled down upon Beethoven, and every piano was for him mute, and he, the maker of sweet sounds, could not hear his own voice, or catch the words that fell from the lips of those he loved, Fate seemed to have done her worst ❧ ❧

And so he wrote: " Forgive me then if you see me turn away when I would gladly mix with you. For me there is no recreation in human intercourse, no conversation, no sweet interchange of thought. In solitary exile I am compelled to live. When I approach strangers a feverish fear takes possession of me, for I know that I will be misunderstood. * * * But O God, Thou lookest down upon my inward soul! Thou knowest, and Thou seest that love for my fellowmen, and all kindly feeling have their abode here. Patience! I may get better—I may not—but I will endure all until Death shall claim me, and then joyously will I go! "

The man who could so express himself at twenty-eight years of age must have been a right brave and manly man. But art was his solace, as it should be to every soul that aspires to become.

Great genius and great love can never be separated—in fact I am not sure but that they are one and the same thing. But the object of his love separated herself from Beethoven when calamity lowered. What woman, young, bright, vigorous and fresh, with her face to the sunrising, would care to link her fair fate with that of a

243

man sore-stricken by the hand of God! ¶ And then there is always a doubt about the genius—is n't he only a fool after all!

Art was Beethoven's solace. Art is harmony, beauty and excellence. The province of art is to impart a sublime emotion. Beethoven's heart was filled with divine love— and all love is divine—and through his art he sought to express his love to others.

But his physical calamity made him the butt and byword of the heedless wherever he went. Within the sealed-up casements of his soul Beethoven heard the Heavenly Choir; and as he walked, bareheaded, upon the street, oblivious to all, centered in his own silent world, he would sometimes suddenly burst into song. At other times he would beat time, talk to himself and laugh aloud. His strange actions would often attract a crowd, and rude persons, ignorant of the man they mocked, would imitate him or make mirth for the bystanders, as they sought to engage him in conversation. At such times the Master might be dragged back to earth, and seeing the coarse faces and knowing the hopelessness of trying to make himself understood, he would retreat in terror.

Six months or more of each year were spent in the country in some obscure village about Vienna. There he could walk the woods and traverse the fields alone and unnoticed, and there, out under the open sky, much of his best work was done. The famous " Moonlight

244

LUDWIG VAN BEETHOVEN

Sonata " was shaped on one of these lonely walks by night across the fields when the Master could shake his shaggy head, lift up his face to the sky, and cry aloud, all undisturbed. In the recesses of his imagination he saw the sounds. There are men to whom sounds are invisible symbols of forms and colors.

The law of compensation never rests. Everything conspired to drive Beethoven in upon his art—it was his refuge and retreat. When love spurned him, and misunderstandings with kinsmen came, and lawsuits and poverty added their weight of woe, he fell back upon music, and out under the stars he listened to the sonatas of God. Next day he wrote them out as best he could, always regretting that his translations were not quite perfect. He was ever stung with a noble discontent, and in times of exaltation there ran in his deaf ears the words, "Arise and get thee hence, for this is not thy rest!" ✄ ✄

And so his work was in a constant ascending scale. Richard Wagner has acknowledged his indebtedness to Beethoven in several essays, and in many ways. In fact it is not too much to say that Beethoven was the spiritual parent of Wagner. From his admiration of Beethoven, Wagner developed the strong, sturdy, independent quality of his nature that led to his exile—and his success.

Behold the face of Ludwig Beethoven—is there not something Titanic about it? What selfness, what will,

LUDWIG VAN BEETHOVEN

what resolve, what power! And those tear-stained eyes
—have they not seen sights of which no tongue can
tell, nor tongue make plain?

His life of solitude helped foster the independence of his
nature, and kept his mind clear and free from all the
idle gossip of the rabble. He went his way alone, and
played court fool to no titled and alleged nobility. The
democracy of the man is not our least excuse for honor-
ing him. He was one with the plain people of earth, and
the only aristocracy he acknowledged was the aristocracy of intellect.

In the work done after his fortieth year there is greater
freedom, an ease and an increased strength, with a
daring quality which uplifts and gives you courage. The
tragic interest and intense emotionalism are gone, and
you behold a resignation and the success that wins by
yielding. The man is no longer at war with destiny.
There is no struggle.

We pay for everything we receive—nay, all things can
be obtained if we but pay the price. One of the very few
Emancipated Men in America bought redemption from
the bondage of selfish ambition at a terrible price. Years
and years ago he was in the Rocky Mountains, rough,
uneducated, heedless of all that makes for righteousness.
This man was caught in a snowstorm, on the mountainside. He lost his way, became dazed with cold and fell
exhausted in the snow. When found by his companions
the next day, death had nearly claimed him. But skilful

246

LUDWIG VAN BEETHOVEN

help brought him back to life, yet the frost had killed the circulation in his feet. Both legs were amputated just below the knees.

This changed the current of the man's life. Footraces, boxing-matches and hunting of big game were out of the question. The man turned to books and art and questions of science and sociology.

Thirty summers have come and gone. This gentle, sympathetic and loving man now walks with a cane, and few know of his disability and of his artificial feet. Speaking of his spiritual rebirth, this man of splendid intellect said to me, with a smile, " It cost me my feet, but it was worth the price."

I shed no maudlin tears over the misfortunes of Beethoven. He was what he was because of what he endured. He grew strong by bearing burdens. All things are equalized. By the Cross is the world redeemed. God be praised, it is all good!

GEORGE HANDEL

HANDEL

When generations have been melted into tears, or raised to religious fervor—when courses of sermons have been preached, volumes of criticisms been written, and thousands of afflicted and poor people supported by the oratorio of " The Messiah "—it becomes exceedingly difficult to say anything new. Yet no notice of Handel, however sketchy, should be written without some special tribute of reverence to this sublime treatment of a sublime subject. Bach, Graun, Beethoven, Spohr, Rossini and Mendelssohn have all composed on the same theme. But no one in completeness, in range of effect, in elevation and variety of conception, has ever approached Handel's music upon this one subject.

—*Rev. H. R. Haweis*

GEORGE HANDEL

ID you meet Michelangelo while you were in Rome?" asked a good Roycroft girl of me the other day.

"No, my dear, no," I answered, and then I gulped hard to keep back some very foolish tears. "No, I did not meet Michelangelo," I said, "I expected to, and was always looking for him; but these eyes never looked into his, for he died just three hundred years before I was born." But how natural was this question from this bright, country girl! She had been examining a lot of photographs of the Sistine Chapel, and had seen pictures of "Il Penseroso," the "Night" and "Morning," the "Moses"; and then she had seen on my desk a bronze cast of the hand of the "David"—that imperial hand with the gently curved wrist ✠ ✠

These things lured her—the splendid strength and suggestion of power in it all, had caught her fancy, and the heroic spirit of the Master seemed very near to her. It all meant pulsating life and hope that was deathless; and the thought that the man who did the work had turned to dust three centuries ago, never occurred to this naive, budding soul.

"Did you see Michelangelo while you were in Rome?" No, dear girl, no. But I saw Saint Peter's that he

251

planned, and I saw the result of his efforts—things worked out and materialized by his hands—hands that surely were just like this hand of the " David."

The artist gives us his best—gives it to us forever, for our very own. He grows aweary and lies down to sleep—to sleep and wake no more, deeding to us the mintage of his love. And as love does not grow old, neither does Art. Fashions change, but hope, aspiration and love are as old as Fate who sits and spins the web of life. The Artist is one who is educated in the three H's—head heart and hand. He is God's child—no less are we—and he has done for us the things we would have liked to do ourselves ✤ ✤

The classic is that which does not grow old—the classic is the eternally true.

" Did you meet Michelangelo in Rome? " Why, it is the most natural question in the world! At Stratford I expected to see Shakespeare; at Weimar I was sure to meet Goethe; Rubens just eluded me at Antwerp; at Amsterdam I caught a glimpse of Rembrandt; in the dim cloisters of Saint Mark's at Florence I saw Savonarola in cowl and robe; over Whitehall in London I beheld the hovering smoke of martyr-fires, and knew that just beyond the walls Ridley and Latimer were burned; and only a little way outside of Jerusalem a sign greets the disappointed traveler, thus: " He is risen—He is not here! "

GEORGE HANDEL

N one of his delightful talks—talks that are as fine as his feats of leadership—Walter Damrosch has referred to Handel as a contemporary. Surely the expression is fitting, for in the realm of truth time is an illusion and the days are shadows.

George Frederick Handel was born in Sixteen Hundred Eighty-five, and died in Seventeen Hundred Fifty-nine. His dust rests in Westminster Abbey, and above the tomb towers his form cut in enduring marble. There he stands, serene and poised, accepting benignly the homage of the swift-passing generations. For over a hundred years this figure has stood there in its colossal calm, and through the cathedral shrines, the aisles, and winding ways of dome and tower, Handel's music still peals its solemn harmonies.

At Exeter Hall is another statue of Handel, seated, holding in his hand a lyre. At the Foundling Hospital (which he endowed) is a bust of the Master, done in Seventeen Hundred Fifty-eight; and at Windsor is the original of still another bust that has served for a copy of the very many casts in plaster and clay that are in all the shops.

There are at least fifty different pictures of Handel, and nearly this number were brought together, on the occasion of a recent Handel and Haydn Festival, at South Kensington.

When Gladstone once referred to Handel as our greatest

GEORGE HANDEL

English Composer, he refused to take it back even when a capricious critic carped and sneezed.

Handel essentially belongs to England, for there his first battles were fought, and there he won his final victory. To be sure, he did some preliminary skirmishing in Germany and Italy; but that was only getting his arms ready for that conflict which was to last for half a century—a conflict with friends, foes and fools.

But Handel was too big a man to be undermined by either the fulsome flattery of friends, or the malice of enemies, who were such only because they did not understand. And so always to the fore he marched, zigzagging occasionally, but the Voice said to him, as it did to Columbus, " Sail on, and on, and on." Like the soul of John Brown, the spirit of Handel goes marching on. And Sir Arthur Sullivan was right when he said, " Musical England owes more to Father Handel than to any other ten men who can be named—he led the way for us all, and cut out a score that we can only imitate." ❧ ❧

GEORGE HANDEL

T the Court of George of Brunswick, at Hanover, in Seventeen Hundred Nine, was George Frederick Handel, six feet one, weight one hundred eighty, rubicund, rosy, and full of romp, aged twenty-four. George of Brunswick was to have the felicity of being King George the First of England, and already he was straining his gaze across the Channel.

At his Court were divers and sundry English noblemen. Handel was a prime favorite with every one in the merry company. The ladies doted on him. A few gentlemen, possibly, were slightly jealous of his social prowess, and yet none pooh-poohed him openly, for only a short time before he had broken a sword in a street duel with a brother musician, and once had thrown a basso profundo, who sang off key, through a closed window—all this to the advantage of a passing glazier, who, being called in, was paid his fee three times over for repairing the sash. It's an ill wind, etc.

Handel played the harpsichord well, but the organ better. In fact, he played the organ in such a masterly way that he had no competitor, save a phenomenal yokel by the name of Johann Sebastian Bach. These men were born just a month apart. Saint Cecilia used to whisper to them when they were wee babies. For several years they lived near each other, but in this life they never met.

Handel was an aristocrat by nature, even if not exactly

255

GEORGE HANDEL

so by birth, and so had nothing to do with the modest
and bucolic Bach—even going so far, they do say, as to
leave, temporarily, the City of Halle, his native place,
when a contest was suggested between them. Bach was
the supreme culminating flower of two hundred fifty
years of musical ancestors—servants to this Grand
Duke or that. But in the tribe of Handel there was not a
single musical trace. George Frederick succeeded to the
art, and at it, in spite of his parents. But never mind
that! He had been offered the post as successor to
Buxtehude, and Buxtehude was the greatest organist of
his time. He accepted the invitation to play for the
Buxtehude contingent. A musical jury sat on the case,
and decided to accept the young man, with the proviso
that Handel (taught by Orpheus) should take to wife
the daughter of Buxtehude—this in order that the
traditions might be preserved.

Young Handel declined the proposition with thanks,
declaring he was unworthy of the honor.

Young Handel had spent two years in Italy, had visited
most of the capitals of Europe, had composed several
operas and numerous songs. He was handsome, gracious
and talented. Money may use its jimmy to break into
the Upper Circles; but to Beauty, Grace and Talent that
does not shiver nor shrink, all doors fly open. And now
the English noblemen requested—nay, insisted—that
Handel should accompany them back to Merry
England ✄ ✄

256

GEORGE HANDEL

He went, and being introduced as Signore Handello, he was received with salvos of welcome. There is a time to plant, and a time to reap. There is a time for everything —launch your boat only at full of tide. London was ripe for Italian Opera. Discovery had recently been made in England that Art was born in Italy. It had traveled as far as Holland, and so Dutch artists were hard at work in English manor-houses, painting portraits of ancestors, dead and living. Music, one branch of Art, had made its way up to Germany, and here was an Italian who spoke English with a German accent, or a German who spoke Italian—what boots it, he was a great musician!

Handel's Italian opera, "Rinaldo," was given at a theater that stood on the site of the present Haymarket. The production was an immense success. All educated people knew Latin (or were supposed to know it), and Signore Handello announced that his Italian was an improvement on the Latin. And so all the scholars flocked to see the play, and those who were not educated came too, and looked knowing. In order to hold interest, there were English syncopated songs between the acts— ragtime is a new word, but not a new thing.

Handel was very wise in this world's affairs. He assured England that it was the most artistic country on the globe. He wrote melodies that everybody could whistle. Airs from " Rinaldo " were thrummed on the harpsichord from Land's End to John O'Groat's. The grand march was adopted by the Life Guards, and at least one air from that far-off opera has come down to us—the " Tascie Ch'io Pianga," which is still listened to with emotion unfeigned. The opera being uncopyrighted, was published entire by an enterprising Englishman from Dublin by the name of Walsh. At two o'clock one morning at the " Turk's Head," he boasted he had cleared over two thousand pounds on the sale of it. Handel was present and responded, " My friend, the next time you will please write the opera and I will sell it." Walsh took the hint, they say, and sent his check on the morrow to the author for five hundred pounds. And the good sense of both parties is shown in the fact that they worked together for many years, and both reaped a yellow harvest of golden guineas.

On the birthday of Queen Anne, Handel inscribed to her an ode, which we are told was played with a full band. The performance brought the diplomatic Handel a pension of two hundred pounds a year.

Next, to celebrate the peace of Utrecht, the famous " Te Deum " and " Jubilate " were produced, with a golden garter as a slight token of recognition.

But Good Queen Anne passed away, as even good queens do, and the fuzzy-witted George of Hanover came over to be King of England, and transmit his fuzzy-wuzzy wit to all the Georges. About his first act was to cut off Handel's pension, "Because," he said, " Handel ran away from me at Hanover."

GEORGE HANDEL

A time of obscurity followed for Handel, but after some months, when the Royal Barge went up the Thames, a band of one hundred pieces boomed alongside, playing a deafening racket, with horse-pistol accompaniments. The King made inquiries and found it was " Water-Music," composed by Herr Handel, and dedicated in loving homage to King George the First.

When the Royal Barge came back down the river, Herr Handel was aboard, and accompanied by a great popping of corks was proclaimed Court Musician, and his back-pension ordered paid.

The low ebb of art is seen in that, in the various operas given about this time by Handel, great stress is made in the bills about costumes, scenery and gorgeous stage-fittings. When accessories become more than the play— illustrations more than the text—millinery more than the mind—it is unfailing proof that the age is frivolous. Art, like commerce and everything else, obeys the law of periodicity. Handel saw the tendency of the times, and advertised, "The fountain to be seen in 'Amadigi' is a genuine one, the pump real and the dog alive." Three hours before the doors opened, the throng stood in line, waiting.

GEORGE HANDEL

BUT London is making head. Other good men and true are coming to town. Handel does not know much about them, or care, perhaps. His wonderful energy is now manifesting itself in the work of managing theaters and concerts, giving lessons and composing songs, arias, operas, and attending receptions where " the ladies refrain from hoops for fear of the crush," to use the language of Samuel Pepys ❧ ❧

In shirt-sleeves, in a cheap seat in the pit, at one of Handel's performances, is a big lout of a fellow, with scars of scrofula on his neck and cheek. Next to him is a little man, and these two, so chummy and confidential, suggest the long and short of it. They are countrymen, recently arrived, empty of pocket, but full of hope. They have a selfish eye on the stage, for the big 'un has written a play and wants to get it produced.

The little man's name is David Garrick; the other is Samuel Johnson.

They listen to the singing, and finally Samuel turns to his friend and says, " I say, Davy, music is nothing but a noise that is less disagreeable than some others." They would go away, would these two, but they have paid good money to get in, and so sit it out disgustedly, watching the audience and the play alternately.

In one of the boxes is a weazened little man, all out of drawing, in a black velvet doublet, satin breeches and silk stockings. At his side is a rudimentary sword. The

260

---

man's face is sallow, and shrewdness and selfishness are shown in every line. He looks like a baby suddenly grown old. The two friends in the pit have seen this man before, but they have never met him face to face, because they do not belong to his set.

"Do you think God is proud of a work like that?" at last asked Davy, jerking his thumb toward the bad modeling in courtly black.

"God never made him." The big man swayed in his seat, and added, "God had nothing to do with him—he is the child of Beelzebub."

"Think 'ee so?" asks Davy. "Why, Mephisto has some pretty good traits; but Alexander Pope is as crooked as an interrogation-point, inside and out." ⚜

"I hear he wears five pairs of stockings to fill out his shanks, and sole-leather stays to keep him from flattening out like a devilfish," said Doctor Johnson.

"But he makes a lot o' money!"

"Well, he has to, for he pays an old woman a hundred guineas a year to dress and undress him."

"I know, but she writes his heroic couplets, too!" ⚜

"Davy, I fear you are getting cynical—let's change the subject."

It surely is a case of artistic jealousy. Our friends locate the poet Gay, a fat little man, who is with his publisher, Rich ⚜ ⚜

"They say," says Samuel, again rolling in his seat as if about to have an apoplectic fit, "they say that

261

GEORGE HANDEL

Gay has become rich, and Rich has become gay since they got out that last book." There comes an interlude in the play, and our friends get up to stretch their legs ❧ ❧

" How now, Dick Savage? " calls Samuel, as he pushes three men over like ninepins, to seize a shabby fellow whose neckcloth and hair-cut betray him as being a poet. " How now, Dick, you said that Italian music was damnably bad! Why do you come to hear it? "

" I came to find out how bad it is," replied the literary man. " Eh! your reverence?" he adds to his companion, a sharp-nosed man with china-blue eyes, in Church-of-England knee-breeches, high-cut vest, and shovel-hat ❧ ❧

Dean Swift replies with a knowing smirk, which is the nearest approach to a laugh in which he ever indulged. Then he takes out his snuffbox and taps it, which is a sign that he is going to say something worth while. " Yes, one must go everywhere, and do everything, just to find out how bad things are. By this means we clergymen are able to intelligently warn our flocks. But I came tonight to hear that rogue Bononcini— you know he is from County Down—I used to go to school with him," and the Dean solemnly passes the snuffbox ❧ ❧

Garrick here bursts into a laugh, which is broken off short by a reproving look from the Dean, who has gotten the snuffbox back and is meditatively tapping it

262

again. The friends listen and hear from the muttering
lips of the Dean, this:

> Some say that Signore Bononcini,
> Compared to Handel is a ninny;
> Whilst others vow that to him Handel,
> Is hardly fit to hold a candle.
> Strange all this difference should be
> 'Twixt tweedledum and tweedledee.

The people are tumbling back to their seats as the
musicians come stringing in. Soon there is a general
tuning up—scrapings, toots, snorts, subdued screeches,
raspings, and all that busy buzz-fuzz business of getting
ready to play.

" The first time we came to the opera Doctor Johnson
thought this was all a part of the play, and applauded
with unction for an encore," says Garrick.

"And I heard nothing finer the whole evening," answers
Doctor Johnson, accepting the defi, and winning by
yielding ॐ ॐ

" Why don't they tune up at home, or behind the
scenes? " asks some one.

" I 'll tell you why," says Savage, and he relates this:
" Handel is a great man for system—he is a strict
disciplinarian, as any man must be to manage musicians,
who are neither men nor women, but a third sex. Often
Handel has to knock their heads together, and once he
shook the Cuzzoni until her teeth chattered."

" That 's the way you have to treat any woman before

GEORGE HANDEL

she will respect you," interrupts the Dean. Nothing else
being forthcoming, Savage continues: " Handel is absolute master of everything but Death and Destiny. Now
he did n't like all this tuning up before the audience;
he said you might as well expect the prima donna to
make her toilet in front of the curtain "——
" I like the idea," says Johnson.
Savage praises the interruption and continues: "And so
ordered every man to tune up his artillery a half-hour
before the performance, and carry his instrument in
and lay it on his chair. Then when it came time to com-
mence, every musician would walk in, take up his
instrument, and begin. The order was given, and all
tuned up. Then the players all adjourned for their
refreshments ✄ ✄
" In the interval a wag entered and threw every
instrument out of key.
" It came time to begin—the players marched in like
soldiers. Handel was in his place. He rapped once—
every player seized his instrument as though it were a
musket. At the second rap the music began—and such
music! Some of the strings were drawn so tight that they
snapped at the first touch; others merely flapped; some
growled; and others groaned and moaned or squealed.
Handel thought the orchestra was just playing him a
scurvy trick. He leaped upon the stage, kicked a hole in
the bass-viol, and smashed the kettledrum around the
neck of the nearest performer. The players fled before
264

the assault, and he bombarded them with cornets and French horns as they tumbled down the stairs.

" The audience roared with delight, and not one in forty guessed that it was not a specially arranged Italian feature. But since that evening all tuning-up is done on the stage, and no man lets his instrument get out of his hands after he gets it right."

" It 's a moving tale, invented as an excuse for a man who writes music so bad that he gets disgusted with it himself, and flies into wrath when he hears it," says Johnson ⚘ ⚘

A subdued buzz is heard, and the master comes forth, gorgeous in a suit of purple velvet. His powdered wig and the enormous silver buckles on his shoes set off his figure with the proper accent. His florid face is smiling, and Garrick expresses a regret that there are to be no impromptu tragic events in way of chasing players from the stage.

" Would you like to meet him? " asks the sharp-nosed Dean ⚘ ⚘

Garrick and Johnson have enough of the rustic in them to be lion-hunters, and they reply to the question as one man, " Yes, indeed! "

" I 'll arrange it," was the answer. The leader raps for attention. Johnson closes his eyes, sighs, and leans back resignedly.

The others look and listen with interest as the play proceeds ⚘ ⚘

GEORGE HANDEL

HE other day I read a book by Madame Columbier entitled, "Sara Barnum." Only a person of worth could draw forth such a fire of hot invective, biting sarcasm and frenzied vituperation as this volume contains. When I closed the volume it was with the feeling that Sara Bernhardt is surely the greatest woman of the age; and I was fully resolved that I must see her play at the first opportunity, no matter what the cost. And as for Madame Columbier, why she isn't so bad, either! The flashes of lightning in her swordplay are highly interesting. The book was born, as all good books, because its mother could not help it. Behind every page and between the lines you see the fevered toss of human emotion and hot ambition —these women were rivals. There were digs and scratches, bandied epithets in falsetto, and sounds like a piccolo played by a man in distress, before all this; and these are not explained, so you have to fill them in with your imagination. But the Bernhardt is the bigger woman of the two. She goes her splendid pace alone, and all the other woman can do is to bombard her with a book ✄ ✄

The excellence of Handel is shown in that he achieved the enmity of some very good men. Read the "Spectator," and you will find its pages well peppered with thrusts at "foreigners," and sweeping cross-strokes at Italian Opera and all "bombastic beaters of the air, who smother harmony with bursts of discord in the

266

GEORGE HANDEL

name of music." ¶ These battles royal between the
kings of art are not so far removed from the battles of
the beasts. Rosa Bonheur has pictured a duel to the
death between stallions; and that battle of the stags—
horn-locked—with the morning sun revealing Death as
victor, by Landseer, is familiar to us all. Then Landseer
has another picture which he called " The Monarch,"
showing a splendid stag, solitary and alone, standing on
a cliff, overlooking the valley. There is history behind
this stag. Before he could command the scene alone, he
had to vanquish foes; but in the main, in some way, you
feel that most of his battles have been bloodless and he
commands by divine right. The Divine Right of a King,
if he be a King, has its root in truth.

One mark of the genius of Handel is shown in the fact
that he has achieved a split and created a ruction in the
Society of Scribblers. He once cut Dean Swift dead at a
fashionable gathering—the doughty Dean, who delighted in making men and women alike crawl to him—
and this won him the admiration of Colley Cibber, who
immortalized the scene in a sonnet. People liked Handel,
or they did not, and among the Old Guard who stood by
him, let these names, among others, be remembered:
Colley Cibber, Gay, Arbuthnot, Pope, Hogarth, Fielding
and Smollett.

People who through incapacity are unable to comprehend or appreciate music, are prone to wax facetious
over it—the feeble joke is the last resort of the man who

does not understand. ¶ The noisy denizens of Grub Street, drinking perdition to that which they can not comprehend, always getting ready to do great things, seem like fussy pigmies beside a giant like Handel. See the fifth act ere the curtain falls on the lives of Oliver Goldsmith, Doctor Johnson, Steele, Addison and Dean Swift (dead at the top, the last), and the others unhappily sent into Night; and then behold George Frederick Handel, in his seventy-fifth year, blind, but with inward vision all aflame, conducting the oratorio of " Elijah " before an audience of five thousand people! ¶ The life of Handel was packed with work and projects too vast for one man to realize. That he deferred to the London populace and wrote down to them at first, is true; but the greatness of the man is seen in this—he never deceived himself. He knew just what he was doing, and in his heart was ever a shrine to the Ideal, and upon this altar the fires never died.

Handel was a man of affairs as well as a musician, and if he had loved money more than Art, he could have withdrawn from the fray at thirty years of age, passing rich ⚜ ⚜

Three times in his life he risked all in the production of Grand Opera, and once saw a sum equal to fifty thousand dollars disappear in a week, through the treachery of Italian artists who were pledged to help him. At great expense and trouble he had gone abroad and searched Europe for talent, and, regardless of outlay,

GEORGE HANDEL

had brought singers and performers across the sea to England. In several notable instances these singers had, in a short time, been bought up by rivals, and had turned upon their benefactor.

But Handel was not crushed by these things. He was philosopher enough to know that ingratitude is often the portion of the man who does well, and a fight with a fox you have warmed into life is ever imminent. At fifty-five, a bankrupt, he makes terms with his creditors and in a few years pays off every shilling with interest, and celebrates the event by the production of " Saul," the " Dead March " from which will never die.

The man had been gaining ground, making head, and at the same time educating the taste of the English people. But still they lagged behind, and when the oratorio of " Joshua " was performed, the Master decided he would present his next and best piece outside of England. Jealousy, a dangerous weapon, has its use in the diplomatic world.

Handel set out for Dublin with a hundred musicians, there to present the " Messiah," written for and dedicated to the Irish people. The oratorio had been turned off in just twenty-one days, in one of those titanic bursts of power, of which this man was capable. Its production was a feat worthy of the Frohmans at their best. The performance was to be for charity—to give freedom to those languishing in debtors' prisons at Dublin. What finer than that the " Messiah " should give deliverance? ¶ The Irish heart was touched. A fierce scramble ensued for seats, precedence being emphasized in several cases with blackthorns deftly wielded. The price of seats was a guinea each. Handel's carriage was drawn through the streets by two hundred students. He was crowned with shamrock, and given the freedom of the city in a gold box. Freedom even then, in Ireland, was a word to conjure with. Long before the performance, notices that no more tickets would be sold were posted. The doors of the Debtors' Prison were thrown open, and the prisoners given seats so they could hear the music—thus overdoing the matter in true Irish style ♖ ♖

The performance was the supreme crowning event in the life of Handel up to that time.

Couriers were dispatched to London to convey the news of Handel's great triumph to the newspapers; bulletins were posted at the clubs—the infection caught! On the return of the master a welcome was given him such as he had never before known—Dublin should not outdo London! When the "Messiah" was given in London, the scene of furore in Dublin was repeated. The wild tumult at times drowned the orchestra, and when the "Hallelujah Chorus" was sung, the audience arose as one man and joined in the song of praise. And from that day the custom has continued: whenever in England the "Messiah" is given, the audience arises and sings in the "Chorus," as its privilege and right. The proceeds

GEORGE HANDEL

of the first performance of the " Messiah " in England
were given to charity, as in Dublin. This act, with the
splendor of the work, subdued the last lingering touch of
obdurate criticism. The man was canonized by popular
acclaim. Many of his concerts were now for charity—
" The Foundlings' Home," " The Seamen's Fund,"
" Home for the Aged," hospitals and imprisoned
debtors—all came in for their share.

Handel never married. That remark of Dean Swift's,
" I admire Handel—principally because he conceals his
petticoat peccadilloes with such perfection," does not
go. Handel considered himself a priest of art, and his
passion spent itself in his work.

The closing years of his life were a time of peace and
honor. His bark, after a fitful voyage, had glided into
safe and peaceful waters. The calamity of blindness did
not much depress him—" What matters it so long as I
can hear? " he said. And good it is to know that the
capacity to listen and enjoy, to think and feel, to
sympathize and love—to live his Ideals—were his, even
to the night of his passing Hence.

GIUSEPPE VERDI

GIUSEPPE VERDI

Of all the operas that Verdi wrote,
   The best, to my taste, is the Trovatore;
And Mario can soothe, with a tenor note.
   The souls in purgatory.

The moon on the tower slept soft as snow;
   And who was not thrilled in the strangest way,
As we heard him sing while the lights burned low,
   " Non ti scordar di me " ?

＊   ＊   ＊   ＊   ＊   ＊   ＊   ＊   ＊   ＊   ＊

But O, the smell of that jasmine-flower!
   And O, the music! and O, the way
That voice rang out from the donjon tower,
   " Non ti scordar di me,
      Non ti scordar di me! "

                                    —*Bulwer-Lytton*

GIUSEPPE VERDI

E sort of clung to the iron pickets, did the boy, and pressed his face through the fence and listened. Some one was playing the piano in the big house, and the windows with their little diamond panes were flung open to catch the evening breeze. He listened.

His big gray eyes were open wide, the pupils dilated—he was trying to see the music as well as hear it.

The boy's hair matched the yellow of his face, being one shade lighter, sun-bleached from going hatless. His clothes were as yellow as the yellow of his face, and shaded off into the dust that strewed the street. He was like a quail in a stubble-field—you might have stepped over him and never seen him at all. He listened. Almost every evening some one played the piano in the big house. He had discovered the fact a week before, and now, when the dusk was gathering, he would watch his chance and slide away from the hut where his parents lived, and run fast up the hill, and along the shelving roadway to the tall iron fence that marked the residence of Signore Barezzi. He would creep along under the stone wall, and crouching there would wait and listen for the music. Several evenings he had come and waited, and waited, and waited—and not a note or a voice did he hear. ¶ Once it had rained and he did n't mind it much, for he expected every moment the music would strike up, you know—and who cares for cold, or wet, or even hunger, if one can hear good music! The air grew chill and the boy's threadbare jacket stuck to his bony form like a postage-stamp to a letter. Little rivulets of water ran down his hair and streamed off his nose and cheeks. He waited—he was waiting for the music ✄ He might have waited until the water dissolved his insignificant cosmos into just plain, yellow mud, and then he would have been simply distributed all along the gutter down to the stream, and down the stream to the river, and down the river to the ocean; and no one would ever have heard of him again.

But Signore Barezzi's coachman came along that night, keeping close to the fence under the trees to avoid the wet; and the coachman fell over the boy.

Now, when we fall over anything we always want to kick it—no matter what it is, be it cat, dog, stump, stick, stone or human. The coachman being but clay (undissolved) turned and kicked the boy. Then he seized him by the collar, and accused him of being a thief. The lad acknowledged the indictment, and stammeringly tried to explain that it was only music he was trying to steal; and that it really made no difference because even if one did fill himself full of the music, there was just as much left for other people, since music was different from most things.

276

GIUSEPPE VERDI

The thought was not very well expressed, although the idea was all right, but the coachman failed to grasp it. So he tingled the boy's bare legs with the whip he carried, by way of answer, duly cautioning him never to let it occur again, and released the prisoner on parole. But the boy forgot and came back the next night. He sat on the ground below the wall, intending to keep out of sight; but when the music began he stood up, and now, with face pressed between the pickets, he listened. ¶ The wind sighed softly through the orange-trees; the air was heavy with the perfume of flowers; the low of cattle came from across the valley, and on the evening breeze from an open casement rose the strong, vibrant, yet tender, strains of Beethoven's "Moonlight Sonata." The lad listened.

" Do you like music? " came a voice from behind. The boy awoke with a start, and tried to butt his head through the pickets to escape in that direction. He thought it was the coachman. He turned and saw the kindly face of Signore Barezzi himself.

" Do I like music? Me! No, I mean yes, when it is like that! " he exclaimed, beginning his reply with a tremolo and finishing bravura.

" That is my daughter playing; come inside with me." The hand of the great man reached out, and the urchin clutched at it as if it were something he had been longing for.

They walked through the big gates where a stone lion

GIUSEPPE VERDI

kept guard on each side. The lions never moved. They walked up the steps, and entering the parlor saw a young woman seated at the piano.

"Grazia, dear, here is the little boy we saw the other day—you remember? I thought I would bring him in." The young woman came forward and touched the lad on his tawny head with one of her beautiful hands—the beautiful hands that had just been playing the "Sonata."

¶ "That's right, little boy, we have seen you outside there before, and if I had known you were there tonight, I would have gone out and brought you in; but Papa has done the service for me. Now, you must sit down right over there where I can see you, and I will play for you. But won't you tell us your name?"

"Me?" replied the little boy, "why—why my name is Giuseppe Verdi—I am ten years old now—going on 'leven—you see, I like to hear you play because I play myself, a little bit!"

GIUSEPPE VERDI

OR over a hundred years three-fourths of Italy's population had been on reduced rations. Starvation even yet crouches just around the corner.

In his childhood young Verdi used to wear a bit of rope for a girdle, and when hunger gnawed importunately, he would simply pull his belt one knot tighter, and pray that the ravens would come and treat him as well as they did Elijah. His parents were so poor that the question of education never came to them; but desire has its way, so we find the boy at ten years of age running errands for a grocer with a musical attachment. This grocer, at Busseto, Jasquith by name, hung upon the fringe of art, and made the dire mistake of mixing business with his fad, for he sold his wares to sundry gentlemen who played in bands. This led the good man to moralize at times, and he would say to Giuseppe, who had been promoted from errand-boy to clerk: " You can trust a first violin, and a 'cello usually pays, but never say yes to a trombone nor an oboe; and as for a kettle-drum, I would n't believe one on a stack of Bibles! "

¶ Over the grocer's shop was a little parlor, and in it was a spinet that young Giuseppe had the use of four evenings a week. In his later years Verdi used to tell of this, and once said that the idea of prohibition and limit should be put on every piano—then the pupil would make the best of his privileges. In those days there was a tax on spinets, and I believe that this tax has never been

GIUSEPPE VERDI

rescinded, for you are taxed if you keep a piano, now, in any part of Italy. Several times the poor grocer's spinet stood in sore peril from the publicans and sinners, but the bailiffs were bought off by Signore Barezzi, who came to the rescue.

The note of thrift was even then in Verdi's score, for he himself has told how he induced the Barezzi household to patronize the honest grocer with musical proclivities. ¶ When twelve years of age Verdi occasionally played the organ in the village church at Busseto. It will be seen from this that he had courage, and even then possessed a trace of that pride and self-will that was to be his disadvantage and then his blessing. Signore Barezzi's attachment to the boy was very great, and we find the youngster was on friendly terms with the family, having free use of their piano, with valuable help and instruction from Signorina Grazia. When he was seventeen he was easily the first musician in the place, and Busseto had nothing more to offer in the way of advantages. He thirsted for a wider career, and cast longing looks out into the great outside world. He had played at Parma, only a few miles away, and the Bishop there, after hearing him improvise on the organ, had paid him a doubtful compliment by saying, " Your playing is surely unlike anything ever before heard in Parma." Fair fortune smiled when Signore Barezzi secured for young Verdi a free scholarship at the Conservatory at Milan.

280

GIUSEPPE VERDI

The youth went gaily forth, attended by the blessings of the whole village, to claim his honors.

Arriving at the Conservatory, the directors put him through his paces, after the usual custom, to prove his fitness for the honor that had been thrust upon him. He played first upon the piano, and the committee advised together in whispered monotone. Then they asked him to play on the organ, and there was more consultation, with argument which was punctuated by rolling adjectives and many picturesque gesticulations. Then they asked him to play the piano again. He did so, and the great men retired to deliberate and vote on the issue ❧ ❧

Their decision was that the youth was self-willed, erratic, and that he had some absurd mannerisms and tricks of performance that forbade his ever making a musician. And therefore, they ruled that his admission to the Conservatory was impossible.

Barezzi, who was present with his protege, stormed in wrath, and declared that Verdi was the peer of any of his judges; in fact, was so much beyond them that they could not comprehend him.

This only confirmed the powers in the stand they had taken, and they intimated that a great musician in Busseto was something different in Milan—Signore Barezzi had better take his young man home and be content to astonish the villagers with noisy acrobatics. There being nothing else to do, the advice was first

GIUSEPPE VERDI

flouted and then followed. They arrived home, and
Grazia and the grocer were informed that the Conservatory at Milan was a delusion and a snare—" a
place where pebbles were polished and diamonds were
dimmed." Shortly after, the townspeople, to show faith
in the home product, had Verdi duly installed as organist of the village church at a salary equal to forty dollars
a year ✠ ✠

Under the spell of this good fortune, Verdi proposed
marriage to the daughter of Jasquith, the grocer, his
friend and benefactor. Gratitude to the man who had
first assisted him had much to do with the alliance; and
in wedding the daughter, Verdi simply complied with
what he knew to be the one ardent desire of the father.
¶ The girl was a frail creature, of fine instincts, but her
intellect had been starved just as her body had been.
Her chief virtue seems to have been that she believed
absolutely in the genius of Verdi.

The ambition of Verdi began to show itself. He wrote
an opera, and offered it to Merelli, the impresario of
" La Scala " at Milan. The impresario had heard of
Verdi, through the fact that the Conservatory had
blackballed him. This of itself would have been no
passport to fame, but the Committee saw fit to defend
themselves in the matter by making a public report of
the considerations which had moved them to shut the
doors on the young man from Busseto. This gave the
subject a weight and prominence that simple admission

282

GIUSEPPE VERDI

never would have given. ¶ Merelli, the Major Pond of
Milan, saw the expressions " bizarre," " erratic,"
" peculiar," " unprecedented," and kept his eye on
Verdi. And so when the opera was written he pounced
upon it, thinking possibly a new star had appeared on
the horizon. The opera was accepted. Verdi, feverish
with hope, moved his scanty effects to Milan, and there,
with his frail and beautiful girl-wife and their baby-boy,
lived in a garret just across from the theater.

Preparations for the performance were going on apace.
The night of November Seventeenth, Eighteen Hundred
Thirty-nine came, and the play was presented. The
critics voted it a failure. Merelli, the manager, saw that
it was not strong enough with which to storm the town,
and so decided to abandon it. He liked the young composer, though, and admired his work; and inasmuch as
he had brought him to Milan, he felt a sort of obligation
to help him along. So Verdi was given an order for an
opera bouffe. That's it! Opera bouffe!—the people
want comedy—they must be amused. Even Verdi's
serious work ran dangerously close to farce—bouffe is
the thing!

Merelli's hope was infectious. Verdi began work on the
new play that was to be presented in the Spring. The
winter rains began. There was no fire in the garret where
the composer and his frail girl-wife lived. They were so
proud that they did not let the folks at Busseto know
where they were: even Merelli did not know their place

of abode. Under an assumed name Verdi got occasional work as an underling in one of the theaters, and also played the piano at a restaurant. The wages thus earned were a pittance, but he managed to take home soup-bones that the baby-boy sucked on as though they were nectar ❧ ❧

Another baby was born that winter. The mother was unattended, save by her husband—no other woman was near. Verdi managed to bring home scraps of food by stealth from the restaurant where he played, but it was not the kind that was needed. There was no money to buy goat's milk for the new-born babe, and the famishing mother, ever hopeful, assured the husband it was n't necessary—that the babe was doing well. The child grew aweary of this world before a month had passed, and slept to wake no more.

But the opera bouffe was taking shape. It was rehearsed and hummed by husband and wife together. They went over it all again and again, and struck out and added to. It was splendid work—subtle, excruciatingly funny, and possessed a dash and go that would sweep all carping and criticism before it.

Food was still scarce, and there was no fuel even to cook things; but as there was nothing to cook, it really made no difference. Spring was coming—it was cold, to be sure, but the buds were swelling on the trees in the park. Verdi had seen them with his own eyes, and he hastened home to tell his wife—Spring was coming!

284

GIUSEPPE VERDI

The two-year-old boy did n't seem to thrive on soup-bones. The father used to hold him in his arms at night to warm the little form against his own body. He awoke one morning to find the child cold and stiff. The boy was dead.

The mother used to lie abed all day now. She was n't ill she said—just tired! She never looked so beautiful to her husband. Two bright pink spots marked her cheeks, and set off the alabaster of her complexion. Her eyes glowed with such a light as Verdi had never before seen. No, she was not ill—she protested this again and again. She kept to her bed merely to be warm; and then if one did n't move around much, less food was required—don't you see?

Spring had come. The opera was being rehearsed. The title of the play was " Un Giorno di Regno." Merelli said he thought it would be a success; Verdi was sure of it ❧ ❧

The night of presentation came. After the first act Verdi ran across the street, leaped up the stairs three steps at a time, and reached the garret. The play was a success. The worn woman there on her pallet, the pale moonlight streaming in on her face, knew it would be. She raised herself on her elbow and tried to call, " Viva Verdi! " But the cough cut her words short. Verdi kissed her forehead, her hands, her hair, and hurried back in time to see the curtain ascend on the second act. This act went without either applause or disapproval.

GIUSEPPE VERDI

Verdi ran home to say that the audience was a trifle critical, but the play was all right—it was a success! He said he would remain at home now, he would not go to hear the third and last act. He would attend his wife until she got well and strong. The play was a success! ❧ She prevailed upon him to leave her and then come back at the finale and tell her all about it.

He went away.

When he returned he stumbled up the stairway and slowly entered the door.

The last act had not been completed—the audience had hissed the players from the stage!

Upon the ashen face of her husband, the stricken woman read all. She tried to smile. She reached out one thin hand on which loosely hung a marriage-ring. The hand dropped before he could reach it. The eyes of the woman were closed, but upon the long, black lashes glistened two big tears. The spirit was brave, but the body had given up the great struggle.

GIUSEPPE VERDI

HE calamities that had come sweeping over Verdi well-nigh broke his proud heart. He was only twenty-six, but he had had a taste of life and found it bitter.

He lost interest in everything. All his musical studies were abandoned, his excursions into science went by default, and he was quite content to bang the piano in a concert saloon for enough to secure the bare necessaries of life. Suicide seemed to present the best method of solving the problem, and the various ways of shuffling off this mortal coil were duly considered. Meanwhile he filled in the time reading trashy novels—anything to forget time and place, and lose self in poppy-dreams of nothingness ✄ ✄

Two years of such blankness and blackness followed. He was sure that the desire to create, to be, to do, would never come again—these were all of the past. One day on an idle stroll through the park he met Merelli. As they walked along together, Merelli took from his pocket a book, the story of " Nabucco," and handing it to Verdi, asked him to look it over, and see if he thought there was a chance to make an opera out of it. Verdi responded that he was not in the business of writing operas—he had quit all such follies. He took the volume, however, but neglected to look at it for several days. At last he read the pages. He laid the book down and began to pace the floor. Possibilities of creation were looming large before him—a rush of thought was upon

GIUSEPPE VERDI

him. His soul was not dead—it had only been lying fallow ✄ ✄

He secured the loan of a piano and set to work. In a month the opera was completed. Merelli hesitated about accepting it—twice he had lost money on Verdi. Finally he decided he would put the play on, if Verdi would waive all royalties for the first three performances, if it were a success, and then sell the opera outright " at a reasonable price," if Merelli should chance to want it. The "reasonable price" was assumed to be about a thousand francs—two hundred dollars—pretty good pay for a month's work.

Verdi took no interest in the production of the piece. He had come to the conclusion that the public was a fickle, foolish thing, and no one could tell what it would hiss or applaud. Then he remembered the blackness of the night when only two years before his other opera was produced ✄ ✄

He made his way to his dingy little room and went to bed ✄ ✄

Very early the next morning there was a loud pounding on his door. It was Merelli. "How much for your opera?" asked the impresario, pushing his way into the room ✄ ✄

" Thirty thousand francs," came a voice, loud and clear out of the bedclothes.

" Don't be a fool," returned Merelli—" why do you ask such a sum!"

GIUSEPPE VERDI

" Because you are here at five o'clock in the morning—
the price will be fifty thousand this afternoon." ¶ Ten
minutes of parley followed, and then Merelli drew his
check for twenty thousand francs, and Verdi gave his
quitclaim, turned over in bed, and went to sleep again.

289

GIUSEPPE VERDI

HE success of "Nabucodonosor" was complete. Its author had his twenty thousand francs, but Merelli made more than that. From Eighteen Hundred Forty-two to Eighteen Hundred Fifty-one may be called the First Verdi Period. A dozen successful operas were produced, and simultaneously at Rome, Naples, Venice, Milan, Genoa and Florence, Verdi's compositions were being presented. The master was a businessman, as well as an artist—the combination is not so unusual as was long believed—and knew how to get the most for the mintage of his mind. Money fairly flowed his way.

Verdi married again in Eighteen Hundred Fifty. His life now turns into what may be called the Second Verdi Period. After this we shall see no more such curious exhibitions of bad taste as a ballet of forty witches in " Macbeth," capering nimbly to a syncopated melody, with " Lady Macbeth " in a needlessly abbreviated skirt singing a drinking-song to an absent lover. In strenuous efforts to avoid coarseness Verdi may occasionally give us soft sentimentality, but the change is for the best ॐ ॐ

His mate was a woman of mind as well as heart. She was his intellectual companion, his friend, his wife. For nearly fifty years they lived together. Her dust now lies in the " House of Rest," at Milan, a home for aged artists, founded by Verdi. This " House of Rest " was a Love-Offering, dedicated to the woman who had

290

GIUSEPPE VERDI

given him, without stint, of the richness of her nature; who had bestowed rest, and peace, and hope and gentle love. She had no feverish ambitions and petty plans and schemes for secretly corralling pleasure, power, place, attention, or selfish admiration. By giving all, she won all. She devoted herself to this man in whom she had perfect faith, and he had perfect faith in her. She ministered to him. They grew great together. When each was over eighty years of age, Henry James met them at Cremona, at a musical festival in honor of the birthday of Stradivari. And thus wrote Henry James: " Verdi and his wife were there, admired above all others. And why not? Think of whom they are, and what they stand for—nearly a century of music, and a century of life! The master is tall, straight, proud, commanding. He has a courtly old-time grace of bearing; and he kissed his wife's hand when he took leave of her for an hour's stroll. And the Madame surely is not old in spirit; she is as sprightly as our own Mrs. John Sherwood, who translated 'Carcassonne' so well that she improved on the original, because in her heart spring fresh and fragrant every day the flowers of tender, human, Godlike sympathy."

GIUSEPPE VERDI

IGOLETTO," produced in the year Eighteen Hundred Fifty-one at Venice, is founded on Victor Hugo's " Le Roi s'Amuse "; and the music has all the dramatic fire that matches the Hugo plot. Verdi's devotion to Victor Hugo is seen again in the use of " Hernani " for operatic purposes. " Il Trovatore " and " La Traviata " followed " Rigoletto," and these three operas are usually put forward as the Verdi masterpieces. The composer himself regarded them with a favor that may well be pardoned, since he used to say that he and his wife collaborated in their production—she writing the music and he looking on. The proportion of truth and poetry in this statement is not on record. But the simple fact remains that " Il Trovatore " was always a favorite with Verdi, and even down to his death he would travel long distances to hear it played. A correspondent of the " Musical Courier," writing from Paris in Eighteen Hundred Eighty-seven, says: " Verdi and his wife occupied a box last evening at the Grand Opera House. The piece was ' Il Trovatore,' and many smiles were caused by the sight of the author and his spouse seemingly leading the claque as if they would split their gloves."

The flaming forth of creative genius that produced the " Rigoletto," " Il Trovatore," and " La Traviata," subsided into a placid calm.

The serene happiness of Verdi's married life, the fortune that had come to him, and the consciousness of having

292

GIUSEPPE VERDI

won in spite of great obstacles, led him to the thought of quiet and well-earned rest. The master interested himself in politics, and was elected to represent the district of Parma in the Italian Parliament. He proved himself a man of power—practical, self-centered and business-like—and as such served his country well.

The sentiment of the man is shown in his buying the property at Busseto, his old home, which was owned by Signore Barezzi. He removed the high picket fence, replacing it with a low stone wall; remodeled the house and turned the conservatory into a small theater, where free concerts were often given with the help of the villagers. The adjoining grounds and splendid park were free to the public.

The master's attention to music was now limited to enjoying it. So passed the days.

Ten years of the life of a country gentleman went by, and the Shah of Persia, who had been on a visit to Italy and met Verdi, sent a command for an opera. The plot must be laid in the East, the characters Moorish, and the whole to be dedicated to the immortal Son of the Sun—the Shah.

It is a little doubtful whether the Shah knew that operas are produced only in certain moods and can not be done to order as a carpenter builds a fence. But it was the way that Eastern Royalty had of showing its high esteem.

Verdi smiled, and his wife smiled, and they had quite a

merry little time over the matter, calling in the neighbors and friends, and drinking to the health of a real live Shah who knew a great musical genius when he found one. But suddenly the matter began to take form in the master's mind. He set to work, and the result was that in a few weeks "Aida" was completed. The stories often told of the long preparation for composing this opera reveal the fine imagination of the men who write for the newspapers. Verdi seized upon knowledge as a devilfish absorbs its prey—he learned in the mass ✣ "Aida" was first produced at Cairo in Eighteen Hundred Seventy-one, with a grand setting and the best cast procurable. A new Verdi opera was an event, and critics went from London, Paris, and other capitals to see the performance.

The first thing the knowing ones said was that Verdi was touched with Wagnerism, and that he had studied "Lohengrin" with painstaking care. If Verdi was influenced by Wagner it was for good; but there was no servile imitation in it. The "Aida" is rich in melody, reveals a fine balance between singers and orchestra, and the "local color" is correct even to the chorus of Congo slaves that was introduced at the performance in Cairo ✣ ✣

All agreed that the rest had done the master good, and the correspondents wrote, "We will look anxiously for his next." They thought the stream had started and there would be an overflow.

GIUSEPPE VERDI

But they were mistaken. Sixteen years of quiet farming followed. Verdi was more interested in his flowers than his music, and told Philip Hale, who made a pious pilgrimage to Busseto in Eighteen Hundred Eighty-three, that he loved his horses more than all the prima donnas on earth.

But in Eighteen Hundred Eighty-seven, the artistic and music-loving world was surprised and delighted with "Otello." This grand performance made amends for the mangling of "Macbeth." James Huneker says: "The character-drawing in 'Otello' is done with the burin of a master; the plot moves in processional splendor; the musical psychology is subtle and inevitable. At last the genius of Verdi has flowered. The work is consummate and complete."

"Falstaff" came next, written by a graybeard of eighty as if just to prove that the heart does not grow old. It is the work of an octogenarian who loved life and had seen the world of show and sense from every side. Old men usually moralize and live in the past—not so here. The play flows with a laughing, joyous, rippling quality that disarmed the critics and they apologized for what they had said about Wagnerian motives. There were no sad, solemn, recurring themes in the full-ripened fruit of Verdi's genius. When he died, at the age of eighty-seven, the curtain fell on the career of a great and potent personality—the one unique singer of the Nineteenth Century.

WOLFGANG MOZART

WOLFGANG MOZART

Mozart composed nine hundred twenty-two pieces of which we know. He is considered the greatest composer the world has ever seen, judged by the versatility and power of his genius. In every kind of composition he was equally excellent. Beside being a great composer he was a great performer, being the most accomplished pianist of his day. He was also an excellent player on the violin.

—*Dudley Buck*

WOLFGANG MOZART

POLOGY: The Mozart " Little Journey " was written, and as over a month had been taken to do the task, the result was something of which I was justly proud. It was quite unlike anything ever before written. The printers were ready to take the work in hand, but I begged them to allow me two more days for careful revision; and as I was just starting away to give a lecture at Janesville, Wisconsin, I took the manuscript with me, intending to do the final work of revision on the train.
¶ All went well on the journey, the lecture had been given with no special tokens of disapproval on part of the audience, and I was on board the early morning train that leaves for Chicago. And as my mind is usually fairly clear in the early hours, I began work retouching the good manuscript. We were nearing Beloit when I bethought me to go into the Buffet-Car for a moment. ¶ When I returned the manuscript was not to be seen. I looked in various seats, and under the seats, asked my neighbors, inquired of the brakeman, and then hunted up the porter and asked him if he had seen my manuscript. He did not at first understand what I meant by the term " manuscript," but finally inquired if I referred to a pile of dirty, dog-eared sheets of paper, all

marked up and down and over and crisscross, ev'ry-which-way.

I assured him that he understood the case.

He then informed me that he had " chucked the stuff," that is to say, he had tossed it out of the window, as he was cleaning up his car, just as he always did before reaching Chicago.

I made a frantic reach for the bell-cord, but was restrained. A sympathetic passenger came forward and explained that five miles back he had seen the sheets of my precious manuscript sailing across the prairie. We were going at the rate of a mile a minute and the wind was blowing fiercely, so there was really no need of backing up the train to regain the lost goods.

" I hope dem scribbled papers was no 'count, boss!" said the porter humbly, as I stood sort of dazed, gazing into vacancy.

I shook myself into partial sanity. " Oh, they were of no value—I was looking for them so as to throw them out of the window myself," I answered.

" Brush ? " said he.

" Yes," said I.

I placed the expected quarter in his dusky palm, still pondering on what I should do.

To reproduce the matter was impossible, for I have no verbal memory—something must be written, though. I decided to leave Chicago in an hour by the Lake Shore Railroad, and have the copy ready for the Roycroft boys when I reached home. ¶ This I did, and as I had no reference-books, maps or memoranda to guide me, the matter seems to lack synthesis. I say seems to lack— but it really does n't, for the facts will all be found to be as stated. Still the form may be said to be slightly colored by the environment, so some explanation is in order—hence this apology to the Gentle Reader. And further, if the Reader should find in these pages that, at rare intervals, I use the personal pronoun, he must bear in mind that I live in the country, and that it is the privilege and right, established by long precedent and custom of country folk, to talk about themselves and their own affairs if they are so minded.

WOLFGANG MOZART

HICAGO: Talent is usually purchased at a high price, and if the gods give you a generous supply of this, they probably will be niggardly when it comes to that. But one thing the artist is usually long on, and that is whim. Let us all pray to be delivered from whim—it is the poisoner of our joys, the corrupter of our peace, and Dead-Sea fruit for all those about us.

Heaven deliver us from whim!

I am told by a famous impresario, who gained some valuable experience by marrying a prima donna, and therefore should know, that whim is purely a feminine attribute. This, though, is surely a mistake, for there have lived men, as well as women, who had such an exaggerated sense of their own worth, that they lost sight, entirely, of the rights and feelings of everybody else. All through life they kept the stage waiting without punctilio. These men thought dogs were made to kick, servants to rail at, the public to be first crawled to and then damned, and all rivals to be pooh-poohed, cursed or feared, as the mood might prompt. Further than this they considered all landlords robbers, every railroad-manager a rogue, and businessmen they bunched as greedy, grasping Shylocks. They always used the word " commercial " as an epithet.

Devotees of the histrionic art can lay just claim to having more than their share of whim, but the musical profession has no reason to be abashed, for it is a good

second. However, the actor's and the musician's art
are often not far separated. In speaking to James
McNeil Whistler of a certain versatile musician, a lady
once said, " I believe he also acts! "

" Madame, he does nothing else," replied Mr. Whistler.
¶ Art is not a thing separate and apart—art is only the
beautiful way of doing things. And is it not most absurd
to think, because a man has the faculty of doing a
thing well. that on this account he should assume airs
and declare himself exempt along the line of morals and
manners? The expression "artistic temperament" is
often an apologetic term, like " literary sensitiveness,"
which means that the man has stuck to one task so long
that he is unable to meet his brother men on a respectful
equality ◢◣ ◢◣

The artist is the voluptuary of labor, and his fantastic
tricks often seem to be only Nature's way of equalizing
matters, and showing the world that he is very common
clay, after all. To be modest and gentle and kind, as we
all can be, is just as much to God as to be learned and
talented, and yet be a cad.

Still, instances of great talent and becoming modesty
are sometimes found; and in no great musician was the
balance of virtues held more gracefully than with
Mozart. He had humor.

Ah! that is it—he knew values—had a sense of proportion, and realized that there is a time to laugh. And a
good time to laugh is when you see a mighty bundle of

303

WOLFGANG MOZART

pretense and affectation coming down the street.
Dignity is the mask behind which we hide our ignorance;
and our forced dignity is what makes the imps of
comedy, who sit aloft in the sky, hold their sides in
merriment when they behold us demanding obeisance
because we have fallen heir to tuppence worth of talent.

WOLFGANG MOZART

APORTE: Mozart had a sense of humor. He knew a big thing from a little one. When yet a child the tendency to comedy was strong upon him. When nine years of age he once played at a private musicale where the Empress, Maria Theresa, was present. The lad even then was a consummate violinist. He had just played a piece that contained such a tender, mournful, minor strain that several of the ladies were in tears. The boy seeing this, relentingly dashed off into a " barnyard symphony," where donkeys brayed, hens cackled, pigs squealed and cows mooed, all ending with a terrific cat-fight on a wood-shed roof. This done, the boy threw his violin down, ran across the room, climbed into the lap of the Empress and throwing his arms around the neck of the good lady, kissed her a resounding smack first on one cheek, then on the other. It was all very much like that performance of Liszt, who one day, when he was playing the piano, suddenly shouted, " Pitch everything out of the windows! " and then proceeded to do it—on the keyboard, of course.

On the same visit to the palace, when Mozart saluted Maria Theresa in his playful way, he had the misfortune to slip and fall on the waxed floor.

Marie Antoinette, daughter of Maria Theresa, just budding into womanhood, ran and picked him up and rubbed his knee where it was hurt. " You are a dear, good lady," said the boy in gratitude, " and when I grow up I am going to marry you." Liszt never made any such promise as that. Liszt never offered to marry anybody. But it is too bad that Marie Antoinette did not hold the lad to his promise. It would have probably proved a valuable factor for her in the line of longevity; and her husband's circumstances would have saved her from making that silly inquiry as to why poor people don't eat cake when they run short of bread. These moods of merriment continued with Mozart, as they did with Liszt, all his life—not always manifesting themselves, though, in the way just described.

As a companion I would choose Mozart—generous, unaffected, kind—rather than any other musician who ever played, danced, sang or composed—excepting, well, say Brahms.

WOLFGANG MOZART

OUTH BEND: We take an interest in the lives of others because we always, when we think of another, imagine our relationship to him. " Had I met Shakespeare on the stairs I would have fainted dead away," said Thackeray.

Another reason why we are interested in biography is because, to a degree, it is a repetition of our own life There are certain things that happen to every one, and others we think might have happened to us, and may yet. So as we read, we unconsciously slip into the life of the other man and confuse our identity with his. To put yourself in his place is the only way to understand and appreciate him. It is imagination that gives us this faculty of transmigration of souls; and to have imagination is to be universal; not to have it is to be provincial. Let me see—would n't you rather be a citizen of the Universe than a citizen of Peoria, Illinois, which modest town the actors always speak of as being one of the provinces?

As I read biography I always keep thinking what I would have done in certain described circumstances, and so not only am I living the other man's life, but I am comparing my nature with his. Everything is comparative; that is the only way we realize anything— by comparing it with something else. As you read of the great man he seems very near to you. You reach out across the years and touch hands with him, and with him you hope, suffer, strive and enjoy: your existence is all blurred and fused with his. ¶ And through this oneness you come to know and comprehend a character that has once existed, very much better than the people did who lived in his day and were blind to his true worth by being ensnared in cliques that were in competition with him.

WOLFGANG MOZART

LKHART: I intimated a few pages back that I would have liked to have Mozart for a friend and companion. Mozart needed me no less than I need him. " Genius needs a keeper," once said I. Zangwill, probably with himself in mind. We all need friends—and to be your brother's keeper is very excellent if you do not cease being his friend. And poor Mozart did so need a friend who could stand between him and the rapacious wolf that scratched and sniffed at his door as long as he lived. I do not know why the wolf sniffed, for Mozart really never had anything worth carrying away. He was so generous that his purse was always open, and so full of unmixed pity that the beggars passed his name along and made cabalistic marks on his gateposts. Every seedy, needy, thirsty and ill-appreciated musician in Germany regarded him as lawful prey. They used to say to Mozart, " I can not beg and to dig I am ashamed —so grant me a small loan, I pray thee."

Yes, Mozart needed me to plan his tours and market his wares. I 'm no genius, and although they say I was an infant terrible, I never was an infant prodigy. At the tender age of six, Mozart was giving concerts and astonishing Europe with his subtle skill. At a like age I could catch a horse with a nubbin, climb his back, and without a saddle or bridle drive him wherever I listed by the judicious use of a tattered hat. Of course I took pains to mount only a horse that had arrived at years

---

of discretion, matronly brood-mares or run-down plow-horses; but this is only proof of my practical turn of mind. Mozart never learned how to control either horse or man by means of a tattered hat or diplomacy: music was his hobby, and it was long years after his death before the world discovered that his hobby was no hobby at all, but a genuine automobile that carried him miles and miles, clear beyond all his competitors: so far ahead that he was really out of shouting distance.

Indeed, Mozart took such an early start in life and drove his machinery so steadily, not to say so furiously, that at thirty-five all the bearings grew hot for lack of rebabbitting, and the vehicle went the way of the one-horse shay—all at once and nothing first, just as bubbles do when they burst.

At the age which Mozart died I had seen all I wanted to of business life, in fact I had made a fortune, being the only man in America who had all the money he wanted, and so just turned about and went to college. This I firmly hold is a better way than to be sent to college and then go into trade later and forget all you ever learned at school. I had rather go to college than be sent. Every man should get rich, that he might know the worthlessness of riches; and every man should have a college education, just to realize how little the thing is worth ✄ ✄

Yes, Mozart needed a good friend whose abilities could have rounded out and made good his deficiencies. Most certainly I could not do the things that he did, but I should have been his helper, and might, too, had not a century, one wide ocean, and a foreign language separated us.

WOLFGANG MOZART

ATERLOO: Friendship is better than love for a steady diet. Suspicion, jealousy, prejudice and strife follow in the wake of love; and disgrace, murder and suicide lurk just around the corner from where love coos. Love is a matter of propinquity; it makes demands, asks for proofs, requires a token. But friendship seeks no ownership—it only hopes to serve, and it grows by giving. Do not say, please, that this applies also to love. Love bestows only that it may receive, and a one-sided passion turns to hate in a night, and then demands vengeance as its right and portion.

Friendship asks no rash promises, demands no foolish vows, is strongest in absence, and most loyal when needed. It lends ballast to life, and gives steadily to every venture. Through our friends we are made brothers to all who live.

I think I would rather have had Mozart for a friend than to love and be loved by the greatest prima donna who ever warbled in high C. Friendship is better than love. Friendship means calm, sweet sleep, clear brain and a strong hold on sanity. Love I am told is only friendship, plus something else. But that something else is a great disturber of the peace, not to say digestion. It sometimes racks the brain until the world reels. Love is such a tax on the emotions that this way madness lies. Friendship never yet led to suicide.

312

WOLFGANG MOZART

OLEDO: Yes, just at the age when Mozart wrote and played his "Requiem," getting ready to die, I was going to school and incidentally falling in love. I was thirty-four and shaved clean because there were gray hairs coming in my beard. Love has its advantages, of course, and the benefits of passionate love consist in scarifying one's sensibilities until they are raw, thus making one able to sympathize with those who suffer. Love sounds the feelings with a leaden plummet that sinks to the very depths of one's soul. This once done the emotions can return with ease, and so this is why no singer can sing, or painter paint, or sculptor model, or writer write, until love or calamity, often the same thing, has sounded the depths of his soul. Love makes us wise because it makes room inside the soul for thoughts and feelings to germinate; but passionate love as a lasting mood would be hell. Henry Finck says that is why Nature has fixed a two-year limit on romantic or passionate love. "War is hell," said General Sherman. "All is fair in Love and War," says the old proverb. Love and War are one, say I. Love is mad, raging unrest and a vain, hot, reaching out for nobody knows what. Of course the kind which I am talking about is the Grand Passion, not the sort of sentiment that one entertains towards his grandmother. ¶ "But it is good to fall in love, just as it is well to have the measles," to quote Schopenhauer. Still, there is this difference: one only has the measles once, but the man

WOLFGANG MOZART

who has loved is never immune, and no amount of pledges or resolves can ere avail.

Just here seems a good place to express a regret that the English language is such a crude affair that we use the same word to express a man's regard for roast-beef, his dog, child, wife and Deity. There are those who speedily cry, " Hold! " when one attempts to improve on the language, but I now give notice that on the first rainy day I am going to create some distinctions and differentiate for posterity along the line just mentioned ✄

WOLFGANG MOZART

LYRIA: As intimated in a former chapter, I was a successful farmer before I went to college. I was also a manufacturer, and made a success in this business, too. I made a fortune of a hundred thousand dollars before I was thirty, and should have it yet had I sat down and watched it. If you go into a railroad-car and sit down by the side of your valise (or manuscript), in an hour your valuables will probably be there all right.

But if you leave the valise (or the manuscript) in a seat and go into another car, when you come back the goods may be there and they may not. That is the only way to keep money—fasten your eye right on it. If you leave it in the hands of others, and go away to delve in books, the probabilities are that, when you get back, certain obese attorneys have divided your substance among them ♫ ♫

However, there is good in every exigency of life, and to know that your fortune is gone is a great relief. When the trial is ended and the prisoner has received his sentence, he feels a great relief, for it is only the unknown that fills our souls with apprehension.

WOLFGANG MOZART

CLEVELAND: In all the realm of artistic history no record of such extremes can be found in one life as those seen in the life of Mozart. The nearest approach to it is found in the career of Rembrandt, who won fame and fortune at thirty, and then holding the pennant high for ten years, his powers began to decline. It took twenty-six years of steady down grade to ditch his destinies in a pauper's grave.

But Rembrandt, during his lifetime, was scarcely known out of Holland, whereas Mozart not only won the nod of nobility, and the favor of the highest in his own land, but he went into the enemy's country and captured Italy. Mozart's art never languished: he held a firm grip on sublime verities right to the day of his death. The high-water mark in Mozart's career was reached in those two years in Italy, when in his thirteenth and fourteenth years. The arts all go hand in hand, for the reason that strong men inspire strong men, and each does what he can do best. In painting, sculpture and music (not to mention Antonio Stradivari of Cremona) Italy has led the world. A hundred years ago no musician could hope for the world's acclaim until Italy had placed its stamp of approval upon him.

Savants in Milan, Florence, Padua, Rome, Verona, Venice and Naples, tested the powers of young Mozart to their fullest; and although he had to overcome doubt and the prejudice arising from being " a barbaric

316

WOLFGANG MOZART

German," yet the highest honors were at the last ungrudgingly paid him. He was enrolled as an honorary member of numerous musical societies, old musicians gave their blessings, proud ladies craved the privilege of kissing his fair forehead, and the Pope conferred upon the gifted boy the Order of the Golden Spur, which gave him the right to have his mail come directed to " The Signor Cavaliere Mozarti."

At Naples the result of his marvelous playing was ascribed to enchantment, and this was thought to be centered in a diamond ring that had been presented to the lad by a fair lady in a mood of ecstasy. To convince the Neapolitans of their error Mozart was obliged to accept their challenge and remove the ring. He wrote home to his mother that he had no time to practise, as in every city where he went artists insisted on his sitting for his portrait.

The acme of attention and applause was reached at Milan, where he was commissioned to write an opera for the Christmas festivities. The production of this opera at La Scala was the most glorious item in the life of Mozart. A boy of fourteen conducting an opera of his own composition before enraptured multitudes is an event that stands to the credit of Mozart, and Mozart alone. " Evviva the Little Master—Evviva the Little Master! "cried the audience. " It is music for the stars," and against all precedent aria after aria had to be repeated. The boy, always rather small for his age,

WOLFGANG MOZART

stood on a chair to wield his baton, and the flowers
that were rained upon him nearly covered the lad
from view.

18

WOLFGANG MOZART

SHTABULA: The place of a man's birth does not honor him until after he is dead, and every man of genius has been distrusted by his intimate kinsmen. If he is granted recognition by the outside world, those who have known him from childhood wink slyly and repeat Phineas T. Barnum's aphorism, a free paraphrase of which the Germans have used since the days of the Vandals.

Leopold Mozart returned home with his wonderful boy not much richer than when he went away. He had left the management of finances to others, and was quite content to travel in a special carriage, stop at the best hotels, and have any "label" he might order, just for the asking.

Reports had reached Germany of the wonderful success of the youthful Mozart in Italy, but Vienna smiled and Salzburg sneezed.

WOLFGANG MOZART

ORTH EAST: It is not so very long ago that all the beautiful things of earth were supposed to belong to the Superior Class. That is to say, all the toilers, all the workers in metals, all the bookmakers, authors, poets, painters, sculptors and musicians, did their work to please this noble or that. All bands of singers were singers to His Lordship, and if a man wrote a book he dedicated it to His Royal Highness. At first these thinkers and doers were veritable slaves, and no court was complete that did not have its wise man who wore the cap and bells, and made puns, epigrams and quoted wise saws and modern instances for his board and keep. This man usually served as a clerk or overseer, during his odd hours, and only appeared to give a taste of his quality when he was sent for.

It was the same with the musicians and singers—they were cooks, waiters and valets, and when there were guests these performers were notified to be in readiness to " do something " if called upon. It was the same with painters—every court had its own. Rubens, as we know, was looked upon by the Duke of Mantua as his private property, and the artist had to run away, when the time was ripe, to save his soul alive. Van Dyck was court painter to Charles the First, and married when he was told to do so.

There is no such office as " Poet Laureate of England " —the Laureate is poet to the King, and used to dine

WOLFGANG MOZART

with the Master of the Hounds. Later he was allowed
to choose his domicile and live in his own house, like
Saint Paul, the prisoner at Rome. His yearly stipend is
yet that tierce of Canary.

WOLFGANG MOZART

ILVER CREEK: Leopold Mozart, and the son who caused his name to endure, were in the employ of the Archbishop of Salzburg. The Archbishop was a veritable prince, with short breath and a double chin, and no shade of doubt ever came to him concerning the divinity of his succession. He ruled by divine right, and everybody and everything were made to minister to the well-being of his person and estate. The Mozarts were too poor to escape from the employ of the Archbishop, and he took pains to warn all interested persons not to harbor, encourage or entice his servants away on penalty of dire displeasure. Mozart ate with the servants, and we have his letters written to his sister showing how his seat was next below that of the coachman. When he was to play before invited guests he was made to wait in the entry until the footman called him, and there he often stood for hours, first on one foot, then on t' other.
¶ It is easy to ask why a man of such sublime talent should endure such treatment, but the simple fact is Mozart was gentle, yielding, kind—immersed in his music—with no power to set his will against the tide of tendency that 'compassed him round. The Archbishop forbade his playing at concerts or entertainments, and blocked the way to all advancement. The Archbishop did n't have a diplomat like Rubens to cope with, or a fighter like Wagner, or a plotter like Liszt, or a stiletto-bearing man like Paganini, and so Mozart wrote his

WOLFGANG MOZART

music on a table in one corner of a beer-garden, and waltzed with his wife, Constance, to keep warm when there was no fire and the weather was cold, and all the time danced attendance on the Archbishop of Salzburg. All of his feeble, spasmodic efforts at freedom came to naught, because there was no persistency behind them ✄ ✄

Gladly would he have sold his services for three hundred gulden a year, but even this sum, equal to one hundred fifty dollars a year, was denied him. He was always composing, always making plans, always seeing the silver tint in the clouds, but all of his music was taken by this one or that in whom he foolishly trusted, and only debt and humiliation followed him ✄ ✄

When at long intervals a sum would come his way from a generous admirer touched with pity, all the beggars in the neighborhood seemed to know it at once. Then it was that music filled the air at the beer-garden, carking care and unkind fate were for the time forgot, and all went merry as a wedding-bell.

Finally the position of Court Musician to the Emperor of Austria fell vacant, and certain good friends of Mozart secured him the place. But the Emperor was not like Frederick the Great, for he could not distinguish one tune from another, and did not consider it any special virtue so to do. The result was that his musicians were looked after by his valet, and Mozart found that

323

his position was really no better than it had been with
the Archbishop of Salzburg.

And still his mind proved infirm of purpose, and he had
not the courage to demand his right, for fear he might
lose even the little that he had.

WOLFGANG MOZART

UFFALO: Mozart was in his twentieth year when he met Aloysia Weber. She was a gifted singer, surely, and was needlessly healthy. She was of that peculiar, heartless type that finds digression in leading men a merry chase and then flaunting and flouting them. Young Mozart, the impressionable, Mozart the delicate and sensitive, Mozart the Æolian harp, played upon by every passing breeze, loved this bouncing bundle of pink-and-white tyranny &c &c

She encouraged the passion, and it gradually grew until it absorbed the boy and he grew oblivious to all else. He lived in her smile, bathed in the sunshine of her presence, fed on her words, and as for her singing in opera it was not so much what her voice was now but what he was sure it would be.

His glowing imagination made good her every deficiency. He thought he loved the girl. It was not the girl at all he loved: he only loved the ideal that existed in his own heart. His father opposed the mating and hastily transferred the youth from Vienna to Paris; but who ever heard of opposition and argument and forced separation curing love? So matters ran on and letters and messages passed, and finally Mozart made his way back to Vienna and with breathless haste sought out the object of his whole heart's love.

She had recently met a man she liked better, and as she could not hold them both, treated Mozart as a stranger, and froze him to the marrow. ¶ He was crushed, undone, and a fit of sickness followed. In his illness, Constance, a younger sister of Aloysia, came to him in pity and nursed him as a child. Very naturally, all the love he had felt for Aloysia was easily and readily transferred to Constance. The tendrils of the heart ruthlessly uprooted cling to the first object that presents itself.

And so Wolfgang Amadeus Mozart and Constance Weber were married. And they were happy ever afterward. It would have been much better if they had quarreled, but Mozart's gentle, yielding character readily adapted itself to the weaker nature of his wife. In his music she took a sort of blind and deaf delight and guessed its greatness because she loved the man. But when two weak wills combine, the net result is increased weakness—never strength.

Constance was as beautiful a specimen of the slipshod housekeeper as ever piled away breakfast dishes unwashed, or swept dirt under a settee. If they had money she bought things they did not need, and if there was no money she borrowed provisions and forgot to return the loan. Irregularity of living, deprivation and hope deferred, made the woman ill and she became a chronic sufferer. But she was ever tended with loving, patient care by the overburdened and underfed husband.

A biographer tells how Mozart would often arise early in the morning to set down some melody in music that he had dreamed out during the night. On such occasions

326

WOLFGANG MOZART

he would leave a little love-letter for his wife on the stand at the head of the bed, where she would find it on first awakening. One such note, freely translated, runs as follows: " Good-morning, Dear Little Wife. I hope you rested well and had sweet dreams. You were sleeping so peacefully that I dare not kiss your cheek for fear of disturbing you. It is a beautiful morning and a bird outside is singing a song that is in my heart. I am going out to catch the strain and write it down as my own and yours. I shall be back in an hour."

WOLFGANG MOZART

LAST AURORA: Aloysia married the man of her choice—an actor by the name of Lange. They quarreled right shortly, and soon he used to beat her. This was endured for a year or more, then she left him. For a while she lived with Wolfgang and Constance, and Mozart, true to his nature, gave her from his own scanty store and deprived himself for her benefit. He stood godfather to one of her children and was a true friend to her to the last.

After Aloysia lived to be an old woman, and long after Mozart had passed out, and the world had begun to utter his praises, she said: " I never for a moment thought he was a genius—I always considered him just a nice little man."

Mozart's soul was filled with melody, and all of his music is faultless and complete. He possessed the artistic conscience to a degree that is unique. Careless and heedless in all else, if his mood was not right and the product was halting, he straightway destroyed the score. He was always at work, always hearing sweet sounds, always weighing and balancing them in the delicate scales of his judgment.

So absorbed was he in his art that he fell an easy victim to the designing, and never stopped his work long enough to strike off the shackles that bound him to a vain, selfish and unappreciative court.

Worn by constant work, worried by his wife's continued illness, dogged by creditors, and unable to get justice

---

from those who owed it to him, his nerves at the early age of thirty-five gave way.

His vitality rapidly declined and at last went out as a candle does when blown upon by a sudden gust from an open door.

It was a blustering winter day in December, Seventeen Hundred Ninety-one, when his burial occurred. A little company of friends assembled, but no funeral-dirge was played for him, save the blast blown through the naked branches of the trees, as they hurried the plain pine coffin to its final resting-place. At the gate of the cemetery the few friends turned back and left the lifeless clay to the old gravedigger, who never guessed the honor thus done him.

It was a pauper's grave that closed over the body of Mozart—coffin piled on coffin, and no one marked the spot. All we know is, that somewhere in Saint Mark's Cemetery, Vienna, was buried in a trench the most accomplished composer and performer the world has ever known. It was a hundred years afterward before the city made tardy amends by erecting a fitting monument to his memory.

His best monument is his work. The melody that once filled his soul is yours and mine; for by his art he made us heirs to all that wealth of love that was never requited, and the dreams, that for him never came true, are our precious and priceless legacy.

329

JOHANNES BRAHMS

BRAHMS

What is music? This question occupied my mind for hours last night before I fell asleep. The very existence of music is wonderful, I might even say miraculous. Its domain is between thought and phenomena. Like a twilight mediator, it hovers between spirit and matter, related to both, yet differing from each. It is spirit, but spirit subject to the measurement of time: it is matter, but matter that can dispense with space.

—*Heine*

JOHANNES BRAHMS

MERSON has said that, next to the man who first voices a great truth, is the one who quotes it.

Truth is in the air; it belongs to all who can appreciate it; and the difference between the man who gives a truth expression and the listener who at once comprehends and repeats it, is very slight. If you understand what I say, it is because you have thought the same thoughts yourself—I merely express for you that which you already know. And so you approve and applaud, not stopping to think that you are applauding your own thought; and your heart beats fast and you say, "Yes, yes, why didn't I say that myself!"

All conversation is a sort of communion—an echoing back and forth of thoughts, feelings and emotions. We clarify our thoughts by expressing them—no idea is quite your own until you tell it to another.

Music is simply one form of expression. Its province is to impart a sublime emotion. To give himself is the controlling impulse in the heart of every artist—to impart to others the joy he feels—this is the dominant motive in his life.

Hence the poet writes, the artist paints, the sculptor models, the singer sings, the musician plays—all is

333

expression—a giving voice to the Silence. But it is all done for others. In ministering to others the artist ministers to himself. In helping others we help ourselves. We grow strong through exercise, and only the faculties that are exercised—that is to say, expressed—become strong. Those not in use atrophy and fall victims to arrested development.

Man is the instrument of Deity—through man does Deity create. And the artist is one who expresses for others their best thoughts and feelings. He may arouse in men emotions that were dormant, and so were unguessed; but under the spell of the artist-spirit, these dormant faculties are awakened from lethargy—they are exercised, and once the thrill of life is felt through them, they will probably be exercised again and again ✄

All art is collaboration between the performer and the partaker—music is especially a collaboration. It is a oneness of feeling: action and reaction, an intermittent current of emotion that plays backward and forward between the player and his audience. The player is the positive pole, or masculine principle; and the audience the negative pole, or feminine principle.

In great oratory the same transposition takes place. Almost every one can recall occasions when there was an absolute fusion of thought, feeling and emotion between the speaker and the audience—when one mind dominated all, and every heart beat in unison with his. The great musician is the one who feels intensely, and is

334

---

able to express vividly, and thus impart his emotion to others ✄ ✄

Robert Schumann was such a man. In his youth, when he played at parlor gatherings he could fuse the listeners into an absolute oneness of spirit. You can not make others feel unless you yourself feel; you can not make others see unless you yourself see. Robert Schumann saw. He beheld the moving pictures, and as they passed before him he expressed what he saw in harmonious sounds. His many admirers say he gave " portraits " on the piano, and by sounds would describe certain persons, so others who knew these persons would recognize them and call their names.

Sterndale Bennett has told of Schumann's playing Weber's "Invitation to the Dance," and accompanying it with little verbal explanations of what he saw, thus: " There," said the player as he struck the opening chords, " there, he bows, and so does she—he speaks—she speaks, and oh! what a voice—how liquid! listen—hear the rustle of her gown—he speaks, a little deeper, you notice—you can not hear the words, only their voices blending in with the music—now they speak together—they are lovers, surely—see, they understand—oh! the waltz—see them take those first steps—they are swaying into time—away!—there they go—look!—you can not hear their voices now—only see them! "

¶ Schumann studied law, and had he followed that profession he would have made a master before a jury.

335

JOHANNES BRAHMS

He saw so clearly and felt so deeply, and was so full of generosity and bubbling good-cheer, that he was irresistible. As we know, he proved so to Clara Wieck, who left father and mother and home to cleave to this unknown composer ✣ ✣

This splendid young woman was nine years younger than Robert, but she had already made a name and fortune for herself before they were married.

In passing it is well enough to call attention to the fact that this is one of the great loves of history. It ranks with the mating of Robert Browning and Elizabeth Barrett. How strange that such things are so exceptional that the world takes note of them!

Yet for quite a number of years after their marriage, Madame Schumann was at times asked this question: " Is your husband musical? "

But Robert Schumann, like Robert Browning, was too big a man to be jealous of his wife. Jealousy is an acknowledgment of weakness and insecurity. " Robert and Clara," their many dear friends always called them. They worked together—composed, sang, played, and grew great together. And as if to refute the carping critics who cry that domesticity and genius are incompatible, Clara Schumann became the happy mother of eight children, and not a year passed but she appeared upon the concert stage, while a nurse held the baby in the wings. Schumann was very proud of his wife. He was grateful to her for interpreting his songs in a way

336

he could not. His lavish heart went out to every one who expressed the happiness and harmony which he felt singing in his soul.

And so he welcomed all players and all singers, and all who felt the influence of an upward gravitation. Especially was he a friend of the young and the unknown. His home at Dusseldorf was a Mecca for the aspiring— worthy and unworthy—and to these he gave his time, money and influence. " Genius must have recognition— we will discover and bring forth these beautiful souls; we will liberate and give them to the world," he used to say. Not only did he himself express great things, but he quoted others.

Among those who had reverenced the Schumanns from afar, came a young man of twenty, small and fair-haired, from Hamburg. He was received at the regular " Thursday Night " with various other strangers. These meetings were quite informal, and everybody was asked to play or sing. On being invited to play, our young man declined. But on a second visit he sat down at the piano and played. It was several minutes before the company ceased the little buzz of conversation and listened—the fledglings were never taken seriously except by the host and hostess. The youth leaned over the keyboard, and seemed to gather confidence from the sympathetic attitude of the listeners, and especially Clara Schumann, who had come forward and stood at his elbow.

He played from Schumann's " Carnival," and as he

played, freedom came to him. He surprised himself. When he ceased playing, Robert kissed his cheek, and the company were vehement in their applause. Next day Schumann met Albert Dietrich, another disciple who had come from a distance to bask in the Schumann sunshine, and said with an air of mystery: "One has come of whom we shall yet hear great things. His name is Johannes Brahms." ✄ ✄

JOHANNES BRAHMS

E have at least four separate accounts of Brahms' first appearance and behavior when he arrived at the city of Dusseldorf. These descriptions are by Robert and Clara Schumann, Doctor Dieters and Albert Dietrich. All agree that Johannes Brahms was a most fascinating personality. Dieters and Dietrich were about the age of Brahms, and were lesser satellites swinging just outside the Schumann orbit. Very naturally when a new devotee appeared, they gazed at him askance. Many visitors were coming and going, and from most of them there was nothing to fear, but when this short, deep-chested boy with flaxen hair appeared, Dietrich felt there was danger of losing his place at the right hand of the Master

Brahms carried his chin in, and the crown of his head high. He was infinitely good-natured, met everybody on an equality, without abasement or condescension. He was modest, never pushed himself to the front, and was always ready to listen. A talented performer who can listen well, is sure to be loved. And yet when Brahms went forward to play, there was just a suggestion of indifference to his hearers in his manner, and a half-haughty self-confidence that won before he had sounded a note. We always believe in people who believe in themselves.

Young Brahms brought a letter of introduction from Joachim. But that was nothing—Joachim was always giving letters to everybody. He was like the men who sign every petition that is presented; or those other good men who give certificates of character to people they do not know, and recommendation letters to those for whom they have no use.

So the letter went for little with Robert Schumann—it was the way Brahms approached the piano, and settled his hands and great shock-head over the keyboard, that won ♫ ♫

" He is no beginner," whispered Clara to Robert before Johannes had touched a key.

It didn't take Brahms long to get acquainted—he mixed well. In a few days he dropped into that half-affectionate way of calling his host and hostess by their first names, and they in turn called him " Johannes." And to me this is very beautiful, for, at the last, souls are all of one age. More and more we are realizing that getting old is only a bad habit. The only man who is old is the one who thinks he is. Of course these remarks about age do not exactly apply just here, for no member of the trinity we are discussing was advanced in years. Robert was forty-three, Clara was thirty-four, and Johannes was twenty.

Johannes Brahms was thrice well blest in being well born. His parents were middle-class people, fairly well-to-do. They proved themselves certainly more than middle-class in intellect, when they adopted the plan of being the companions and comrades of their children.

340

JOHANNES BRAHMS

Johannes grew up with no slavish fear of " old folks."
He had worked with his father, studied with him;
learned lessons from books with his mother, and played
" four hands " with her at the piano, by the hour, just
for fun.

Then when Remenyi came that way with his violin, and
wanted a pianist, he took young Brahms. When their
lines crossed the line of Liszt, they played for him at his
inn; and then Liszt played for them.

This Remenyi was our own " Ol' Man Remenyi," who
passed over only a year or so ago. I wonder if he was
Ol' Man Remenyi then! He never really was an old
man, and that appellation was more a mark of esteem
than anything else—a sort of diminutive of good-will.
I met Remenyi at Chautauqua, where he spent a month
or more in Eighteen Hundred Ninety-three. He gave
me my first introduction to the music of Brahms, of
whom he never tired of talking. He considered Brahms
without a rival—the culminating flower of modern
music; and if the Ol' Man slightly exaggerated his own
influence in bringing Brahms out and presenting him to
the world, I am not the one to charge it up against his
memory ✠ ✠

In explaining Brahms and his music, Remenyi used to
grow animated, and when words failed he would say,
" Here, it was just like this"—and then he would seize
his violin, the bow would wave through the air, and the
notes would tell you how Brahms transposed Beethoven's

JOHANNES BRAHMS

" Kreutzer Sonata " from A to B flat—a feat he never
could have performed if Remenyi had not told him how.
It was Remenyi who introduced Brahms to Joachim, and
it was Joachim who introduced Brahms to Schumann,
and it was Schumann's article, " New Paths," in the
" Neue Zeitschrift fur Musik," that placed Brahms on a
pedestal before the world. Brahms was not the great
man that Schumann painted, Remenyi thought, but
the idealization caused him to put forth a heroic effort
to be what Clara and Robert considered him. So it was
really these two who compelled him to push on: otherwise he might have relaxed into a mere concert performer or a leader of some subsidized band.

Remenyi always seemed to me like a choice antique
mosaic, a trifle weather-worn, set into the present. He
used to quote Liszt as if he lived around the corner, and
would criticize Wagner, and tell of Moescheles, Haertel,
the Mendelssohns and the Schumanns, as if they might
all gather tomorrow and play for us at the Hall in the
Grove ✄ ✄

Recently I met dear old Herr Kappes, eighty years
young, who knew the Mendelssohns, and admired
Brahms, loved Clara Schumann, and liked Remenyi—
sometimes. They were too much alike, I fear, to like
each other all the time. But the harmony is still in the
heart of Herr Kappes. He gives music-lessons, and
lectures, and will explain to you just how and where
Brahms differs from Schumann, and where Schubert

342

JOHANNES BRAHMS

separates from both. ¶ Herr Kappes can speak five languages, but even with them all he finds difficulty in making his meaning clear, and at times adopts the Remenyi plan, and will just turn to the piano and cry, " It 's like this, see! Schumann wrote it in this way"— and then the strong hands will chase the keys down and back and over and up. " But Brahms took the motif and set it like this "—and Herr Kappes will strike the bass a thunderous stroke—pause, look at you, glide back and down, up and over, and you are carried away in a swirl of sweet sounds, and see a pink face framed in its beautiful aureole of white hair. You listen but you do not " see " the fine distinctions, because you do not care—Herr Kappes is all there is of it, so animated, so gentle, so true, so lovable—because he used to pay court to Fanny Mendelssohn and then transferred his affections to Clara Schumann, and now just loves his art, and everybody.

JOHANNES BRAHMS

CHUMANN'S article, "New Paths," at once determined Brahms' career. He must either live up to the mark that had been set for him—or else run away.

I give below an extract from Robert's estimate of Brahms and his work:

Ten years have passed away, as many as I formerly devoted to the publication of this paper—since I have allowed myself to commit my opinions to this soil so rich in memories. Often in spite of an overstrained productive activity, I have felt moved to do so; many new and remarkable talents have made their appearance, and a fresh musical power seemed about to reveal itself among the many aspiring artists of the day, even if their compositions were only known to the few.

I thought to follow with interest the pathways of these elect; there would—there must—after such a promise, suddenly appear one who should utter the highest ideal expression of the times, who should claim the mastership by no gradual development, but burst upon us fully equipped, as Minerva sprang from the brain of Jupiter. And he has come, this chosen youth, over whose cradle the Graces and Heroes seem to have kept watch ⚘ ⚘

His name is Johannes Brahms; he comes from Hamburg, where he has been working in quiet obscurity, instructed by an excellent, enthusiastic teacher in the most difficult principles of his art, and lately introduced to me by an honored and well-known master. His mere outward appearance assures us that he is one of the elect ⚘ ⚘

344

JOHANNES BRAHMS

Seated at the piano, he disclosed wondrous regions. We were drawn into an enchanted circle. Then came a moment of inspiration which transformed the piano into an orchestra of wailing and jubilant voices. There were sonatas, or rather veiled symphonies, songs whose poetry revealed itself without the aid of words, while throughout them all ran a vein of deep song-melody, several pieces of a half-demoniacal character, but of charming form; then sonatas for piano and violin, string quartets, and each of these creations so different from the last that they appeared to flow from so many different sources. Then, like an impetuous torrent, he seemed to unite these streams into a foaming waterfall; over the tossing waves the rainbow presently stretches its peaceful arch, while on the banks butterflies flit to and fro, and the nightingale warbles her song.

Whenever he bends his magic wand towards great works, and the powers of orchestra and chorus lend him their aid, still more wonderful glimpses of the ideal world will be revealed to us.

May the Highest Genius help him onward! Meanwhile another genius—that of modesty—seems to dwell within him. His comrades greet him at his first step in the world, where wounds may, perhaps, await him, but the bay and the laurel also; we welcome this valiant warrior!

Robert Schumann had been before the public as essayist, poet, pianist and composer for twenty years. He had given himself without stint to almost every musical enterprise of Germany, and his sympathy was ever on tap for every needy and aspiring genius. You may give

345

your purse—he who takes it takes trash—but to give your life's blood and then hope for a renewal of life's lease, is vain.

The public man owes to himself and to his Maker the duty of reserve.

The desert and mountain are very necessary to the individual who gives himself to the public. That any man should so bestride the narrow world like a colossus that the multitude must stop to gaze, and thousands feed upon his words, is an abnormal condition. The only thing that can hold the balance true is solitude. Relaxation is the first requirement of strength. Watch the cat, the tiger or the lion asleep. See what complete absence of intensity—what perfect relaxation! It is all a preparation for the spring.

Schumann had not sought the mountain, nor abandoned himself to the woods in old shoes, corduroys and a flannel shirt. Now he was paying the penalty of publicity. Virtue had gone out of him; and in the article just quoted, there are signs that he is clutching for something. He hails this new star and proclaims him, because in some way he feels that the ruddy, valiant and youthful Brahms is to consummate his work. Brahms is an extension of himself. It is a part of that longing for immortality—we perpetuate ourselves in our children and look for them to accomplish what we have been unable to do.

Johannes Brahms was the spiritual son of Robert

JOHANNES BRAHMS

Schumann. ¶ In less than a year after Brahms and Schumann first met, there were ominous signs and evil portents in the air. " Why do you play so fast, dear Johannes? I beg of you, be moderate! " cried Robert on one occasion. Brahms turned, and his quick glance caught the ashy face and bloodshot eyes of a sick man. His reply was a tear and a hand-grasp.

Soon, to Schumann, all music was going at a gallop, and in his ears forever rang the sound of A. He could hear naught else. Tenderness, patience, and even love were of no avail. Indeed, love is not exempt from penalty—the law of compensation never rests. Nature forever strives for a right adjustment.

The richness and intensity of Schumann's life were bought with a price. The first year after his marriage he composed one hundred thirty-eight songs. Sonatas, scherzos, symphonies and ballads followed fast, and in it all his gifted wife had gloried.

But when, in Eighteen Hundred Fifty-four, Robert had, after sleepless nights, in a fit of frenzy thrown himself into the Rhine, and had been rescued, shattered, unable to recognize even his nearest friends—the loyal and devoted wife saw where she herself had erred ⚜ Writing to Brahms she says: " I encouraged him in his work, and this fired his ambition to do and to become. Oh! why did I not restrain that intensity and send him away into the solitude to be a boy; to do nothing but frolic and play and bathe in the sunshine, and eat and sleep? The life of an artist is death. Kill ambition, my Brother! "

Activity and rest—both are needed. The idea of the " retreat " in the Catholic Church is founded on stern, hygienic science. Wagner's forced exile was not without its advantages, and the " retreats " of Paganini and the " retirements " of Liszt were very useful factors in the devolution of their art.

JOHANNES BRAHMS

OR the malady that beset Robert Schumann, there was no cure save death; his only rest, the grave. When his spirit passed away in Eighteen Hundred Fifty-six, his devoted wife and the loyal Brahms attended him. Owing to the insidious creeping of the disease, Schumann's affairs had got into bad shape; and it was now left to Brahms, more than all others, to smooth the way of life for the stricken wife and her fatherless brood.

The versatility and sturdy commonsense of Brahms were now in evidence. In business affairs he was ready, decisive and systematic. And the delicacy, tact and charming good-nature he ever showed, reveal the man as a most extraordinary figure. Great talent is often bought at a price—how well we know this, especially with musicians! But Brahms was sane on all subjects. He could take care of his own affairs, lend a needed hand with others, but never meddle—smile with that half-sardonic grimace at all foolish little things, weep with the stricken when calamity came; yet above it all the little man towered, carrying himself like the giant that he was. And yet he never made the mistake of taking himself too seriously. " I am trying to run opposition to Michelangelo's ' Moses,'" he once called to Dietrich, as he leaned out of the window in the sunshine, and stroked his flowing beard. In his later years many have testified to this Jovelike quality that Brahms diffused by his presence. No one could come

JOHANNES BRAHMS

into his aura and fail to feel his sense of power. Around such souls is a sacred circle—if you are allowed to come within this boundary, it is only by sufferance; within this space only the pure in heart can dwell.

JOHANNES BRAHMS

OLSTOY in "Anna Karenina" speaks of that quiet and constant light to be seen on the faces of those who are successful—those who know that their success is acknowledged by the world ❧ ❧

Brahms was a successful man by temperament, for success (like East Aurora) is a condition of mind. There is no tragedy for those who do not accept tragedy; and the treatment we receive from others is only our own reflected thought.

Brahms thought well of everybody, if he thought of any one at all. He reveled in the sunshine, and everywhere made friends of children. "We saw Brahms on the hotel veranda at Domodossola," wrote a young woman to me in Eighteen Hundred Ninety-five, "and what do you think?—he was on all-fours, with three children on his back, riding him for a horse!"

For many years Brahms used to make an annual pilgrimage to Italy, and often on these tours at fairs he would fall in with Gipsy bands. At such times he would always stop and listen, and would lustily applaud the performance. On one such occasion, Dietrich tells, the leader recognized Brahms, and instantly rapped for silence. He was seen to pass the whispered word along, and then the band struck up one of Brahms' pieces, greatly to the delight of the composer.

He was a man of the people, and I am glad to know that he hated a table d' hote, smiled a smile of derision at all

351

dress-coats, had small sympathy with pink teas, loved his friends, doted on babies, and was never so happy as when in the country walking along grass-grown lanes in the early summer morning, when the dew was on and the air was melodious with the song of birds. He had a habit of going bareheaded, carrying his hat in his hand; and on these country walks, always with bared head, he would sing or whistle, and unconsciously in his mind the music would be taking shape that was to be written out later in the quiet of his study.

Brahms knew the world—not simply one little part of it—he knew it as thoroughly as any man can, and was interested in it all. He knew the world of workers—the toilers and bearers of burdens. He knew the weak and the vicious, and his heart went out to them in sympathy; for he knew his own heart and realized the narrow margin that separates the so-called " good " from the alleged " bad." He knew that sin is only a wrong expression of life, and reacts to the terrible disadvantage of the sinner.

He was interested in mechanics—bookbinding, printing, iron-working, carpentry, and was well acquainted with all new inventions and labor-saving devices. He knew the methods of farming, the different breeds of cattle; he knew what soil would produce best a certain crop, and understood " rotation." He could call the wild birds by name and imitate their notes, and studied long their haunts and habits. That excellent man and

JOHANNES BRAHMS

talented, George Herschel, in a letter to a friend speaks
of walking with Johannes Brahms along the highway,
and Brahms suddenly calling in alarm, " Look out!
look out! you may kill it! "
It was only a tumblebug, but he shrank from putting
foot on any living thing. Brahms reverenced all life, and
felt in his heart that he was brother to that bug in the
dust, to the birds that chirruped in the hedgerows, and
to the trees that lifted their outstretching branches to
the sun.
He was deeply religious—although he never knew it.
All music is a hymn of praise, a song of thanksgiving, a
chant of faith. Music is a making manifest to our dull
ears the divine harmony of the universe, and thus all
music is sacred music, and all true musicians are priests,
for by their ministrations we are made to realize our
Oneness with the Whole. Through music we read the
Universal ✁ ✁
Music is the only one of the arts that can not be prosti-
tuted to a base use. We hear of bad books, of the
" Index Expurgatorius," and in every State there are
laws against the publication of immoral books and
indecent pictures. We also hear of orders issued by the
courts requiring certain statues to be removed or veiled,
but no indictment can be brought against music. It is
the only one of the arts that is always pure.
Brahms realized this and felt the dignity of his office,
holding high the standard; and yet he knew that the

353

---

toilers in the fields were doing a service to humanity, just as necessary as his own. And possibly this is why he uncovered, walking with bared head. All is holy, all is good—it is all God's world, and all the men and women in it are His children.

JOHANNES BRAHMS

OR forty-two years Brahms was the devoted friend of Clara Schumann. She was thirteen years his senior, yet their spirits were as children together. From the first he was to her, " Johannes," and she was " Clara " to him. A few of their letters have been published in the " Revue des deux Mondes," and this woman, who was a great-grandmother, and had sixty years before captured a world, then in her seventy-fifth year, wrote to her " Dear Johannes " with all the gentle fervor of a girl of twenty, congratulating him on some recent success. In reply he writes back to his "Dear Clara" in gracious banter; mentions rheumatism in his legs as an excuse for bad penmanship; hopes she is keeping up her practise; tells of a " Steinway Grand " that some one has sent him, and regrets that she does not come to try it " four hands," as he has failed utterly to get out of it alone the melody that he knows is there.

Brahms never married—the bond between himself and Clara was too sacred to allow another to sever or share it. And yet the relationship was so high, so frank, so openly avowed, that no breath of scandal has ever smirched it.

The purity and excellence of it all has been its own apology, as love ever should be its own excuse for being. ¶ For about three months every year these two friends dwelt near each other. Together they worked, composed, sang, read, wrote and roamed the woods. " None of

JOHANNES BRAHMS

Madame Schumann's children is as young as she is,"
wrote Doctor Hanslick, when Clara was sixty and
Johannes was forty-seven. " With the hope of passing
for her father, Brahms is cultivating a patriarchal
beard," continues Hanslick.

In his essay on " Friendship," Emerson speaks of the
folly of forcing our personal presence on the friend we
love best, and of the faith that ideality brings. Something of this thought is shown in the letters of Madame
Schumann to Brahms, and in his to her.

Often for six months they would not meet, he doing his
work in his own way, she doing hers, but each ever
conscious of the life and love of the other—feeding on
the ideal—writing or not writing, but glorying in each
other's triumphs—lives linked first by the love of a
third person, cemented by dire calamity, and then
fused by a oneness of hope and aspiration.

Brahms' nature was too decidedly masculine, that is to
say, one-sided, to exist without the love of woman;
Clara Schumann, gentle, generous, motherly, plastic,
needed Johannes no less than he needed her.

When Clara's spirit passed away, in May, Eighteen
Hundred Ninety-six, Brahms attended her funeral at
Frankfort. Hero that he was in body and spirit, the
shock unnerved him. No rebound came—every bodily
faculty seemed to have lost its buoyancy. The doctors
tried to cheer him by telling him that he had no organic
ailment, and that twenty years of life and work were

before him. He knew better, and told them so. Men do not live any longer than they wish to. " Shall I live to see the anniversary of her death ? " asked Brahms of the doctor in March, Eighteen Hundred Ninety-seven. " Oh, undoubtedly—you can live many years if you only will to," was the answer. Three weeks later—on April Third—Max Kalbrech telegraphed to Widmann, this message, " Brahms fell asleep early this morning."

SO HERE ENDETH "LITTLE JOURNEYS TO THE HOMES OF GREAT MUSICIANS," WHICH IS VOLUME FOURTEEN OF THE SERIES OF "LITTLE JOURNEYS TO THE HOMES OF THE GREAT," AS WRITTEN BY ELBERT HUBBARD. THE TYPOGRAPHY, BORDERS AND INITIALS WERE DESIGNED BY THE ROYCROFT ARTISTS AT THEIR SHOPS, WHICH ARE IN EAST AURORA, NEW YORK

INDEX

Abbey, Edwin A., birth of, vi, 305; evolution of the art of, vi, 312; work of, in the Boston Public Library, vi, 323; studio of, vi, 322; George W. Childs and, vi, 309; Henry James on, vi, 311.

Abbotsford, home of Sir Walter Scott, iv, 321.

Abbott, John S. C., iii, 7; his life of Napoleon, vi, 129.

Abbott, Lyman, on H. W. Beecher, vii, 378.

Abildgaard, the painter, Thorwaldsen and, vi, 105.

Ability, a bucolic estimate of, viii, 173.

Abnegation, v, 243.

Abolition, v, 205; in New England, vii, 408.

Abraham, x, 19.

Abraham, Rembrandt's, iv, 63.

Abstinence, v, 248.

Account of the English Poets, Addison, v, 246.

Achievement, the price of, v, 135.

Acton, Lord, i, 60.

Adam Bede, Eliot, i, 59; v, 148.

Adams, Brooks, *The Law of Civilization and Decay*, xii, 89.

Adams, John, iii, 79, 251, 239; quoted, iii, 89.

Adams, John Quincy, mother of, iii, 143; marriage of, iii, 145; president, iii, 146; member of Congress, iii, 146; death of, iii, 146; on business, ix, 131; on Thomas Paine, ix, 158.

Adams, Maude, i, p xxvii; xii, 169.

Adams, Samuel, letter of, to Arthur Lee, iii, 78; politics of, iii, 80; part of, in the Boston uprising, iii, 81; member of the Calkers' Club, iii, 85; as a member of the Congress of the Colonies, iii, 91; characteristics of, iii, 94; place in history of, iii, 95, 251;

typical Puritan, iii, 232; quoted, iii, 240.

Adams, Sarah Flower, v, 48.

Addison, Joseph, iii, 60; birthplace of, v, 239; the perfect English gentleman, v, 239; education of, v, 244; travels of, v, 247; under-secretary of State, v, 252; Parliamentary experience of, v, 252; meeting of, with Steele, v, 254; his connection with the *Tatler* and the *Spectator*, v, 254; referred to, v, 294; on Plato, x, 121.

Adirondack Murray, vii, 375.

Adler, Felix, ix, 282; preaching of, vii, 310.

Adolescence, Dr. Charcot on, xii, 23.

Adoration of the Magi, Botticelli, vi, 70.

Adversity, uses of, i, 110.

Æschines, disciple of Socrates, viii, 29.

Æschylus, ii, 28.

Æsthetic England, Walter Hamilton, xiii, 272.

Affectation, v, 238.

Africa, Petrarch, xiii, 239.

Agassiz, Louis, xi, 419; xii, 407; Darwinism and, xii, 230; Thoreau and, viii, 417; compared with Disraeli, v, 338.

Age, of enlightenment, viii, 271; of Herbert Spencer, viii, 354; of Michelangelo, iv, 6; of Rembrandt, iv, 78.

Age of Reason, The, Thomas Paine, ix, 157, 160, 179.

Agitators, personality of, vii, 409.

Agnosticism, x, 342.

Agnostic School, the, xii, 327.

Agriculture, Humboldt on, xii, 140.

Aida, Verdi, xiv, 294.

Aids to Reflection, Coleridge, v, 313.

Alameda smile, the, viii, 365.

Alaska, population of, iv, 128.

Albert memorial, i, 314.

Alcibiades, Socrates and, viii, 29; Nero compared with, viii, 71.

Alcott, Bronson, viii, 403; Emerson and,

i

ii

iv

▼

Bramante, Italian architect, iv, 26.
Brann the Iconoclast, ix, 97.
Brantwood, i, 88.
Brashear, John, maker of telescopes, xii, 178.
Breathing habit, the, viii, 159.
Breeds in birds and animals, ix, 275.
Breton, Jules, ix, 198.
Bridge of Sighs, Venice, iv, 150; v, 200.
Bright, John, Robert Owen and, ix, 226; Richard Cobden and, ix, 149, 231; Gladstone on, ix, 238; on the Corn Laws, ix, 216; Sir Robert Peel on, ix, 238; on taxation, ix, 228.
Bright, Dr. Richard, physician, ix, 224.
Bright's Disease, iii, 123.
Brisbane, Arthur, x, 338.
British Museum, origin of, i, 124.
Broadway, the village of, vi, 319.
Brockway methods, viii, 72.
Bronco-busting, viii, 328.
Bronte, Charlotte, ii, 239; father of, ii, 98; mother of, ii, 99; death of, ii, 99; home of, ii, 107; sisters of, ii, 108; works of, ii, 112; Thackeray and, i, 240; referred to, v, 294.
Bronze, casting of, vi, 274.
Brooke, Lord, referred to, i, 303.
Brooke, Stopford, quoted, v, 78.
Brook Farm, viii, 402; x, 319; influence of the, viii, 402; Theodore Parker and, ix, 293.
Brookfield and Alfred Tennyson, v, 76.
Brooklyn, Washington at, iii, 24.
Brooks, Phillips, preaching of, vii, 309.
Brooks, Shirley, i, 236.
Brotherhood, of Fine Minds, the, v, 304; of Latter-Day Swine, i, 71; of man, ix, 133; of Saint Luke, Antwerp, iv, 173.
Brougham, Lord, i, 108; ii, 83: Byron and, v, 218.
Brown, Dr. John, xi, 264.
Brown, Ford Madox, ii, 125; v, 18; vi, 11; his description of Elizabeth Eleanor Siddal, xiii, 261.
Brown, John, vii, 409; Theodore Parker and, ix, 300; Major Pond and, vii, 360.
Brown, Osawatomie, vi, 148.
Browning, Elizabeth B., date of birth, ii, 17; early years of, ii, 19; mother of, ii, 19; father of, ii, 20; education of, ii, 21; London home of, ii, 27; friends of, ii, 30; meeting of, with Robert

vi

Browning, ii, 35; marriage of, ii, 37; Italian home of, ii, 38; favorite book of, ix, 376; grave of, v, 64; influence of, on William Morris and Burne-Jones, v, 12; quoted, iv, 5.
Browning, Robert, i, 96, 236; ii, 109; v, 97; appearance of, v, 40; his ancestry, v, 41; grave of, v, 43; parents of, v, 44; life of, by Mrs. Sutherland Orr, v, 40; habits of, v, 42; love for Lizzie Flower, v, 48; gipsy life of, v, 51; his friendship for Fanny Haworth, v, 56; his meeting with Elizabeth Barrett, ii, 35; v, 58; his marriage, v, 61; death of, v, 65; homage rendered his memory, v, 66; Elizabeth Barrett and, xiv, 125; John Stuart Mill compared with, xiii, 170; Rembrandt compared with, vi, 67; Wordsworth compared with, i, 222; on spiritual advisers, viii, 174; quoted, iii, 41; v, 62; love of society, v, 79.
Brown-Sequard, Dr., i, 247.
Bruno, Giordano, xii, 47; Luther and, xii, 54; Sir Philip Sidney and, xii, 51; statue of, ix, 123.
Bryant, William Cullen, iv, 51; v, 97; xi, 258.
Bryce, James, on American institutions, iii, 75; on Parnell, xiii, 204.
Buck, Dudley, on Mozart, xiv, 298.
Bucke, Dr., friend of Whitman, i, 166.
Bucke, Richard Maurice, quoted, xiii, 61.
Buckingham, Duke of, iv, 115.
Buckingham, poet, contemporary of Addison, v, 249.
Buckle, Henry Thomas, the historian, v, 196; grave of, i, 231; noted, iv, 42; quoted, iii, 60; vii, 180; referred to, v, 289.
Buckley, Dr., opinion of, regarding Susan B. Anthony, i, 135; ii, 52.
Buddha, quoted, xiii, 84.
Buffalo Bill, i, 119; ii, 149.
Buffalo Normal School, i, p xvii.
Buffon, French naturalist, xii, 370.
Builder's itch, x, 313.
Bull Run, battle of, iii, 200.
Bulwer-Lytton, and Disraeli, v, 333; on Verdi, xiv, 274.
Bunker Hill, battle of, iii, 140.
Bunsen, Robert, German chemist, xii, 351.
Bunyan, John, and Oliver Cromwell, ix, 331.

viii

Diplomacy, women and, v, 114.
Dipsy Chanty, Kipling's, ii, 75.
Disagreeable girl, the, described, xiii, 113.
Discipline, Thomas Arnold on, x, 231; the parental idea of, vi, 160.
Discontent, xiv, 77.
Discord, uses of, vi, 329.
Disestablishment, i, 114.
Dispute, The, Raphael, vi, 32.
Disraeli, Benjamin, xii, 199; ancestry of, v, 322; education of, 324; personality of, v, 325; literary efforts of, v, 327; political life of, v, 331; marriage of, v, 338; Chancellor of the Exchequer, v, 340; Prime Minister, v, 340; *Coningsby*, v, 341; *Contarini Fleming*, v, 324; *Endymion*, v, 342; *Lothair*, v, 342; *Sybil*, v, 341; *Tancred*, v, 341; *Vivian Gray*, v, 324; attitude toward Free Trade, v, 340; Agassiz compared with, v, 338; Mrs. Austen and, v, 327; Lady Blessington and, v, 333; Bulwer-Lytton and, v, 333; Lord Byron and, v, 324; Froude on, v, 326; Mrs. Wyndham Lewis and, v, 333; Macaulay compared with, v, 197; Mephisto compared with, v, 320; Thomas Moore and, v, 333; Lady Morgan and, v, 333; Napoleon compared with, v, 321; O'Connell and, v, 336; Count d'Orsay and, v, 333; Pitt and, v, 331; Voltaire compared with, viii, 295; N. P. Willis on, v, 329; Mrs. Willyums and, v, 344; on Cobden, ix, 140; on Charles Darwin, v, 341; on democracy, xi, 255; on the Established Church, xii, 155; on initiative, xiv, 152; on Dr. Jowett, viii, 351; on love, xiii, 158; quoted, iv, 160; v, 41; xiii, 408.
Disraeli, Isaac, v, 322.
Dissection, iv, 59.
Divine Comedy, The, Dante, xiii, 134.
Divine passion, the, ii, 36; iv, 242.
Divine right of kings, ii, 83; v, 291.
Divinity, idea of, vi, 49.
Divinity of business, xi, 14.
Division of labor, iii, 99.
Divorce, i, 111; Milton on, v, 130; women and, viii, 133; Voltaire on, viii, 290.
Dixon, photographer of animals, ii, 125.
Dr. Jekyl and Mr. Hyde, Stevenson, xiii, 27.
Doctors, v, 203; Kant on, viii, 162.
Dodo, Edward F. Benson, i, 148.

Dogmatism, vi, 348; x, 292.
Dog-star, influence of, v, 103.
Doll's House, Ibsen, xiii, 112.
Don Juan, referred to, iii, 176; Byron compared with, v, 221.
Donnelly, Ignatius, vi, 65.
Donniges, Helene von, xiii, 363.
Donnybrook Fair, ix, 252; spirit of, xii, 337.
Dore Gallery in London, the, iv, 344.
Dore, Gustave, early life of, iv, 332; " the child illustrator," iv, 336; life in Paris, iv, 338; love for his mother, iv, 339; ability as a musician, iv, 340; decorated with the Cross of the Legion of Honor, iv, 340; characteristics of his art, iv, 341; his visit to England, iv, 344; presented to Queen Victoria, iv, 345; death of, iv, 346.
Dorset, poet, contemporary of Addison, v, 249.
Douglas, Fred, vii, 409.
Draco, laws of, ii, 20.
Drake, Edwin L., xi, 370.
Drake, English admiral, iv, 81.
Draper, J. W., historian, v, 94.
Dream of Fair Women, A, Tennyson, v, 78.
Dream of John Ball, A, William Morris, v, 23.
Droll Stories, Balzac, xiii, 300.
Drummond, Henry, referred to, v, 290.
Drum-Taps, Whitman, i, 175.
Drunkard's home, the, xiv, 234.
Dryden, Addison and, v, 246; Shakespeare and, i, 124; his opinion of Shakespeare, i, 134.
Duality of the human mind, i, 113.
Duane, James, New York's first Continental Mayor, iii, 238.
Dumas, Alexandre, iv, 249; friend of Meissonier, iv, 126; a negro, x, 205; on Garibaldi, ix, 115.
Dunciad, Pope, i, 179; vi, 329.
Dunkards, the, ii, 189.
Duplicity, evils of, vii, 371.
Durer, Albrecht, xii, 119; vi, 259; Martin Luther and, vii, 139; Moses compared with, x, 37; on Erasmus, x, 157.
Duse, Eleanor, xiv, 127.
Dutch, industry of, iv, 42.
Dyer, Mary, execution of, ix, 365; Governor Endicott and, ix, 363; Anne Hutchinson and, ix, 359.
Dynamic force, iv, 193.

xiv

xvi

xxiv

Incandescent lamp, invention of, i, 329.

Incompatibility, iv, 254; v, 129; vii, 68.

Inconsistency, examples of, x, 366.

Independence, vi, 332.

Independence, Declaration of, iii, 75.

Indians, Canada's treatment of, xi, 404; North American, in London, ix, 28; Washington's mission among, iii, 17

Indian, the American, xii, 141; as orator, iii, 189.

Indifference, vi, 325.

Individuality, xiv, 43.

Indulgences, vii, 123.

Infant phenomenon, the, v, 122.

Inferno, Dante, iv, 340.

Infidelity, vi, 13; x, 342.

Influence of women, i, 75.

Ingalls, John J., quoted, vii, 177.

Ingersoll, Ebon, brother of Robert Ingersoll, vii, 249; death of, vii, 235.

Ingersoll, Robert G., xii, 251; birthplace of, vii, 242; parents of, vii, 237; wife of, vii, 259; his great achievement, vii, 268; mental evolution of, vii, 257; H. W. Beecher and, vii, 357; Peter Cooper and, xi, 259; the dictum of, viii, 173; Gladstone's reply to, x, 363; William Godwin compared with, xiii, 87; the Governor of Delaware and, ix, 261; Elbert Hubbard and, vii, 255; on Alexander von Humboldt, xii, 160; Huxley compared with, xii, 319; on love, vii, 232; lecture on the mistakes of Moses, x, 15; opinions regarding, vii, 253; compared with Paine and Bradlaugh, ix, 243; quoted, iii, 288; on Shakespeare, xii, 319.

Initiative, xii, 242.

In Memoriam, Tennyson, v, 82, 88.

Innocent III, Pope, referred to, i, 151.

In Patience, Christina Rossetti, ii, 114.

In Praise of Folly, Erasmus, x, 177.

Inquisition, the Spanish, vi, 171.

Insanity, defined, i, 163; viii, 255; originality and, viii, 197.

Inspiration, vi, 155.

Instrumental music, v, 236.

Insurance, a species of gambling, viii, 300.

Intellect and beauty, x, 277.

Intellectual Life, The, Hamerton, vi, 50.

Intellectual tyranny, x, 348.

Introspection, vii, 118.

Invocation, Tennyson, v, 89.

Iowa, farmers' wives in, ii, 222.

Ireland, American travelers in, i, 155; beauty of, i, 274; Edmund Burke on, vii, 178; Parnell on, xiii, 174; Lord Dufferin on, xiii, 175; Gladstone on, xiii, 176; Henry George on, xiii, 190; Home Rule in, xiii, 199; the Irish and, xi, 335; lawlessness in, i, 277; women of, i, 275.

Irish Church, the, i, 114.

Irish immigration, xiii, 179.

Iron, the consumption of, xi, 296.

Ironsides, Cromwell's regiment, ix, 320.

Irreparableness, E. B. Browning, ii, 16.

Irrigation and religion, ix, 278.

Irving, Henry, ii, 237; at Harvard University, xiv, 177; Seneca compared with, viii, 56; on success, viii, 345.

Irving, Washington, iv, 218; vi, 316; John J. Astor and, xi, 221; on the Jews, viii, 207; quoted, i, 293.

"Isaac Bickerstaff," pseudonym of Dean Swift, i, 149.

Isaiah, the Prophet, i, 317.

Israelites, or Children of Israel, ii, 140; x, 21.

Italian Renaissance, the, xiii, 210.

Italy, senility of, iii, 232.

Itineracy, Wesley on the, ix, 48.

Jacks and Jennies, xi, 20.

Jackson, Andrew, iii, 190, 210, 221.

Jacqueminot roses, ii, 241.

James I, iv, 189; Claudius compared with, viii, 58.

James, Henry, on Edwin Abbey, vi, 311; on Verdi, xiv, 291; on Tyndall, xii, 358.

Jameson, Mrs., quoted, iv, 159.

Jane Eyre, Charlotte Bronte, i, 240; ii, 94, 108.

Jansen, Cornelius, painter, v, 122.

Japanese art, vi, 349.

Jay, John, home of, at Rye, N. Y., iii, 233; legal training of, iii, 236; Samuel Adams regarding, iii, 240; governor of N. Y., iii, 247; his religious nature, iii, 249; genius of, iii, 250; referred to, ii, 77; iii, 89; typical Huguenot, iii, 232.

Jealousy, artistic, vi, 176, 275; Gainsborough's freedom from, vi, 150.

Jefferson, Thomas, education of, iii, 55; appearance of, iii, 55; friends of, iii, 58; Patrick Henry and, iii, 61; as a lawyer, iii, 63; member of Virginia

xxx

Smith, Sydney, iv, 320; grave of, i, 231; on Macaulay, v, 178.

Smollett, Tobias, iv, 302.

Snobs, Thackeray on, vi, 66.

Snuffboxes, iv, 120.

Sobieski, John, xiv, 86.

Social Contract, The, Rousseau, i, 205; vii, 207; ix, 389.

Socialism, xii, 342; William Morris and, v, 22.

Socialists, Christian, v, 22; classes of, xi, 42.

Social ostracism, vi, 172.

Social Statics, Spencer, viii, 336.

Society, fashionable, vi, 170.

Society of Friends, ix, 217.

Society for the Prevention of Cruelty to Children, ii, 20; v, 123.

Socrates, birth of, viii, 11; appearance of, viii, 11; parents of, viii, 11; wife of, viii, 22; death of, viii, 37; referred to, ii, 195; Aspasia and, vii, 32; viii, 20; Bronson Alcott compared with, viii, 27; on character, viii, 27; Confucius compared with, x, 50, 60; the first democrat, x, 112; disciples of, viii, 29; Emerson and, viii, 16; influence of, viii, 204; x, 99; Thomas Jefferson compared with, xi, 97; Samuel Johnson compared with, v, 168; Plato and, viii, 11, 29; x, 102; the Sophists and, viii, 18; Tolstoy and, viii, 22; compared with Walt Whitman, i, 170; his opinion of women, viii, 21; Xenophon and, viii, 11, 29.

Solitude, ii, 285; v, 175, 268.

Solomon's ideal wife, ii, 69.

Somers, Bishop Manners, and George III, vii, 200.

Song of the Open Road, quotation from, i, 162.

Song Without Words, Mendelssohn, vi, 117; xiv, 183.

Sonnets From the Portuguese, E. B. Browning, ii, 36.

Sonnets of Michelangelo, iv, 4.

Sophistication, the art of, viii, 202.

Sophists, Socrates and the, viii, 18; the Stoics compared with, viii, 53.

Sophocles, v, 230.

Sordello, Browning, v, 39.

Sorrow, vii, 84.

Sortie of the Civic Guard, Rembrandt, vi, 66.

Soul, Emerson on the, viii, 403; growth

of the, vi, 109; Plato on the, viii, 403.

Southey, Robert, ii, 225; Greta Hall, home of, v, 279; parents of, v, 279; monument of, v, 281; Lord Byron, v, 281; Coleridge and, v, 301; his sonnet to Robert Emmett, v, 264; his estimate of Jane Austen, ii, 254; Lovell and, v, 301; on Lord Nelson, xiii, 398; Shelley and, v, 283; Mary Wollstonecraft and, xiii, 102, the Wordsworths and, i, 214; v, 303.

Spain, England and, in the 16th century, iv, 81; senility of, iii, 232; under the rule of Philip II, vi, 171; dominion in the Netherlands, iv, 81.

Spalding, Bishop, on Mill, xiii, 162.

Spanish colonies in America, xii, 145.

Spanish Inquisition, the, vi, 171.

Sparrows, Grant Allen on, viii, 400.

Spear, William G., custodian of the Quincy Historical Society, iii, 134; vi, 315.

Specialist, age of the, iv, 120.

Speech for Unlicensed Printing, Milton, xiii, 85.

Speed, Joshua, Lincoln's law partner, iii, 303.

Spelling-bees, iii, 255.

Spencer, Herbert, parents of, viii, 325; personality of, viii, 352; as a civil engineer, viii, 359; as assistant editor *Westminster Review,* viii, 334; *Principles of Psychology,* viii, 342; *Manners and Fashion,* viii, 342; Poultney Bigelow and, viii, 189; Charles Bradlaugh compared with, viii, 334; the Carlyles and, xii, 340; Comte and, viii, 261; Madame Curie and, viii, 259; Mrs. Eddy and, viii, 189; on education, xi, 171; Mary Ann Evans and, viii, 335; on genius, vii, 316; W. E. Gladstone and, xii, 230; Haeckel compared with, xii, 257; on the herding instinct, viii, 149; Huxley and, viii, 345; George Henry Lewes and, viii, 337; on morality, ix, 191; on Sir Isaac Newton, x, 366; quoted ii, 75; v, 70, 109; referred to, i, 56; ii, 290; v, 174, 289; xii, 207; 371; xiii, 85; Michael Rossetti on, viii, 344; on science, xi, 386; *Social Statics,* viii, 336; on Swedenborg, viii, 190; on John Tyndall, xii, 34, 356; on the Unknowable, viii, 173; Prof. E. L. Youmans and, viii, 344.

xlvi

Spencerian system of writing, vi, 134.

Spenser, Edmund, iv, 197; v, 14.

Spinoza, Benedict, xi, 129; excommunication of, viii, 224; Grotius compared with, viii, 228; influence of, viii, 206; on the Mennonites, viii, 211; Novalis on, viii, 233; parents of, viii, 210; philosophy of, viii, 234; Renan on, viii, 229, 233; *Tractatus Theologico-Politicus*, viii, 232; Van der Spijck and, viii, 228.

Spirit, of the hive, vii, 245; of mutual giving, vi, 237.

Spiritism, Alfred Russel Wallace's views on, xii, 392.

Spirits, disembodied, viii, 176.

Spiritual companionship, v, 227; gravity v, 241; relationship, vii, 385.

Spiritualism, x, 342.

Spirituality, religion and, iv, 236; sex and, xiii, 346.

Spirit-world, the, i, 298.

Spirit World, Swedenborg, viii, 172.

Spooner, Rev. Peleg, viii, 45.

Spoons, collecting, iv, 120.

Sport, the college type described, v, 152.

Sporza, Francisco, equestrian statue of, vi, 54.

Sposalizio, Raphael, vi, 27.

Spring, beauties of, iii, 298; the coming of, ix, 286.

Spring, Botticelli, iv, 159; vi, 78.

Springfield, Ill., home of Abraham Lincoln, iii, 287.

Spurgeon, on Darwinism, xii, 228; Gustave Dore and, iv, 343; Talmage compared with, ix, 284; his estimate of Shelley, i, 135.

Stagecoach days, v, 275.

Standard Oil Co., formation of the, xi, 379.

Standish, Capt. Miles, iii, 128.

Stanley, Dean, quoted, iii, 5.

Stanton, Elizabeth Cady, quoted, xiii, 200.

State and Church, separation of, xiv, 231.

Statesman, definition of, vii, 18.

Statistics, vital, v, 96.

Stead, William T., on America, vi, 340.

Steele, Richard, v, 254; regarding women, viii, 130.

Steinheil, friend of Meissonier, iv, 129.

Stephen, George, xi, 423.

Stephen, Leslie, i, p xx; life of Dean Swift, i, 143.

Stephenson, inventor of the steam-locomotive, xi, 246.

Stepmothers, vi, 47; ministrations of, vi, 23.

Sterne, shallowness of, v, 162.

Stevenson, Robert Louis, iv, 178; Edmund Gosse on, xiii, 42; experience of, on shipboard, xiii, 30; experience of, in New York, xiii, 31; on failure, vi, 169; humor of, xiii, 11; Fanny Osbourne and, xiii, 22; quoted, iv, 314; xi, 73; xiii, 19; on relaxation, xiv, 41; on Velasquez, vi, 154; Walt Whitman and, xiii, 18.

Stewart, Alexander T., business methods of, xi, 344; business palace of, xi, 351; Peter Cooper and, xi, 352; wealth of, xi, 352; the apple-woman and, xi, 220; President Grant and, xi, 334; purchaser of Meissonier's *Eighteen Hundred and Seven*, iv, 142; John Wanamaker and, xi, 353.

Stoddard, Charles Warren, iv, 263.

Stoics and Sophists compared, viii, 53.

Stone Age, the, x, 16.

Stoner, Winifred Sackville, ix, 283.

Stones of Venice, Ruskin, i, 89.

Story, Judge, and Daniel Webster, iii, 197.

Story of a Country Town, E. W. Howe, x, 247.

Story of France, Thomas E. Watson, viii, 241; ix, 380.

Story of German Love, Max Muller, viii, 192.

Story of My Life, The, George Sand, xiv, 76.

Story, W. W., sculptor, xi, 327.

Stowe, Harriet Beecher, v, 207.

Strabismus, v, 100.

Strafford, Browning, v, 55.

" Strap-oil," vii, 243.

Stratford-on-Avon, i, 49.

Strawberry Hill, home of Horace Walpole, iv, 302.

Street preaching, ix, 38.

Stupidity, Irish, xii, 336.

Sublime Porte, the, viii, 82.

Submission, religion by, ix, 188.

Substance and Show, Starr King, vii, 328.

Substitution, religion by, ix, 188.

Subterranean Vegetation, Humboldt, xii, 139.

Success in business, xi, 355.

Suicide, Schopenhauer on, viii, 385.

xlvii

lii